WOODSTOK FARLEY

The Judas Coins

This novel is dedicated to my mother, who introduced me to the love of a good mystery.

"Then, when Judas, who had betrayed
Him, saw that He had been condemned, he felt
remorse [μεταμεληθεὶς] and returned
the thirty pieces of silver to the chief
priests and elders,"
—Matthew 27:3 (NASB)
Greek: v. μεταμεληθεὶς = having re-
gretted; [created in him an emotional
remorse].

1

Ever have one of those mysteries that abuse your mind 'til it's too painful to sleep? You try to subdue the abuse with whiskey, but alcohol gets restless, and more and more, it aligns with the abuse. You are being violated by both your mind and the bottle. Eventually, whiskey replaces the evening slumber with an unconsciousness that wakens only for an insistent alarm and the hope that today, you can solve the case. Detectives die a little when they can't solve the case.

Whiskey can hurry the death. Remorse hurries it even faster.

This is a story about that dying.

So, let's see, where do I begin? Let's go back to when I first met Frank.

It was one of those beautiful South Florida days. Sun was shining. A slight tropical breeze blew. Eighty-two degrees and holding. You could smell the salt air coming off the coastline on the ocean side of the islands across the Intercoastal Waterway. South Florida sweat actually cools you as the breezes blow across the sweat on your forehead. It cools you as it blows on the wetness between your shoulder blades and in the middle of your chest. Native Floridians know to leave their shirts untucked so the breeze can blow up and in.

It's nature's air-conditioner.

I decided to leave my car parked on South Flagler Drive and walk while romancing the day and seducing the breeze, inviting it to cool me. I have always been fascinated with this city. I wasn't born here, but as the non-natives are fond of saying, "I got here as fast as I could." It was my father who brought me here. He used to love to walk its streets and back alleys with me in tow. He would tell me of the days he remembered being native-born before the great hurricane of '28 and the depression that moved his family out west. He would gesture to this site and that as we would walk along the Intercoastal Waterway downtown with its ever-insistent lapping of the salt tide against that mainland seawall and its Royal palms reaching heavenward, waving slightly at their Creator. He would tell me that downtown was once graced with majestic Mediterranean Revival-style hotels. He explained that in their day, they attracted the rich and glamorous from the islands across the Intercoastal by ferry and from points far north coming here for the winter.

He said they were grand hotels. The grand hotels began with Henry Flagler. He built the Hotel Royal Poinciana in 1894. At that time, it was touted as "the world's largest resort" and included a dining room that could seat 1,600 guests. His next hotel, The Breakers, was originally called the Palm Beach Inn.

Flagler built it in 1901, but in 1903, it was destroyed by fire. He then rebuilt it and opened it again, but tragedy repeated itself over a decade after Flagler died—The Breakers burnt once more, only to be rebuilt in '26. And, of course, there was the royal dame herself, often referred to as The Breakers West—the Pennsylvania Hotel. Originally, the Pennsylvania was built in 1926 with 216 rooms on the corner of Evernia Street and Narcissa Avenue, facing South Flagler Drive and the Intercoastal Waterway. For a short time, the hotel was known as the Hotel Royal Worth but was renamed the Pennsylvania Hotel by its new owner, a German immigrant who also owned the Hotel George Washington.

The Pennsylvania was my destination. Here I was to meet a man who my grandfather knew growing up on the edge of this southeastern coastline. The man was a semi-retired private investigator, as we would say today, although, in his day, folks would have referred to him as a private dick or a shamus.

His name was Francis Lobeck, or Frank, as he would later introduce himself to me. He had just turned 86 and had now outlived my grandfather. Little did I know at the time that my grandfather had set me up. Little did I realize this meeting would change my life.

You see, I am a private investigator, too.

Now Frank was at the end of his career with an investigator's worst nightmare—an unsolved case. But I did not know that then. All I knew was he was an old friend of my grandfather, and I was, for some unknown reason to me, charged with the task of bringing Frank the bad news that my grandfather had passed. One thing my grandfather passed on to me was that death has its expected remorse and must be realized.

Frank had lived in the Pennsylvania Hotel since the early '40s. And in the mid-60s, the hotel was purchased by the Carmelite Sisters, originally for folks who wanted semi- or full-time retirement. Frank continued to live there. He never officially retired; he just got older.

The entrance to the Pennsylvania was on Evernia Street around the block. Turning off Narcissus Street, I could see the large canvas awning now covering the entrance into the lobby. Upon entering, I looked around and tried to imagine how beautiful this building was in her heyday. The stairs led to the grand mezzanine, which was covered in a 4-inch handmade Spanish tile. The ceilings were high, with columns decorated 4 feet up with more colorful tile in blue, green, and yellow. The lobby once contained both a beauty shop and a barber. It once had a dining room that had seating for 400. But now, the lobby had more of a '60s/70s décor. I didn't appreciate the change. It wasn't just the furnishing style update, but it assaulted my sense of nostalgia for things past. I often romanticized the days of '40s shamus in Fedoras and suits packing heat in a shoulder harness and drinking hard liquor from a silver hip flask. Ah, shades of Sam Spade were everywhere in my imagination as I crossed the lobby to the stairs.

Looking at the address I had written on my notepad, I walked up to the second floor past the mezzanine and, knocking on the door of room 218, I heard a whispered voice telling me to come in. Turning the brass doorknob, I stepped into a dimly lit room. The only light came from an east-facing window, and dust floated on the sunbeam that settled on a plain coffee table with a pair of slipper-covered feet underneath. The feet belonged to the thin legs attached to the thin frame sitting on the overstuffed couch with floral print. The man's emaciation almost gave him up to the couch's eagerness to swallow any who ventured to sit there.

As he looked up, I noticed a surprised gaze giving me the once-over. I imagined I was not the expected guest he was waiting for. I deduced from his layered clothing and the small electric heater at his feet he was expecting maintenance to come and coax more warmth out of the antiquated heating system blowing from the ceiling. I had read somewhere that this magnificent building was in dire need of repair and was slated for demolition soon. The owners were probably not rushing to rejuvenate the system.

It did not take Frank long to realize his mistake in identity. He smiled slightly at the obvious similarity to his old friend since I looked much like my grandfather when he was my age.

"You must be Farley's boy. Name's Frank. Find a seat and have a sit," he said with a wink.

"Grandson. Farley was my grandfather on my mother's side. My name's Thomas Brunson. Folks just call me Brunson," I said as I extended my hand and received a cold, thin hand in return that only hinted at a one-time strength long gone. Then, I scanned the furniture for an unoccupied seat. I noticed what little furniture there was in the small living room was scattered with a woman's apparel. It was as if some lady had rushed in and dropped her clothes on the way to the bedroom. I was told this guy lived alone, and yet the clothing had the look of an apartment that housed a woman, and a young woman at that. Upon closer scrutiny, I realized the clothing, especially the undergarments, belonged to a woman who lived and dressed some 40 or 50 years ago. Draped over the back of a Chippendale wingback armchair with Queen Anne's feet was a full silk peachy slip trimmed with a lace ruffle at the V-neck and the hem. Details. I always notice details, especially when it comes to women's undergarments. I further noted that nothing had been moved since the garments had been tossed there. From my knowledge, women don't usually leave their bras, panties, and slips out where anyone unexpected could see. Besides, it was the dust on the clothing that clued me in; the clothes hadn't been moved in some time.

Can't help it—occupational hazard. I notice everything. Ah,

the details. "Nice place. Housekeeping on vacation this week?"

Frank looked at me, and then he looked around the room as if he had not noticed the condition before. He stared down at the floor with an expression of regret and offered with a sigh as he looked up, "They were her things. I haven't had the heart to move them since I moved into her room."

"How long has that been, Frank?"

Now, looking to the ceiling as if the answers to my questions were found written around the room, he paused, and tears began to form in his eyes. Without looking back at me, he said, "It was about a couple of months after they discovered her body."

"What year was that, Frank?"

"It was the fall of '42."

Then, looking back at me, he started in.

"In her day, she was one fine lady. Built during Prohibition, you see, in that Mediterranean style. She even had a tower on the west side of her," he said as he indicated with an old, thin finger in the general direction. "The rich from the islands and the mainland had magnificent dinners here and charity balls for whatever good cause. They also had debutante parties for those with more money than they knew what to do with. Why, they even had slot machines in the hallways for those who decided to spend the winter on the East Coast."

It took me a minute to realize Frank was not talking about the lady as a woman who had occupied the room but the "grand dame" known as the Pennsylvania. Frank seems to be equally infatuated with both.

I pulled a chair over from the small kitchenette table and sat down, facing the old detective. He smiled as he leaned back into the couch and looked to the ceiling as he reminisced about the *glory days* with my grandfather.

"Your grandfather, Farley, and I met many years ago. We were quite the pair. No port was safe from the two of us."

"Well, I am afraid I got some bad news about my grandfather."

"He's passed on, hasn't he?"

"I'm afraid so. How did you know?"

"He told me he would send you before it was too late."

"Well, I'm afraid it is too late."

"I don't mean too late for Farley; I mean too late for me."

"Too late for you? I'm afraid I don't follow."

"Your grandfather said he would send you when he was gone to help me before they destroyed all the evidence."

"I'm still not following you, Frank. Evidence? What evidence? What are you talking about?"

Indicating with his feeble hands as he swept the room with them."This room! This room is all the evidence I got left on who killed her. They're going to tear down the hotel soon, and I haven't solved the case yet."

"I'm still afraid I'm not following you. Maybe you better start from the beginning. Beginning with who is the murdered lady you have been talking about since I arrived."

"This is going to be a long story. Maybe you should pour us a drink," Frank said as he indicated with that shaky finger to the one lone bottle sitting on top of a Spanish-carved, dark walnut, Tuscan 2-drawer credenza next to the apartment's front door.

Rising, I walked over and noticed the bottle, much like the other items in the room, had not been moved in quite some time. Dust everywhere. There were two glasses upside down, sitting next to the bottle on a cloth napkin. Picking it up, I noticed it was a bottle of I. W. Harper Bourbon Whiskey. The seal had not been broken. I remembered it was my grandfather's favorite whiskey.

"This bottle's been sittin' here a long time, Frank. When's the last time you saw my grand—uhmm, when did you see Farley last?"

Looking up at me with a squint from his clouded blue-grey eyes and a smile, he said, "I haven't seen Farley in many, many years. Bought that bottle for him back in '47, I believe it was. We never got to open it. He always said he would come for a visit one day, but it never happened for some reason or another. We did talk on the phone occasionally. That's how I knew about you."

"Sure you want me to break this seal?"

"We'll drink to your grandfather. It woulda' pissed him off, makin' such a fuss with such a fine whiskey, but, well, he shoulda' been here to open it himself. His fault. Go ahead and pour us a couple."

Twisting the corked lid to break the seal was almost a solemn occasion for me. I hadn't had a drink in over six months, not since it failed my marriage. I wasn't sure this was a good idea and even thought I ought to tell Frank that me and drink don't get along so well anymore. It almost took my life. It did take my wife.

Blowing the dust away from the edge of the glasses, I slowly poured a healthy drink for each of us and then pushed the cork back into the bottle. Turning to Frank, I handed him a glass and raised mine in toast of my grandfather. Taking a very slight sip, I said, "Here's to Farley. A good man gone too early."

"To Farley. I'll see ya soon, my friend."

Throwing back the whiskey in one swallow, Frank grimaced from the burn as he coughed again and again. I silently prayed Frank wasn't joining Farley at this particular moment in time.

"You ok there, Frank? You need some water?"

Waving me off, he coughed out, "I'm fine. I'm fine. Just . . ." coughing and clearing his throat, he stopped for a moment to gain control of the liquor. "Just haven't had a drink in many a day. Think that whiskey put some weight on sittin' over there all these years."

Holding his glass to me, he said with a smile, "Why don't cha pour me another so I can steady the last one."

Grabbing the bottle, I hesitated over mine and realized I hadn't taken more than a sip and did not need a refill. So I filled Frank's and set the bottle on the coffee table for him to reach if he wanted more. I didn't need to be in charge of pouring.

"So, Frank, you gonna tell me about this lady and the case? You got me interested now."

Draining his glass in one swallow again and giving me a wink, Frank eased back into the couch and closed his eyes. I thought for a moment he had gone to sleep, but soon, he began to talk in reverent whispers about the lady and the days that only existed in his memories.

He began slowly, "It was late summer in '42 . . ."

2

The phone rang twice before Marla picked up the receiver, and in a sensuous voice that her employer suggested she use to attract the male clientele, she answered, "Frank Lobeck Investigations, how may I help you?"

"Uh-huh. Uh-huh. Sure. Let me connect you to Mr. Lobeck," she said to the voice on the other end; then, covering the receiver with her hand, she turned and said over her shoulder to the inner office, "Frank, pick up. Sounds like you might have a case."

Inside the inner office, Frank, who looked to be in his mid-thirties with a deep Florida tan, quickly took his feet off the desk and sat upright while grabbing the black desk phone.

"This is Frank Lobeck. Who am I talking to?" pausing while the voice on the other end responded, Frank continued, "Mr. Wilson, what can I do for you?"

Listening for a few minutes, Frank suggested, "There's an old gin mill on the corner of Okeechobee and Dixie. Yeah, meet me there in twenty. I'll be at the bar."

Hanging up the phone, Frank stood and grabbed his dark

gray wool felt Frederick Fedora from his coat rack while he combed a shock of dark brown hair back out of his eyes with his fingers, and walking out of the office and up behind Marla, he placed his hands suggestively on her shoulders. Leaning down and eagerly breathing in the sweet aroma of her perfume, Frank whispered in her ear as he massaged the office romance tension, saying, "Gotta go out to meet a client. Be back in an hour or two."

Marla looked up longingly at Frank into his piercing blue-grey eyes and then rested her cheek against his right hand and said with a smile, "Have one for me, boss."

As he headed to the office door, he looked back while fitting his hat on and winked, saying, "Sure thing, baby. Sure thing."

Now, as Frank entered the bar, the small crowd of established afternoon patrons all greeted him with raised glasses and cheers.

Bill, one of several retired police officers at the table, said with a laugh, "Missed ya for lunch today, Frank. Marla, gotcha takin' out the trash?"

Everyone joined in the laughter.

"Nah, had some paperwork to catch up on a case," and tipping his Fedora, Frank quipped, "Besides, you know the only one Marla can get to take out the trash is you, Bill."

Again, everyone laughed as Bill turned red-faced and offered a few profanities to the crowd, then he broke out into a grin and offered a "tocatto goombah" to Frank, as he headed straight to the forty-two-foot mahogany Brunswick bar that Kelsey, the bartender was polishing to its standard gloss.

Setting himself up while sitting on the dark green leather bar stool with his foot on the brass foot rail, he nodded his chin at

Kelsey. Tapping the bar with his right index finger, he ordered:

"Let me have a Brooklyn there, Kelsey."

"Can do, Frank. Comin' right up."

Kelsey's one of those bartenders that knows his regulars, and he knows what they like to drink. Grabbing a bottle of Old Crow Straight Pure Rye, Kelsey began to work his magic. He added vermouth and some maraschino liqueur along with a quarter ounce of Amer Picon and, out of habit, garnished with a maraschino cherry, but then pulled it back out by the stem, remembering that Frank thought the cherry made his drink too much like a dame's drink. As he set the drink on a cocktail napkin in front of Frank, Kelsey threw the fruit over his left shoulder backward into the wastebasket. Two points! Bob Feerick, his old teammate back in Santa Clara College, would be proud. Kelsey grinned as he tipped his head to the left at the what-did-you-expect basket, bowed to the crowd's riotous cat-calls and applause, and then went back to polishing the bar.

As Frank sipped his drink, he took a small, blue-covered notepad from his inside coat pocket and glanced at what he had written from the phone call so as to be sharp when his prospective client arrived. He silently repeated the client's name, Albert Wilson, and that he lived in Marietta, Ohio and that he worked for over twenty years at a local paint company. Frank always prided himself on the gathering of details that, at the moment, might seem irrelevant to others. He quickly calculated the miles the man must have driven to get to West Palm from Marietta. This was sort of a hobby for Frank, something his dad had made into a game on family vacations. Frank smiled from the memory. He continued reading that Mr. Wilson has a wife and that he had one daughter, Betty Lou.

Just then, the door to the bar opened and let the prohibited sunlight that hid the afternoon drinkers and moseyed in, along with a man in his mid to late-forties who walked weighted down with the sadness of someone much older, keeping his eyes to the floor. Slowly, the man raised his head while his eyes adjusted to the dominant darkness the brief sunlight could not banish, and he quickly scanned the room, looking for the detective who said he would be at the bar. Frank raised his glass in the man's direction and waved him over, recognizing the expected slump of a troubled client. With a slight nodding of his chin in Frank's direction, the man almost limped toward the bar, oblivious of the bar patrons who welcomed one and all.

A voice that was unsure and, to Frank, lacking in sleep, asked, "You, Frank Lobeck?" "Most times," Frank replied as he stood up and offered his hand. "Have a sit. You must be Mr. Wilson. What can I get ya?" he asked as he nodded again to Kelsey, shaking his own empty glass.

Wiping the length of the bar as he made his way over, Kelsey, from his years of listening and solicited advice offerings, addressed cautiously an obviously broken man, "Whatta you have there, mister?"

"I don't drink much anymore, so just a glass of water or a club soda, please."

"Come on, I'm buyin'. You look like a beer guy to me. Am I right?" Frank said, noticing the hard callouses of the sad man's hands. Crusts of dried paint showed around the sad man's fingers.

Staring down at the bar, then slowly looking nervously from side to side as if the patrons all knew his plight, and then up at Kelsey, he responded almost as if he were frightened of something no one could see, "Alright, I'll have a beer."

Kelsey patiently asked, "Bottle or draft?"

"Give him a draft there, Kelsey, and while you're at it, mine needs a refill," Frank said with a wink while again shaking his empty glass at the bartender.

When Kelsey moved to fill the order, Frank asked, "So, Mr. Wilson, you wanna tell me what this is all about?"

Looking down at the bar again, the man slowly filled his chest with air through his nose. As he inflated himself, his head came up and looked at Frank with eyes that expressed a sense of deep sadness and terror at the same time. Holding Frank's stare for a minute as if to secure a confidence from this person he had never met, Mr. Wilson began slowly as he deflated:

"Three days ago, my daughter, Betty Lou," Wilson hesitated as tears filled his eyes; he pushed hard to get the next few words out, "well, . . . she . . . she was murdered at the Pennsylvania Hotel," pausing while looking back down at the bar, he continued slowly, "she was only twenty- three years old."

Frank had sensed that this heartbroken man was dealing with great loss before he even heard the word murder. He knew this from experience. All he ever seemed to get were cases that took him to the dark side of people's lives and their shattered emotions. Just once, he hoped he'd get a case that ended with everyone happy, especially himself. Why didn't anyone ever ask him to find their lost dog? Or, maybe, assist in reuniting family members. Instead, it seemed all his cases were about people who cheat one another or, people who cheat *on* one another, or people who destroy other people's lives with their selfish, misguided cheating. Why couldn't he get a happy-ever-after ending? But it looked like, at least today, that was certainly not going to be the case. It's no wonder private dicks drink, he thought to himself. It's sometimes the only happiness they can find. Lately, Frank has been unhappy a lot.

Giving Mr. Wilson a moment to collect himself, Frank continued his observation of the shattered man next to him. He noticed the man's clothes appeared to be on their second or third day of being worn. He noticed stains on the shirt from spilling coffee while probably driving. He also noticed the man had not shaved in several days and thus concluded that Mr. Wilson probably drove straight through to here from Ohio without stopping to rest or eat a sit-down meal. He most likely only stopped for gas and drank filling station coffee during the over one-thousand-mile trip. If he left right after receiving the phone call from the police, then he had been in town for the last two days. He probably spent his first day at the police station, and Frank concluded that his inside man there, Officer Gregory, tipped Mr. Wilson the name of a local private investigator. Gregory had known Frank since they were in high school together and often sent work Frank's way out of respect for Frank's dad, who had been a police officer for over twenty years before being shot on duty during a hold-up of a liquor store.

Kelsey moved down to the other end of the bar after placing the men's drinks in front of them so as to give Frank some privacy with this apparent client. Kelsey knew Frank's routine was to use the alcohol to loosen up the client to get as much info as he could before taking a case. Frank had told Kelsey if a client doesn't spill, then it makes it harder to close. Closing is the most important part, Frank said, because then he got paid, and so did Kelsey.

Raising his glass toward Wilson, Frank said, "Please continue and don't leave anything out, no matter how insignificant it might appear. Every detail is important if I am to help you."

Drawing another deep breath after taking an obligatory sip of the beer in front of him, Mr. Wilson began:

3

"I was at work when I got the call from the police, like I said, three days ago. They said…" Wilson swallowed hard before he continued, "They said they were sorry to inform me that Betty Lou was found dead." He stopped and stared down at the bar, then, taking another swig from his beer, he started again, "They said she was found apparently murdered in her room at the Pennsylvania, where she worked as a singer." Looking at Frank, he whispered, "She loved to sing." Then, looking up at the ceiling as the tears filled his eyes, "Betty Lou . . . Betty Lou was always singing around the house. She was singing since before she could walk, it seems. I remember her standing on the kitchen chair at the table while we ate, holding a spoon in her hand as if it were a microphone. We knew then, my wife and I, that this little angel would go places with her voice. She sang in church. She even sang in the school choir as a soloist. She was such a good girl, an innocent girl. She had never been outside of Marietta except to visit my sister in Columbus. She didn't know . . . anything . . . didn't know a thing of the world." Again, he lowered his tear-filled eyes to the bar. A drop splashed and pooled with the water ring from his beer glass.

Shaking his head slowly from side to side, he continued, "When they told me, it was as if it was a dream. I couldn't believe what they were sayin'. I kept asking them to repeat it. Each time, the news sounded like it was for someone else."

Looking back at Frank, Wilson just stared with trembling lips and with eyes that hadn't known sleep, real sleep in days. Turning back to his beer for courage, he started again:

"They told me I needed to come down and identify the body. I broke down right there and fell to my knees on the plant floor. My boss came over, and I managed to repeat what the police had told me. He told me to leave and go home to be with my wife. I walked out to the parking lot, got into my car, and drove straight through to here. I never even went home. I never told my wife; I just drove straight here. When I got to the police station, they told me my wife had called in a panic because I never came home. Guess my boss called her and broke the news. It was like I was looking at all this from somewhere outside my body. A detective and an officer took me to a room, and they pulled open a drawer with a body covered by a sheet, and then they pulled it back, and there was my baby. My Betty Lou. She was all grey and lifeless. Her eyes were closed. Her voice was gone." Wilson paused again for courage, and then, "They said she had been strangled and stabbed. I fell on her and cried, oh my God, why? Why? Please, God, why did you take my baby from me? Please give her back," Wilson broke again, and more tears fell to the bar. Pulling his handkerchief from his back pocket, he wiped his eyes and continued, "The men with me held me up as they led me from her into another room. I heard the drawer close shut behind me. It was then I knew she was singin' with the angels." He then looked up to the ceiling as if he was seeing something that no one else could see.

After a period of reverenced silence, he continued. "Someone brought me a phone and said I should call my wife. When she answered, we both just sat in silence, not knowing what to do or say or even how to grieve over a phone. Finally, my wife said, 'Frank, come home and bring our baby home. Please, Frank, just come home.'

"I asked the detective how soon could I have Betty Lou's body to take her home and bury her. They said it might take days, even weeks, before they could release the body. They suggested I get a hotel and let them know where I was staying and that they would call as soon as they knew something. That's when Officer Gregory told me about you. He also suggested the name of a priest that he said Betty Lou might have seen. It seems that she had written the priest's name down on some stationery in her room. Officer Gregory assumed it was because she had seen him or intended to call him for something."

Then Wilson broke down again. He laid his head in his hands on the bar and sobbed great, hard sobs that raised his shoulders up and down. His sobbing turned to wailing, and Frank moved over to console what he knew could not be consoled. The bar patrons, out of respect for the man's grief, got up silently and left, leaving Frank and Kelsey alone with Mr. Wilson. Kelsey kept his distance even though he had seen many men break over the years of tending bar. Men of all walks of life, men who never cried in public, much less private, before. Men who lost it all and came to drown their emotions with liquor and confessions to Kelsey. Yeah, Kelsey had seen it all; Kelsey had heard it all, but never had he witnessed firsthand the depth of grief this man poured into his bar top. Frank had seen it all, too, but he didn't have the ability to comfort. All he could offer was his talent for finding the responsible party and holding them accountable. This he would do for this man. He vowed silently that he would find Betty Lou's killer. He would never quit until he did. Somehow and for some strange reason, at that moment, Frank took on the grief of losing Betty Lou, and it would be his motivation from that day forward.

After what seemed like an hour or more, although actually, it was only minutes, Mr. Wilson composed himself, and, using the bar towel Kelsey offered, he turned to Frank and apologized for his emotional breakdown. Frank patted the broad shoulders of this hard-working man and assured him he would have done the same thing if he had lost a daughter. In fact, the secret no one knew is that Frank had, but he buried it so deep that not even Marla knew about it for the first couple of years they had been together.

Sliding the beer toward Wilson, Frank encouraged him to take a couple of sips and let the alcohol steady him. Then Frank continued carefully to see if there was perhaps more to the story that Wilson could elaborate on.

Wilson began slowly, "I left the police station and went to talk to that priest Officer Gregory told me about. Gregory had given me directions to the church, and I walked since it was only a few blocks from the station. The church was St. Ann's, and the priest's name was Father Peter. He told me he didn't know Betty Lou all that well since she had just started coming to mass. Father Peter told me the only way he knew her at all was as he greeted her once when she was leaving; he remembered her voice from confession. He said she sounded both sad and frightened at the same time and that she sounded like she was from up north, not at all like a local. When he asked what was troubling her, she said she'd save that for her next confession. Father Peter said he never saw her again from that day at mass. He said he was so sorry to hear about her death and that he would pray for both her and me and my wife in Mass on Saturday. I left the church and called you."

Frank scribbled notes as fast as he could. It was easy since Wilson spoke deliberately and paused often. He made a mental note to see this Father Peter as soon as he could. But right now, he needed to visit the crime scene and see what the coppers missed. He was good at that.

Throwing back the last of his allotted drink, he knew that Marla would be keeping strict accounts of his expenses, especially when it came to the afternoon greasing of a client. Frank rose and, placing another consolatory hand on Mr. Wilson's back, he leaned close to the man's ear and said with his best sympathy, "Listen, I got enough to get started for now. Why don't you go and use that hotel room of yours and I'll be in touch as soon as I have anything more to add. Come on, why don't you get a shower and some sleep."

Then, patting him one last time, Frank reached for his notebook and asked, "Give me your hotel and room number, and like I said, I'll let you know of any new developments."

Looking up at the detective with hope in his voice Wilson said, "I'm in room sixteen at the Southlands Motor Lodge on South Dixie," and then, with his jaw set, he leaned in close to Frank and said, "You catch that sonofabitch what murdered my baby girl. I don't care what it costs me; you find him, you hear, and then you turn him over to me. You hear!" Those last words were punctuated with Wilson's finger stabbing Frank in the chest several times to emphasize his meaning. Frank caught his meaning without the punctuation, and he knew that Wilson meant every finger jab. Hell, he thought he would have done the same thing if someone had hurt his little girl. The fact is—he did.

4

Frank's first step was to pay a visit to Officer Gregory and thank him for pointing Wilson in his direction. He needed to keep the relationship with Gregory, his childhood friend from the old days at school, indebted, working it both ways. Frank was aware that maybe half of his investigative skills came from favors people owed him. Even though Marla didn't like it, Frank would occasionally do someone a pro bono courtesy. That way, when folks know they are obliged to you for something, they are more apt to return it with information. He likewise needed to reciprocate so that folks didn't feel used. Frank knew he was gonna need to check out the crime scene to see if he could find anything the police might have missed, and Gregory was his usual way in. A problem happened the last time Frank walked in without permission at a crime scene. Lieutenant Jacobs, Gregory's superior, had him thrown out.

You see, Harold Jacobs held a grudge against Frank for quite some time, and there had been no indication that he was going to relent. At least not lately. It seems that Frank solved one of Jacobs' most difficult cases within ten minutes of being on the scene. Jacobs had been working the case for some nine months without so much as a single clue as to who was involved or guilty of the crime. Not even the slightest hint as to a lead to chase down. The case involved the murder of one of the girls who worked the brothel for Nora Taylor, a well-known madam out of Jacksonville who supplied prostitutes throughout the state for the wealthy men coming to Florida in the winter without their wives. Pleasure sells often, and wealth often masks the trail to that pleasure. The crime happened at an apartment building known as Sunrise Hall in Fort Lauderdale. During the thirties and into the forties, this three-story brothel was a wooden structure with balconies on all sides that gave itself over to the corrupt side of society, which included drugs, gambling, and prostitution.

Jacobs had begun his career back in the twenties as a young detective there in Ft. Lauderdale, so as a favor to the police chief there, Jacobs was brought down from West Palm to work the case. He had moved up to West Palm to better his chances for advancement, and he knew providing a favor for his former employer would certainly bolster any decision toward that promotion.

As was said, Jacobs was getting nowhere on this particular case. What little evidence he managed to put together seemed to point to a possible "john" who went too far and slashed the girl's throat, probably in the heat of passion, he thought. There were too many fingerprints, no weapons were found, and apparently, no witnesses would come forward if, indeed, there were any. Jacobs floated the idea that it might have been an inside job executed by Hector, the man whom Nora hired to watch the comings and goings of important clientele for future blackmail. It seems that Hector had a reputation for manhandling the girls;

at least, that's what his arrest record indicated.

But Hector had a solid alibi from Tina, his steady girl, who gave a detailed account of Hector's whereabouts during the time the young prostitute was killed. Tina said that Hector was occupied with her, which took him away from his position at the front door when the girl took a customer upstairs. The girl, giggling, hollered into the back office to Tina, "Tell Hector I'm going to work." You see, Tina said she and Hector were practicing their eventual honeymoon, hoping that if Nora released her from her contractual obligation, they could marry. With Hector cleared, that left Jacobs with only the possibility of a client going too far.

When Frank, who just happened to be working another case involving the Sunrise Hall, stumbled into the wrong room looking for an informant who was known to frequent the brothel, he was stopped by an officer guarding the crime scene from any locals looking for an unoccupied room to sleep off their previous night's revelry. He kept Frank at the door and wouldn't allow him to enter.

Intrigued, Frank looked past the young officer into the room and noticed a blood- spattered copy of Botticelli's *The Birth of Venus* on the wall. He remembered a conversation he had had with a friend the night before while bowling at the Star Lane Bowling Alley. It was his league night, and a teammate, Brad Peterson, a realtor for West Palm Beach, told him of a wealthy client from up around New Jersey who had bragged about killing a prostitute at the Sunrise and that the blood had shot all the way up the wall splashing a painting hanging above the bed. The client said the painting was of a naked broad standing in a seashell. Frank figured this painting was what the murderous braggart was talking about while he quickly scanned the room from the doorway. Always looking to promote some favor, Frank thought as long as he was here, he might as well provide some useful information. He told the officer to let the one in charge know about a certain Bartholomew Herrington visiting from New Jersey who had shot off his mouth about whacking a pro skirt and the blood-spattered painting. Frank also said to check with Nora and that she would have records of clients even though they usually didn't use their real names. He continued by telling him he might check with Hector, who worked the door, and that he might be able to offer a physical description since Hector's job was to provide security for the girls, although this particular time, that security didn't pan out. When the officer told Jacobs what Frank had relayed, it didn't take Jacobs long to locate Herrington, who was staying at the Pennsylvania. When questioned, Herrington broke immediately and confessed. He was feeling way too guilty, and the breakfast of Bloody Marys probably helped to loosen his conscience. Later, when Jacobs interviewed Hector, he found that Hector was absent from the door that night and never saw the girl's client go in. Still, the confession was enough to put Herrington in the electric chair. Jacobs thought it was too easy once he had a suspect, and it bothered him at the effortlessness that Frank seemed to use to put the pieces together. Frank never told Jacobs how he knew what he knew; he just hoped Jacobs would be grateful for putting another case to bed.

But that's not how it turned out for Frank. Yeah, he got some of the credit for solving the case, but this embarrassed Jacobs in front of his fellow officers and especially his former boss, the police chief of Lauderdale, so Jacobs took it out on Frank. He was heard to say that "no two- bit private dick was gonna show him up in front of everyone," and he meant it.

So Frank figured for now, until he got back into Jacobs' good graces if he ever did, he might as well go through Gregory just in case there were still hostile feelings around with some of the other officers.

"Whataya mean I cain't go check out the crime scene? Come on, Gregory. It's me, your ol' pal from the old days. Come on, you owe me. Remember? I figured out for you your wife was plannin' a surprise party for your fifth and not runnin' around on you. Hell, I even came to the party, and I didn't even charge you a damn cent for my trouble. I even took the heat from Marla for that expense and didn't lay any grief on you. Gregory, my friend, what gives?"

"It's outta my hands, Frank. It's comin' from somewhere up top," Gregory emphasized by pointing his finger up toward the second floor and then holding it to his lips. Then whispering, he continued, "I can't do nuthin' about it. They say no one touches the evidence, and they won't even let you see the autopsy report without a court injunction, and that's that. Guess you're gonna have to do some detecting." Gregory laughed at his attempt at defusing the situation, but Frank didn't see the humor in it.

"Well, detecting takes examination. Hell, how can I discover anything if I cain't examine? Why don't tell that to your superiors? Geez! Damnit to hell, Gregory! I gotta get in there," then, looking around the station, Frank said angrily under his breath, "I bet that damn Jacobs is behind this. Man, that guy sure knows how to hold a grudge."

"I told ya there's nuthin' I can do about it, Frank." Then, looking slowly from side to side, Gregory pulled Frank in closer with a beckoning index finger. He leaned in and whispered so only Frank could hear, "They say there's some Feds diggin' around the case, somethin' about some German fella, and it's them what says no one can go in. What I can tell ya is the autopsy report says the girl was strangled and then cut in the belly sometime after she was dead." Then, shrugging his shoulders and grimacing, Gregory whispered, "Why would anyone want to mutilate a body once they already killed it. Cain't figure some people out. No sir, people got no scruples when it comes to killin' folks nowadays."

Standing up, Gregory looked again around the room to make sure no one had heard his previous comments, and then he said out loud for everyone to hear, "I told ya, Frank, no one can go snoopin' around the crime scene unless I say so, and that's that. Now, if you can't handle that, damn it, that's your problem, not mine. You'll have to find another sap to get what you want," then Gregory grinned at the others, who had lifted their heads to see what all the commotion was about. They all smiled, knowing one of their own was sticking it to some two-bit gumshoe.

Frank knew his friend well. He knew that Gregory was only protecting both of them in this public forum. "Another sap" was Gregory's way of saying that Frank should use his own methods of getting into the crime scene. Those saps were what Gregory used to refer to Frank's informants outside the police station. He gave Gregory a sly wink and headed to the Pennsylvania.

Now, Frank prided himself on his contacts and the many relationships he had built up in this town over the years. As he told Gregory, those who were willing to spill some behind-closed-door secrets or unlock those same doors were all part of the detecting game. He knew at the Pennsylvania he could pull favors because of the many bellhops and staff that allowed him something at one time or another. Sometimes, Frank had to garner favor by greasing some palms. That was an expense that Marla always gave Frank the hardest time about. She was convinced, and sometimes rightly so, that the payoffs coming for the Pennsylvania were mostly payoffs to the many slot machines that graced the hallways. Frank told her that some of that was true, but he said it was sometimes necessary to blend into a crowd and to loosen a few lips with a few drinks. The way Frank figured it was, "Some things just come from paper grease."

5

"How's it hangin', Harry?" Frank asked the young, over-tanned bellhop in the lobby of the Pennsylvania.

Harry was watering one of the many potted Bottle Palms that graced the entrance to the hotel. It seemed the management chose young athletic men to attract the rich female clientele that wintered at the Pennsylvania every season—sometimes with their husbands, sometimes without. Remember, wealth masks the trail to pleasure. Harry's Florida tan was crowned with a head full of sun-bleached hair neatly groomed around the ears but just enough length on top to present a roguish and slightly alluring persona. His starched, deep burgundy bellhop jacket with its some thirty-plus gold buttons in three vertical rows on the front cut an impressive, almost military look about him. Harry, unlike the other bellhops, refused to wear the matching burgundy round brimless cap with its golden braided rope that banded the cap just above the ears. He said it made his head sweat and restricted the blood flow to his hair. The real reason, Frank thought, was that Harry didn't want anything messing with his hair. Harry said his hair was like his business card, and he didn't want anything interfering with business.

"Hangin' enough to keep me in the management's good graces and the women's warm embraces," Harry quipped, looking up at Frank with an overly white toothy smile. "Business is good!"

"Well, look at who's become a poet," Frank replied with a wink and a slap on Harry's left uniform shoulder board with one hand while slipping a fiver into his breast pocket with his other.

Then, being so close, Frank leaned into Harry's ear and whispered, "Can you help a fella Cassanova out? I really need to take a look inside that murdered girl's room for just a bit."

Patting the jacket pocket with his left hand, Harry smiled and looked around at the late-to-rise crowd slowly filling the lobby. He didn't want to overlook today's agenda or perhaps tonight's entertainment. Without saying a word, Harry cocked his head to the right, motioning Frank to follow discreetly up the stairs to the level above the mezzanine.

While slowly ascending the stairs and watering along the way as if his duties were taking him there, Harry smiled, ran his fingers through his hair to enhance his roguish appeal, and nodded at the women who happened to look his way. He made several mental notes for later this evening when his shift ended. The ladies all smiled back with their own discrete nod or the fluttering of eyelashes, hoping Harry had selected them. Frank followed at a distance, pretending to go in the same direction. He stopped to solidify the illusion by slipping a nickel into a random slot machine. Harry set his watering can down on a Mahogany Spider Leg Two-Tier end table, then quickly snatched it up while looking around to see if housekeeping saw the potential ring stain that would certainly draw some criticism from Enid, a large black woman who ran housekeeping like a German war camp. Harry knew his job would be lucky to survive any minor infraction to housekeeping regulations. Enid had that kind of power. Enid was one of the rare employees that had been with the Pennsylvania long before Harry and any other staff, it seems. Enid was an institution, and management relied on her to help keep the rest of the staff in line.

She controlled her people like they were her children who were caught sneaking out the bedroom window past curfew. No one got anything over on Enid. Harry thought that it was good Enid didn't interfere with his off-the-books activities with the lady patrons, although he was never quite sure why she didn't impose herself on him and the other bellhops. Maybe it was because the management looked the other way as well. Harry quickly wiped any evidence from the table with his handkerchief and then set the watering can on the floor behind the end table.

Reaching into his front pants pocket for his unlawful master room key, Harry kept looking over his shoulder for Enid or any of her loyal minions who would gladly rat him out to replace him with a cousin in need of employment.

Opening the door, Harry nodded Frank inside the room with the admonition, "Make it quick and be sure to lock up after. I don't know you if'n ya get caught." Then, with sincerity, Harry added, "Sure hope you find the SOB who done this to that girl . . ." and then he added with a sad smile, "Betty Lou. She didn't deserve to go out this way. She was all right in my book," then, broadening the smile, he added, "and she was a real looker." Sticking his head out into the hallway and looking right and left, he slipped out coolly, retrieved his watering can and headed back down to the lobby to secure his hopeful evening appointments.

Frank stood just inside the doorway and quickly scanned the room to orient himself before his search. He had to make sure he left no evidence that he had been there, or there would be hell to pay from Jacobs. He noticed that it appeared Betty Lou had been undressing as she headed to her bedroom. Her clothes were scattered over the furniture and upon the floor in places. There was a window that was locked on the wall left of the door. Frank figured whoever came in came in through the door and not the locked window. Either Betty Lou knew and allowed her guest entrance, or someone had a passkey. He turned and examined the door lock for any signs of lock picking or prying. There was none.

Frank then moved cautiously into the darkened bedroom and reached instinctively for the light switch on the wall inside and opposite the door as it stood open. As his eyes adjusted, he first noticed the bloodstains on the unmade bed in front of him. He thought that Betty Lou either ignored housekeeping or that the bed was used prior to all that blood. The image that was formulating in Frank's head of the young singer was running contrary to the image her distraught father had believed earlier. Continuing to look around the room from the doorway, Frank couldn't see any signs of struggle, so he again thought that the visitor was known to Betty Lou. He thought that anyone following the young singer stripping as she headed toward her bed was invited. Frank knew he needed to look into whether or not Betty Lou had a steady or did she "entertain" a lot.

Backing out of the bedroom, Frank again scanned the living room for any indication that the visitor might be a longed-for guest. Framed photographs usually show how much one is admired and thought of. There were none. It now seemed possible to Frank the visitor was someone new in the relationship with the young singer.

Getting down on his knees, Frank began the search that the police sometimes miss, and that's the search for what is under the furniture. He noticed something under the couch and reached under to grab whatever the lost item was.

Holding the small round metal object between his thumb and index finger, Frank moved it up close to his left eye as he squinted the right and noticed it appeared to be a coin and possibly an old coin at that. It looked to be made of silver with the image of a man's head graced with a crown of leaves on one side and, on the other side, a majestic bird.

As Frank held the coin, he noticed a tingling in his fingers radiating up his arm and then coursing throughout his entire body. Then, an overwhelming sense of guilt and despair exploded into his thoughts and weighed heavily, almost to the point of bursting in his heart. All at once, all the moments of disappointment, guilt, betrayal, and deceitfulness of a lifetime came vividly into his memory. It was more than he could bear. He trembled and heaved great groans from the pain of letting others down. The weight of all the many emotions racing through his head drove his mind to think about taking out his .38 1911 Colt Detective Special and ending it all at that very moment in Betty Lou's living room there, kneeling on the floor behind the couch. As he reached for the pistol in his shoulder harness, he dropped the coin in his shaking right hand, and the feelings began to fade rapidly. Placing both hands on the carpet in that kneeling position, Frank breathed deeply between subsiding chest-expanding sobs that just moments ago threatened to destroy him.

Looking down at the small round object, Frank wondered

what could have brought on the tremendous wave of emotion and guilt. His first instinct was it was just coincidence, but looking down at the coin, he felt a sense of dread coming from it mixed with an overwhelming lust for coveting this object, which could possibly be surrendered for all the hard work that often went uncompensated. At that moment, he thought the little silver object seemed to have tremendous value. It screamed into his head to possess it; it begged him to ease his many financial burdens; it whispered to him that Marla would never again bother him about his expenses; it told his mind that all the years of working hand to mouth and doing so much for others deserved a little reward; it told him there was no shame in fortune. With trembling and selfish fingers, he slowly picked it up again and again; within moments, the emotionally destructive guilt came in wave upon wave. His whole body trembled, and his eyes filled with the tears of sorrow for the life he had led that was intertwined with so many others. He felt the pain they experienced that he alone was responsible for. Frank sensed the coin laughing at him about deserving a reward.

This time, he threw it down and fell back into a sitting position, looking at the magical coin. Again, the damaging guilt faded a little more slowly this time. He asked himself could it be this coin was somehow playing a role in his affecting his mind and bringing on this gut- wrenching grief. How was that possible? Just how could anything so little wield such great power over a man's emotions and bring him to the edge of suicide? What was this coin? Where did it come from? Frank knew instinctively he would have to seek answers about the strange coin, and he also knew there was only one person who would know anything if there was anything to know. That one person frightened him more than the coin did at that moment.

Frank pulled out his handkerchief and tentatively picked up the coin. He noticed that the power of guilt did not overwhelm him, and he figured that as long as he didn't touch it with his skin, he was okay. He wrapped the coin in his handkerchief and put it in his pocket, and then, using the back of the couch to help him get up from his sitting position, he made his way slowly to the door, still shaken by the experience and slipped out into the hallway unnoticed. Making sure he locked up as Harry asked him to, he took a deep breath that drew him up to full height. Frank slowly let the air out as he composed himself. He reached inside his jacket and patted the wood grips of his .38. The action surprised him as he looked down at the hand still inside his jacket and still lightly ran his fingers over the wood. He drew another deep breath, steeled his resolve, and then headed back downstairs. When he made eye contact with Harry, he nodded his chin up as his bottom lip pushed against his top and held back his expected wink so that no one would suspect he and Harry were somehow in cahoots with one another.

Frank reluctantly headed out to Flamingo Park to face his greater fear.

6

Whirlpools sometimes happen when two fast-flowing currents are traveling in opposing directions. When these forces of nature come into contact with one another, they are obliged to interact by swirling around each other. Sometimes, one current will form a downdraft, creating a vortex and drawing objects in and under the water's surface. Known as maelstroms, these powerful currents are often found in the ocean, forming as the currents created by tides are present near inlets that empty their water into the deeper body, especially during strong ocean winds.

Life sometimes creates maelstroms between two opposing people.

The one place Frank did not want to be at this moment was standing outside the Mission Revival-style house in Flamingo Park, downtown West Palm Beach. The smooth stucco and arched entryways, all shaded by overhanging eaves and cooled by a red clay tile roof, were a painful memory for him. However, this was the residence of the only expert in archaeology that he knew personally. It is the home of Archibald Forester, or the Reverend Archibald Forester, a retired Episcopal priest with a Ph.D. in Archaeology from Harvard. He also happened to be the former father-in-law of one Frank Lobeck, private eye.

Reverend Forester did not like Frank; in fact, it could be said he hated Frank. As far as he was concerned, Hell was not hot enough for the likes of one Frank Lobeck. He blamed Frank for the divorce of his daughter, Lilly, and her eventual destruction from alcohol, which resulted in the death of his only granddaughter, Beth. Lilly's grief and bitterness over separating from Frank led her to drive drunk one night with Beth in the backseat of the car. As Lilly was about to cross the bridge over Boynton Beach inlet on SR 140 heading south out of Manalapan, she swerved to miss a dog, she thought, the alcohol causing her to overcompensate. Then, her car went airborne off the east side of the highway just before the bridge, plunging into the strong dark current of the inlet. As the saltwater poured in through the rolled-down window of the driver's side door, Lilly's drunken panic went into action as her instinct to survive pushed her out the window and into the outgoing tide waters that rushed her decision to get free of the sinking tomb. She barely managed to keep her head above water as the determined current pushed her more and more toward the swirling whirlpool that made its home where the ocean's east winds met the outgoing current at the entrance to the inlet. Adrenaline gave her the strength to wrestle the current and forced it to lose its hold momentarily as she reached out and clung to the barnacle-covered jetty. The razor-sharp shells of the tidal crustaceans crowding the jetty wall sliced through the skin of her hands like a surgeon's knife. The current reclaimed its powerful capture on Lilly and rolled her along the jetty wall, tearing small pieces of flesh as well as shredding clothing as it did, but suddenly, the movement toward the whirlpool ceased as her body slammed into the steel cable with one end attached to an iron post cemented into the jetty's boardwalk and the other end anchored to the bottom of the jetty's man-made wall that held firmly a buoy marking the dangers of the wall for boats coming in and out of the inlet. As she clung to the cable, she did not notice her car speeding below her feet toward the ocean's bottom.

Somehow, the alcohol still numbed the pain, and Lilly pulled herself out and onto the jetty's broad walkway. The darkness of the water now matched the darkness of her vision as she lay there gasping for breath and unable to remember what was so important in the backseat of her car.

The next morning, Lilly woke screaming, remembering through the alcoholic haze what she had left in the back seat of the car.

Morning fishermen found Lilly bleeding and weeping on the jetty boardwalk. Later, divers found Beth still in the back seat about a hundred yards out and away from the inlet's northside jetty. The car was lying upside down, jammed into the coral reef twenty-five feet down on the ocean floor during low tide. It lay among the ruins of several boats that did not navigate the currents safely over the years.

There was more than just wreckage of wood and metal. In the distance, lying purposefully on the ocean floor, facing away from the wreckage, was a large object more dangerous than the currents.

Standing there in the doorway, Frank wished silently for another way to get the answers he needed. But he didn't have a choice because he needed answers, and he needed them now.

This coin might be a clue as to what happened in Betty Lou's room that fateful night. And he knew Archie well enough to know that the mystery of the coin would be enough to get him focused on its otherworldly powers and not focusing on the hatred he had toward Frank.

Frank hesitated at first, but then he knocked on the heavy oak door as he noticed the curtain on the window next to the door moved slightly.

A voice from within shouted, "What the hell brings you to my door? I thought I made it clear I didn't ever want to see you again."

"I remember, Archie, and I don't care to see you either, and if it wasn't important, I wouldn't be here. You can bet on that," Frank responded with his best contempt and at a level that the neighbors could hear. He knew Archie wouldn't be able to go on shouting, letting everyone know his business in this nosy community. Frank was counting on Archie's reputation as a former pastor to force him to open the door. And it worked.

Both men stood in the doorway, staring at each other, trying not to be the first one to blink. Frank was good at stare-downs; it came with the occupation, but he didn't want to get into a stare-down with this man. He knew from experience that it would only lead to more blame and more hatred. Frank looked deep into the cold, hard eyes of this former *man of God* and one-time relative and wondered where all the lectured forgiveness went and just how long would it be lost. He wondered if Archie would ever see the events of divorce and the loss of an only child were just as hard, no . . . even harder for Frank. But Frank was not here to dredge up the past, so he got right to the reason for the unannounced visit.

"Listen, Archie,I didn't come here to fight with you; I came because I got something that I figure you're the only one around who could know something about this," Frank said as he reached into his front pocket and carefully took out the wrapped coin. He opened the handkerchief slowly, being careful not to touch its contents.

It was as if the coin spoke to Archie. It whispered for him to lean in close and examine it with the delicacy of observation that made him an honored archaeologist. Just as the lure to possess the object swept over Archie, he reached out to pluck the coin from Frank's handkerchief, and immediately, the lure was snatched away as Frank quickly closed his draped hand around it and shoved the coin back into his trouser pocket.

Standing back up quickly, Archie leered at Frank and swore, "What the hell, you bastard! You want me to examine it or not? I can't very well tell you anything from inside your pocket."

Frank steadied himself from the verbal insult and looked hard at Archie, but a tone of skepticism was in his voice. "Archie, before I let you examine the coin, I got to warn you about its somewhat, I don't know, somewhat special powers.I mean, the coin ain't natural. It seems it has this ability or bizarre power to expose your deepest guilts and break you down till you no longer want to live. I know this all sounds strange, but I'm just warning you before you touch it with your bare skin."

Archie looked at Frank with an expression of disbelief at first, but then his countenance changed, and he began to smile. It was as if he recognized something in what Frank had said. Something from years ago in some forgotten textbook stuck away in the myth section of his library. Then he asked, "Frank, you say this coin when you touch it, causes one to feel the guilt and shame of one's sins?"

"Yeah, I know it sounds weird,and I can't explain it any other way, but that's exactly what happened when I touched it."

Archie's smile was no longer out of amusement for his perceived lunacy in his former son-in-law; he now speculated that Frank had stumbled on to something that had been hinted at among archaeologist for many, many years.

Looking at Frank without his usual disgust, Archie said with a suppressed glee in his voice, "What you have here is possibly one of the original thirty pieces of silver received for the betrayal of Jesus. I believe what you have is one of the Judas coins."

7

"Frank, you ol' gum-shoe. What's doin'? Come join us and have asmell from the barrel," Joe declared in a loud voice over the crowd at the table while he raised his glass to the detective.

The rest of the crowd raised their glasses as Frank moved across the room. Tipping his hat with a wink, Frank smiled at the table of regulars and said, "Maybe later, Joe, but I got folks to meet," and then he headed to the bar.

Nodding his chin to Kelsey, he ordered, "A Brooklyn there, my friend. Got some folks comin'. Could we set them up in back?"

Pointing with his thumb to the back room, Kelsey said, "They're already set up and waitin', and they already started drinkin'. They been drinkin' since before I opened up, Frank. You better get in there and corral them before they get out of hand. Say, Frank, you know who is hangin' back there? It's Hemingway his-self!"

"Yeah, I know. I invited him to help me figure out some things about the case that aren't coming together. Put his tab on mine, ok, Kelsey."

43

"Marla ain't gonna like that."

"An extra drink ain't goin'to kill the office budget. Besides, Marla knows I use the office coffers to sweeten clients' wallets and to get snitches to spill."

"I know that Frank, but it ain't just one guy back there. There's several gents back there drinkin'. He's got the whole Crook Factory with him. Go on back; I'll bring ya yur drink in a sec."

Entering the back room, Frank was immediately struck by the amount of noise that whiskey and rum produced. It seemed everyone was talking at once, and each one shouting louder to be heard over the next voice. Seated at a large round oak table was the man himself, Papa Hemingway, holding court and out shouting everyone.

He was dressed in a lightweight cotton Khaki-colored safari jacket with the sleeves rolled up and secured by the Swiss tabs. Under the jacket, he wore an untucked multi-colored Viyella button-down shirt with the sleeves pushed up to where the jacket sleeves stopped at the elbows. Below the table, Hemingway wore pleated, double-belted Gurkha shorts and traditional espadrilles, a casual canvas slipper. Frank made a mental note that Hemingway not only created a style in his minimalist novels but in his appearance as well. Frank knew Marla would ask about Hemingway's appearance after she berated him for not bringing her along to meet her favorite author. Frank cared too much for Marla to allow her to be subject to this well-known womanizer.

Raising his glass in the direction of Frank as he entered the room, Hemingway acknowledged, "Welcome, Frank. You better get in here and catch up. I'm afraid the boys here are very advanced in their liquor. Come sit here," Hemingway shouted as he pulled out the chair next to him while lambasting the occupant, a Basque seaman nicknamed Sinbad, for not rising quick enough to relinquish his place at the round table. The table was round, but Hemingway was clearly the head. That is the way Hemingway's Camelot operated.

Waving his hand around the table, Hemingway boasted with a wide grin, "Allow me to introduce you to the Crook Factory. These are my compatriots in crime and espionage during this damned war! Next to me, here we got Winston Guest," Hemingway said, pointing at the man to his left. "My boys labeled him Wolfie, and next to him, we have Gregorio, my first mate and cook. And that's Patchi, a former Basque pelota player, who just informed us he has a cousin here who works in a brothel." Then, leaning back on two legs of his chair, Hemingway laughed so hard his barreled chest managed to test the buttons on his shirt as he proclaimed, "Man, the company I keep." Setting his chair back down on four legs, he whispered to Frank, "Pelota is like the game jai alai." He winked then continued, "and next to him is Marine Sergeant Don Saxon, my radio operator. And that gentleman is Sinbad, whose real name is Juan Dunabeitia," Hemingway said, raising his glass to the disgruntled man who had to give up his seat of honor. "And finally, that young one over there," he said as he pointed to a dark-haired boy no more than eleven years old drinking along with the rest of the Crook Factory, "is my youngest son, Gregory. His brother, Patrick, is back home in Cuba with Martha."

Slapping Frank on the back with his right hand, Hemingway shouted for everyone to lower the volume, signaling his drunken compadres with his left hand as one would conduct an orchestra; then, he turned to Frank with a grin that broadened his beard, and he bellowed, "Well, you ol' shamus how's the case coming? You catch that bastard that murdered that young lady?"

"Still trying to put the pieces together, Mr. Hemingway."

Laughing from deep in his barreled chest, Hemingway slapped the table hard with both hands at once. "Did you hear that, boys, Mr. Hemingway? Finally, some respect around here." Then, turning to Frank as he continued to laugh, he demanded, "Just call me Papa. Everyone else always calls me Papa."

Kelsey arrived with Frank's drink and began to take orders for refills. Making eye contact with Frank, Kelsey used his chin to circle the crowd and then, pursing his lips together, glanced down at the order book to remind Frank of the tab and then nodded his head up and down till he saw that Frank got his meaning. Marla!

"What's that you're drinking there, Mr., eh, Papa?

"It's something I came up with while we spend all that time on the *Pilar* at sea. I call it the Papa Doble. You see, we drink a lot, and some of us need to cut back," Hemingway said with a smile as he nodded to Saxon.

Saxon raised his glass to the captain of the *Pilar* and smiled back as he quickly downed another of the many already emptied in front of him.

"It's a bit of rum and a little grapefruit juice with a slice of lime, maraschino, and some crushed ice. Quite refreshing, but a little slow in bringing the head that comes quicker with whiskey." Then, lowering his voice as he leaned close to Frank's face, Hemingway spoke carefully, "But sacrifices have to be made for the sake of the crew. Like I said, we drink a lot," then, throwing his head back, he let out a thunderous laugh that everyone joined in on even if they didn't know why they were laughing.

Frank smiled to himself as he thought that being a member

of this crew would do him no good. Unlike Hemingway, Frank wouldn't be able to sacrifice for the sake of his friends. The only one to keep him in dry dock lately was Marla, and even then, she often wrestled the glass from his hand by distracting him with her feminine wiles.

"So, tell me, Papa, about this venture you all are on. Just what is it you hope to accomplish? And what about this sighting you made the other night off the coast of Palm Beach?"

Leaning back into his chair and tucking his bearded chin into his chest while sipping his drink, Hemingway looked over the rim of his glass around the table and smiled with admiration. Admiration that a father might have over his children. Then, slowly, Hemingway began:

"There were several events that sparked the idea in me. First, you remember the torpedoing of that British tanker, the Eclipse, right outside of the inlet at Boynton Beach last May? It was a German U-boat laying on the bottom of the ocean just off the reef near a bunch of wreckage so that no one noticed."

Frank winced at his own dark memory of Boynton Beach.

"Well, that was not the only ship or transport sunk off the coast, and the Florida Straight on into the Gulf and down around Cuba. Hell, there's been sinkings throughout the Caribbean down to South America." Then, leaning forward with his arms on the table and emphasizing with his finger stabbing Frank in the chest, Hemingway continued in a somber tone.

"These Nazi sonsabitches would also surface on private fishing boats and order the hands off into lifeboats and then raid the boats of any supplies and fresh food and water and then blast the boats with their big deck guns and sink it. Sometimes, they would even murder the crew, who were only just making a living for their families. Well, hell! I just couldn't stand it anymore, and then our government put out the call for any private boats to patrol the seas close to shore and to report any sightings. You remember the Q-boats used in WWI for luring U-boats to the surface and then breaking all hell on them with their hidden guns. Well, that's what got me to thinkin', and so I assembled the Crook Factory to do the reconnaissance and then loaded up the *Pilar* with weapons to do the same thing. Lure them into the surface and then blast them to hell!"

Hemingway raised his glass to the men and the boy around the table, and everyone joined suit and lifted their glasses with a shout, "Blow all the Nazis' sonsabitches to hell!"

Turning his attention back to Frank, Hemingway continued, "I got a hold of the embassy down in Cuba and got them to provide us with bazookas, grenades, and Thompson machine guns. Hell, we even got us a bomb shaped like a coffin with handles on the flying bridge. Patchi there will toss the bomb along with some hand grenades down the conning tower once we pull alongside and rid the bridge of any Nazis that come out on deck with our Thompsons. You see, the *Pilar* looks like it's just out fishing, and when the Nazis surface looking for fresh supplies, we strike!" Hemingway shouted as he slapped the table, upsetting several drinks.

"I aim to kill as many Nazis as I can for what they are doin' to innocent Americans just out here botherin' no one. Damn it! We just want to be left alone so we can fish for marlin. You fish there, Frank?" Hemingway asked but didn't allow Frank to respond before continuing:

"You ever hooked a beautiful marlin and fought her for hours and hours to dominate her as she resists your every move and advance? And when she finally gives up out of exhaustion, she then offers herself up to you. Then when you bring her carefully but quickly on board before she could change her mind and run away again, you admire her form as she lay there in all her beauty and majesty, just lookin' up at you while she relinquished her entire being to you, you then realize that you are the master of this damn creature. Man! That's the most beautiful experience ever." Hemingway then smiled at something that only he understood as he raised his glass again to the crowd in salute. The Crook Factory raised their glasses to support whatever it was their leader was celebrating even when they didn't know and many times didn't care as long as the liquor kept pouring.

Frank raised his eyebrows instead of his glass as he thought that Hemingway was not talking about just fishing for marlin. He knew the man's reputation. Again, he was glad Marla was not here. Frank knew married or not, Hemingway saw everything in life as a sport. There was always game to pursue and dominate.

"So what about this sighting you fellas had the other night off Palm Beach? Tell me about that."

"Yeah, that was interesting. I was bringing the *Pilar* up to Rybovich's boat works for some work on the driveshaft and for them to do some work on the engine and the rings that needed replacing. I've known ol' John and his boys for some time now, and they do a first-rate job. They know boats, and they know fishing. We were coming north up the coast towards the Breakers Hotel, and it was already dark. I was trying to get to the Palm Beach inlet to cut back into the Intercoastal Waterway and to Rybovich's dock when I saw this raft beaching just below the south side of the hotel. Like I said, it was already dark, and I was in a hurry, but I did notice the someone getting out of the raft was in what looked like a suit jacket or could have been a uniform with brass buttons and all. Not real sure. The lights from the *Pilar* weren't really aimed at him good, but he looked like he didn't want to be seen. He kept crouching low, and then he ran into the scrub brush and disappeared. I didn't think too much about it at the time, but later, I figured that he could have been a German spy dropped off out at sea by a U-boat. I had heard about that happening up in Jacksonville, but they eventually caught those Krauts. The next thing I know is I'm sittin' in the lobby of the Pennsylvania, and I run into you, and now here we are."

8

St. Ann's has been located on North Olive Avenue since 1902. The original location was on the corner of Rosemary and Datura Street. It was later moved by church members with a team of oxen to its permanent location on the North Olive property donated by railroad magnate and oil tycoon Henry Flagler. After some time had passed, a much larger sanctuary was built, and the older building became the St. Ann School in 1925. The sanctuary is graced with spectacular ornamental stained-glass windows made by the artisans of Franz Mayer of Munich, who made the stained-glass windows of countless Roman Catholic churches around the world. The current religious order priest, Father Peter, had arrived at the church less than a year ago from Ohio as a temporary appointment while it was decided by the bishops who would run the parish. There was a reservation about Father Peter and his ordination by one of the bishops within the council, but unfortunately, that bishop died suddenly, and no one among the council knew why there was an objection, so Father Peter remained without question.

After spending any amount of time with Archie, Frank needed to clear his head and his heart. His pain of loss for Beth had driven him to dark depths that almost destroyed him once. A darkness that Frank had never been able to relinquish. It haunted him in the depths of night when sleep evaded him and nightmares abounded. It haunted him with unfathomed depths of guilt that the Church was unable to release him from. It even haunted him in the arms of Marla, who tried unsuccessfully to soothe his demon-fueled fever of contrition. Frank had blamed Lilly for his loss of Beth, yet he martyred himself with shame for his part in the divorce. Lilly's fate was punishment enough for her crime of negligence. She was locked away forever upstate in a mental institution, having forgotten and still trying to remember what she had left in the back seat of her car as it plunged into the dark waters of Boynton Inlet. But Frank always believed it was not enough. He wanted her suffering to equal his or perhaps surpass his own. And Archie . . . well, Archie helped compound Frank's guilt. He had a way of sending Frank back into the hopelessness of his soul, floundering in a bottle and then pushing and holding Frank's head under until the liquor drowned him as well.

Beth drowned once; Frank drowns daily.

But this time, Betty Lou had provided him with a reason not to drown again, at least for the present. Right now, he needed to understand the reason for the coin Archie had believed to be an ancient religious myth and what it was doing in Betty Lou's room. He also needed to visit with Mr. Wilson again. Frank had a lot of questions that he needed Wilson to answer. He knew he would need to be delicate when it came to Betty Lou's character. Fathers often don't see or believe their little girls can be women—women with their own set of needs, their own set of desires. But instead, he found himself standing in front of St. Ann's. Frank knew he needed to talk with Father Peter, but the shadow of the cross from the sanctuary roof glared down at him, accusing him of betrayal. The coin in his pocket agreed with the church. Somehow, Archie had managed to align with the church and long ago stole away Frank's childhood faith. Lilly had a hand in that, too. Frank worried Father Peter would also point his finger at him, but the questions wouldn't wait.

"Excuse me, could you tell me where I might find Father Peter?" Frank asked a young nun who was headed in the direction of St. Ann's school.

Pointing to the church, she replied as she hurried along without stopping, "Try the main church. He's probably in the sanctuary praying before confessions." Then she continued her hurry and was gone.

Frank walked hesitantly into the vestibule and wondered how many years it took to void the practice of using the sign of the cross. Still, instinct and old habit kicked in, and he found himself doing the sign without conscious thought. Looking at the votive stand of candles before the statue of St. Ann, the mother of the Blessed Virgin Mary, the mother of Christ, Frank noticed a kneeling priest with his head bowed in prayer. Out of respect for something he no longer practiced, Frank took a seat in a back pew and waited for the priest to finish his prayers.

When the priest rose and headed to the sacristy room behind the altar, Frank, too, rose and made his way quietly down to the front to make his inquiries. He found the priest attending to his vestments in preparation for the next mass.

"Father Peter?" Frank asked.

Startled, the priest turned and showed signs of guilt that the confessional prayers had not erased.

"Sorry, I wasn't aware anyone was in the building. You gave me a fright."

"Why would a priest have reason to be afraid? Guilty of something there, Father?" Frank said with an added smile and a wink.

The priest did not smile back.

"Name's Frank Lobeck. I'm a private investigator lookin' into the murder of one Betty Lou Wilson. I understand from her father you were one of the last ones to see her alive. Mind if I ask a few questions?"

With what appeared to be a deliberate hesitation, Father Peter then offered his own contrived smile and responded with, "Miss Wilson? Yes, I remember her attending at least one mass and, before that, a confessional, but beyond that, I'm afraid I don't know anything about her. I met her father, Mr. Wilson, but as I told him, I really didn't know the young woman. I'm afraid, Mr. Lobeck, I can't help you any more than that."

Frank noted that the priest dismissed him awfully quick as if he knew more than he was telling or perhaps willing to tell. He was not sure as to the exact reason why he became suspicious of any and all clergy, but nevertheless, it was how he viewed the world now. Again, he blamed Archie and sometimes Lilly for his jaded view of the Church.

"I'm just trying to establish a reason why someone would want to kill a nice young girl like Betty Lou. Surely you would want to help bring some peace to her loved ones who are suffering for some answers, wouldn't you, Father Peter? I mean, ain't that the business you're in, bringing peace to troubled souls?" Frank asked with a twist of sarcasm.

"Like I told Mr. Wilson, we just exchanged pleasantries after Mass one time, and what she shared in the confessional is sacred and cannot be disclosed. But I will tell you this she was troubled over someone she had recently met, but that's all I can say about it. Now, if you would excuse me, I have to get ready for confessions."

And again, Frank noticed he was being dismissed by this priest. Frank instinctively thought Father Peter knew more than he was telling. Using the sanctity of the confessional was too easy, Frank thought. Still, he had an uneasiness about this priest, and he didn't believe it came strictly from his jaded view of the Church.

As Frank turned to leave, Father Peter said suddenly, "Listen, Frank, is it? I know that Mr. Wilson needs some comfort from his loss. Anyone who has lost loved ones needs release, or they might do harm to those who they believe deserve it." Father Peter looked off toward the ceiling as if perhaps he was remembering his own loss. "So, if it helps, Betty Lou had recently met a German where she worked. But that's all I'm going to say about that. Good day, Frank; I really have to be going."

And with that, Father Peter slipped out into the sanctuary and entered the confessional booth. There was already a line of penitents waiting to feel better about their choices in life.

Frank now had a lead—a German.

Heading west a block from the church and down South Dixie to the Southlands Motor Lodge, Frank arrived at the motel Wilson had said he was staying at when they had met earlier at the bar. A green 1940 four-door Dodge Sedan with Ohio plates was parked out front of the room. Frank noticed road-salt rust on the bottom of the driver's side front door. He understood then Wilson as a hard-working man and remembered Wilson's "whatever it costs" was more from deep love and desperation than easy ability. He knocked on the motel door number sixteen. The door faced Dixie. Mr. Wilson came to the door after the first knock; he didn't appear to have slept any. A towel on the bathroom floor showed he at least had showered.

"Sorry to bother you, Mr. Wilson, but I got a couple of questions if you don't mind?" "Come on in," Wilson said from a voice that was weary for over three days without proper sleep and then looking at Frank with the face of a desperate man capable of destroying anyone who harmed his own, he asked, "Did you learn who murdered my baby girl?"

"I've talked to the police and other folks chasin' down leads, but I need to ask if Betty Lou ever mentioned meeting anyone new? Perhaps a man?"

Walking over to the bed and sitting on its edge, Wilson bent from the waist and leaned his tired frame on his arms, which were resting on his legs. He bowed his head as if he were asking God for an end to this nightmare and then looked up at Frank with tear-filled eyes; he said slowly and softly, "She mentioned once the last time my wife spoke with her that she had met a fella. I didn't like not knowin' who this fella was seein' my girl, but I couldn't do nuthin' about it then. My wife said I had to trust her and remember how we raised her." Locking eyes with Frank so that there was no chance he was misunderstood, he continued, "We raised her right. She wouldn't uh got mixed up with no one who wasn't on the up and up, you understand. She was a good girl!"

"Did she say anything to your wife about this guy? Did she mention his name or, where he was from, or what he did for a living? Anything would be helpful."

Looking down again at the gray and white checkered tile floor in the motel room, Mr. Wilson appeared to be thinking hard before he raised his head and said, "All she told my wife was that she was in love with this guy and his name was Hans," and then staring off into the ceiling he added with regret, "and that he was from Germany."

9

"Hmmm, you're the second one to mention a German. Father Peter also said Betty Lou had recently met a man who was German," Frank said absently, almost as if he were talking out loud to himself, running the pieces over in his mind as was his habit. He knew that he would have to find this German and see how the pieces fit. Everything had to fit in Frank's mind, or he couldn't rest until it did. It's what made him a good detective.

Turning and interrupting Frank's meditation, Wilson asked, "You think it was him what hurt my little girl?" Then putting his fatigue aside and rising with renewed determination like a wounded soldier who refuses to give ground, Wilson clinched his fists, and with verbal obscenities, he vowed, "I'll kill that damned Kraut sonofabitch for killing my Betty Lou. The only good German is a damn dead German, as far as I'm concerned. I might be too old to fight over there, but I still can take 'em out when they come here and threaten harm on my family."

Then, looking at Frank, he continued as he headed to the door, "You know where we can have a conversation with this so-called German bastard?"

Frank grabbed Wilson by the arm and spun him around where they were facing each other. He saw the rage in Wilson's eyes. He knew if he didn't choose his words carefully, he could have this damaged father looking for revenge—evidence be damned!

"Listen, Mr. Wilson, we can't go out and bang heads until we know more. Let me do my job, and I'll track down this German fella and see what's what. Okay? Besides, we don't know yet if he had anything to do with Betty Lou's death. I'll find out, and you stay put. I'll be in touch. I promise."

Frank left the dejected man standing in the doorway of the motel room. He checked his rearview mirror several times for the green sedan to make sure Wilson hadn't decided to follow him. Wilson must have stayed put, but Frank knew he had to work fast and get some answers. He wasn't sure how long he could keep that broken father at bay.

Frank figured that he needed to talk to Harry at the Pennsylvania Hotel to see if he knew anything about this so-called German. Harry knew the comings and goings of everyone at the hotel, and he had told Frank that he admired Betty Lou, if only from a distance. Harry always said he kept his distance from the hired help; he only focused on those with the means to advance him to the lifestyle he envied.

"Yeah, I remember Betty Lou was seein' some guy, and he weren't from around here. Spoke with some kinda accent, could of been German, I reckon, but I ain't sure for certain. All I know is Enid didn't take to him right away. She never said why, just that she didn't trust him when she first met him. But later, it seemed she came around and decided he was alright. Again, I ain't sure what changed her mind on him, just that eventually, she said he was okay for Betty Lou. That was enough for me. You know Enid. If she likes you, you're okay; if she don't, then

Katie bar the door. Ya know what I mean, don't ya, Frank," he said, lifting his chin and grinning. " You might wanna ask Enid about him."

"Thanks, Harry. I owe ya. Where can I find Enid?"

"Think she's down in the laundry right now. Either that or she's workin' on some new hire, makin' sure they get it right. She sure runs a tight ship. That Enid don't nuthin' get by her. She'll know ifn' that guy was German or not." Then, looking over Frank's shoulder, he said as he patted Frank's arm, "Gotta go there, Frank. Mrs. Carlisle is on the prowl, and I need a dinner date for Thursday."

Frank smiled as he headed toward the laundry. He wished he had half of Harry's energy and charm when he was around Marla. It seems all he could bring to the relationship was a shoulder rub as a prelude to a dinner at the hash house and then off to Marla's apartment for his own selfishness. Frank never stayed till morning. Marla always wished he would. She made good pancakes.

As he approached the laundry, Frank heard voices arguing. He thought he recognized one voice he hadn't heard in quite some time. It sounded like Hector from the Sunrise Hall down in Fort Lauderdale from a case he had worked on a while back. Frank remembered the Cuban whose job it was to protect the girls at the brothel, but for some reason, the night of the murder, he was preoccupied with one of the other girls who worked there.

Frank had a good memory; it's what made him a good detective.

As he entered the laundry, he saw Hector towering over a

frightened girl in a maid's uniform, crouching with her arms raised up over her head in a defensive position as she warded off blows from Hector. Frank rushed to intercede and grabbed Hector's arm to prevent the blow to the girl just as Enid entered. She, too, must have heard all the noise and grabbed Hector from behind and slung him into the wall away from Frank and the horrified girl.

"I warned you before, Hector 'bout comin' round here botherin' my girls. I told you what I'd do if'n I caught you here again." Then, grabbing a mop from a nearby bucket, Enid began to let loose some serious blows on Hector's back, sending the man to his knees and crying out for her to stop.

Frank was surprised at Enid's rage in protecting one of her girls.

"Now get the hell outta my hotel, and don't you come back," Enid shouted with fury in her voice. "If I catch you here again, Hector, you're gonna wish your mama had scraped you out of her after your daddy knocked her up. Now get!"

Hector crawled slowly to the door as he whimpered in pain. He grabbed the door handle and pulled himself up slowly, and then he surprised everyone as he reached into his belt and pulled out a gun, pointing it at Enid.

"I'll kill you, you damn bitch! No one's gonna beat me like that and get away with it. No one you hear!"

Frank had been kneeling and attending to the broken girl when he saw her eyes grow wider with fear, looking over his shoulder. From his crouched position, he spun around to face Hector and, without hesitation, pulled his gun and pointed it at Hector's chest. Demanding as he cocked the hammer, he said slowly, "Lose the heater unless you want to gain some weight!"

Hector looked past Enid into Frank's eyes, and what he saw

convinced him to lower his weapon as he backed out of the doorway. Then he snarled, "This ain't over, Enid, not by a long shot. You better sleep with one eye open 'cause some night I'll come creepin' in and finish this. You're gonna regret this, Enid." And then he turned his anger on Frank, and pointing his index finger with his thumb raised cocked like a pistol, he threatened, "And you better watch your back, tough guy. I'm gonna finish this between us. You mark my word; I'm gonna finish it!" And then he smiled as he mimicked the sound, "Bang! Bang!" He raised his finger to his lips and blew on the end.

Then he ran off down the hallway and out a side door and was gone.

Enid bent down to check on the girl's battered face. She pulled a soft cotton handkerchief from her apron pocket and, wetting it with her tongue, gently wiped the tears and blood with all the tenderness a mother would use on her child, who had come running to her after being accosted by some neighborhood bully. Frank couldn't hear what Enid was muttering under her breath to the girl, but he knew she was offering comfort and absolute protection from the threat. He stood and went down the hallway to make sure Hector was not hiding in the alleyway, plotting his revenge. When he was sure the Cuban bully had left, he went back to check on Enid and her charge. Enid had gotten the girl to her feet and had her sitting in a chair. She gently brushed the girl's hair out of her eyes with her fingers, and Frank smiled at the tenderness of this large and powerful black woman. He chuckled to himself, thinking that he would not want to tangle with her. He wasn't convinced he'd come out on top.

"I take it you knew him from somewhere. Mind filling me in?"

Not taking her eyes off the trembling girl, Enid spoke without turning her head. "Yeah, I knowed him. His name being Hector, and he used to work here a while back. He was no good then, and he ain't got no better. Damn bastard comin' 'round here messin' with my girls." Then she turned and looked Frank in the eyes with her own, revealing her resolute will, "He come 'round, here again, I aim to kill him! Mark my word; I aim to kill him dead!"

"Tell me more about this Hector."

Helping the girl to her feet, Enid whispered in her ear to go home and take a few days off. She reassured her that everything would be okay when she came back. Watching the girl as she shuffled slowly and looking right then left down the hallway before she headed out the doorway, Enid then turned and faced Frank. She eyed him slowly as she cocked her head to one side and thought about what she would reveal to Frank. It's true Frank had interceded with Hector, but Enid was being careful with what all she knew; Frank could tell she held back something, and his gut told him that what she knew was more than just about this Hector guy. He figured he better tread lightly with Enid; he didn't want to get between her and her mop.

Sitting down heavily in the chair as if the weight of the memories she carried were more than she could bear at times, Enid first looked down at her hands. It was then Frank saw that the beating she gave Hector came from hands that were scared and calloused. This truly was a woman who knew hardships and hard living. She turned her hands over, examining both sides as if they carried responsibilities she refused to allow others to carry for her. Then, as if she were washing away the stain of vengeance, she rubbed them clean on her apron front and looked up at Frank.

"Hector worked here a few years back. Worked as a gardener, and I thought at first he had promise. But I noticed not long after he started here he started makin' the girls nervous. I asked around, but no one would tell me what he said or did. I figured he was threatening them if they told. So I made me a trap and watched him from outta sight. I heard him use that smooth talk on some of the girls. You know the kind a man will use when he wants something more than a body is willin' to give. I started to notice the girls were at first smilin' at his charm, but later, they was more frightened by him. He seemed to find somethin' against them, but I still wasn't sure. Finally, there was this young gal named Tina," Enid paused and breathed in slow and deep when she pronounced the name. Frank thought he noticed her eyes begin to water. Continuing, "This girl Tina, she came to work here. Hector took a real keen interest in her. She was a real good worker. Always came in early and never turned her back, even on the nastiest clean-up jobs. But one day, she just up and quit. She didn't give no reason, just didn't show up. I went by her house where she stayed, and when she came to the door, I noticed she had had a beaten. I figured it was Hector, so I just out and asked if'n he done that to her. She said it weren't none of my business, and then Hector came to the door and told me to get. He said he and Tina was movin' to Lauderdale and that they was gonna work for some other place run by a lady named Nora. I knew Tina wasn't wantin' to go; I could tell it in her eyes, but she just smiled a little, and then Hector shut the door on me. Ever once in a while, he would come slinkin' back up here from Lauderdale, and I'd catch him talkin' up one of my girls, and I'd run him off, but the next thing I knowed, they'd be gone. I swore that one day I'd catch his sorry ass and give him a beatin', but until today that never did happen."

Enid then stood up and pressed her apron with her scared hands as if reading herself for whatever job was in need of doing, then she said without looking at Frank, "And that's the story of that bastard, Hector. Now, if'n you'll pardon me, I gots to check on my girls. This place don't run itself."

Then, without giving Enid a chance to exit, Frank asked, "What can you tell me about the German and Betty Lou?"

Enid stopped and turned slowly back to Frank and looked hard at him as if he didn't have the right to ask such a question. Then she asked cautiously, "Who told ya he was German?"

10

"Who told ya he was German?" Enid asked with suspicion in her voice and clinching her fists while facing Frank.

Frank glanced around the room for the mop she used on Hector before he would answer her.

He was hesitant at first. His profession made him that way, but he told Enid, "I been hired by Betty Lou's father to look into her death. He told me Betty Lou's mother told him about a German named Hans, who Betty Lou said she was seein'. What can you tell me about him?"

Enid looked hard into this man in front of her, wondering just how much she could trust him, how much she could reveal without telling him everything, and whether or not she needed to tell him anything. She knew there were some things that needed to be kept quiet; things best not revealed just yet, if ever. Things she promised to the desperate dying. There were people Enid felt it was hers alone to protect.

Enid let out the breath she had been holding as she looked for a chair that could support her burden. The memories that seemed from so long ago came like a summer squall out on the

Atlantic. Not quite as destructive as a full-blown hurricane, but still, there could be some damage if one doesn't prepare against the rising waters. She chose her words carefully and slowly.

"His name was Hans Metzger. Betty Lou she tells me he came to America to escape the war."

"And you believed her?"

"No, not at first. Betty Lou said she first laid eyes on him on the beach one night below the Breakers Hotel. She liked to walk there, you know, along the water there while the sun set before she had to be on stage. She was a singer, you know, and a damn good singer too. Oh, she had a fine voice. Ain't no one in Hollywood could sing the way that gal could sing," Enid said with pride in her voice as if Betty Lou was her only child. "That's how come she to be here at the Pennsylvania. She told me she answered an ad for evening entertainment at a place down in Lauderdale called the Sunrise Hall run by that no-good whore, Nora Taylor," Enid let out a snort as she uttered the woman's name. "That woman is trash, and it wouldn't harm heaven any if someone put a bullet in that woman's head. Now I'm a God-fearin' woman, you understand, and I don't reckon God takes kindly to folks what wants to hurt other folks, but the fact is, I'd be willin' to pull the trigger myself."

Enid's rage showed on her face. She breathed deep and hard through her nose while wringing her hands together as if she were wringing the neck of a chicken. Frank believed her about pulling the trigger. She clearly didn't have any love lost for Nora Taylor.

"Anyhow, where'd I quit? Oh, yeah. Betty Lou told me she had come down to Florida because of some ad she found in a trade magazine. Like I said, she was a singer, and she thought if'n she could just get a start somewhere's, she could hit the big time. Between you and me, I don't think her parents were too keen on her comin' here, but they loved their little gal and gave her five dollars that she pinned to the inside of her hat, and they put her on a bus and sent her here. Well, she knew right away that that place in Lauderdale weren't no place for the likes of her. She didn't know much of the world, but she figured it out before they got their hooks in her and skedaddled out of there and found a ride that brung her here to West Palm. That's when I found her sittin' on a bus bench cryin' to beat the band with nuthin' but a secondhand suitcase, and can you believe it, she still had that five dollars pinned inside her hat. She was a cute thang. Cute as a bug's ear, she was. Sittin' there all teary-eyed with her nose a runnin' and mumblin' 'bout how she didn't have enough money to get her back to Ohio, and she couldn't bring herself to admittin' she had been tricked and was never gonna be no singer now.

"Well, sir, I just couldn't walk away and leave her a sittin' there all night long cryin' the way she was, so I brung her to the hotel and set her up for the night in my room what I use for an office. Got her some coffee and a sandwich and tucked her in on the couch, and she just cried herself to sleep that night. The next mornin', I figured if'n she was to get back to Ohio, she'd need to get herself a job, so I up and hired her to work with my girls cleanin' rooms and workin' the laundry. She was a damn good worker too. She just jumped in and never complained about nuthin' and made me so proud. Yes, sir, she was a fine worker, that gal. Good lookin', too. The boys was just crazy 'bout her. I can see why that Taylor woman wanted her so badly. Why she even sent that Hector fella up to the hotel to try and get her to come back to Lauderdale, but I ran him off then just like I run him off today.

"Now that Betty Lou, like I said, she was a singer and a damn good singer too. She was a singin' all over this here hotel." Enid leaned back in her chair and smiled with her whole face at the memory of Betty Lou singing in those earlier days. She sat for a moment and then continued looking at the memories off in the ceiling. "You could hear her down in the laundry like she was a whole choir of angels singin' a heavenly chorus. The management heard her, too. Why they went and offered her a job a-singin' in the lounge on weeknights, and I'm tellin' you, that gal just lit up and took right off. The hotel gave her a regular salary and a room to stay in, and she got her some pretty things to wear and did her hair up. Man, she was a looker! Like I said, all da boys came round a sniffin' like a pack a hounds tryin' to tree a purty little pigeon dove. I tried to warn her 'bout them boys, but she was a likin' the attention. That's when that boy, Hans, started showin' her some interest."

Enid's face stopped smiling, and she could no longer hear the beautiful music.

Frank knew if he didn't keep Enid on track, she would wander back through her happy and sad memories and never get to what she knew about this German named Hans.

"You said you didn't trust this Hans character at first. Why is that?"

"Well, sir, ya see, it was kinda the way he up and showed up on the beach that night. Betty Lou told me she seen him a rowin' a shore in a raft straight out of the Atlantic. She said he was all bent over actin' kinda suspicious-like 'specially when he made shore. She said it was like he didn't want no one seein' him comin' in that way. Betty Lou said there was another boat comin' up the coast but that that boat was after the fact of the raft comin' in. She said that other boat was a big fishin' boat full of folks, and they slowed down a mite but kept a goin' and didn't seem to pay that raft no mind after all.

"She figured at first he must have been fishin', but he weren't dressed like no fisherman, and she didn't see him haulin' no tackle out of that there raft, just boxes, and maybe a suitcase. Betty Lou said he was dressed in a suit jacket, if you can imagine that. She said that at first, in the dim light, it almost looked like a uniform with brass buttons and such. Said he had a tie on around his neck like he was a-goin' to a dance or somethin' important. Why, Betty Lou said, he even had a hat on. Then she thought maybe he was someone from the Breakers who decided to go out for a row on the ocean. Only a damn fool or a Yankee would go out in the ocean for a row dressed in a suit jacket. Them damn Yankees! If it weren't for the money they bring ta us here, I'd say send 'em all home. Betty Lou, too, figured he probably was someone who weren't from around here and had never seen the ocean afore and decided on a whim to go out a rowin'. Only an idiot would do such a thing, but that's mostly what we gets from the North.

"Then she said that that there fella turned and saw her, and it scared her 'bout half to death as he fixed his eyes on her like he was a tryin' to memorize her, and just before she lit out back to the highway, she turned and took one more good look at him and noticed he was holdin' a gun. But for the life of her, Betty Lou couldn't understand why he was all secret 'bout it."

"So, was this guy in the raft Hans?"

"Yeah, but I'm getting' to that. It was the next night while Betty Lou was doin' her show at the Pennsylvania that she noticed the fella from the raft was sittin' in the crowd, and he was lookin' straight at her just like the other night, and this made her somewhat nervous all over again. But that Betty Lou, she's got spunk. Durin' her break, she said she just up and went straight at him to see just what he was doin' and why he had his eye on her. But as she made her way through the crowd, he up and disappeared. Then she said it was two days later, while she eatin' her dinner at the bar, that someone tapped her on the shoulder, and when she turned 'round, it was him. He just stood there lookin' at her, not sayin' a word at first. And when he spoke, said his name was Hans. Hans Metzger he told her. Betty Lou knew right away from bein' from up North his last name was German. Said he also spoke with an accent. She said that the area she was from had lots of folks that was German, and she knew a German when she heard one."

Frank asked, "So Betty Lou figured he was German, and you say that initially, she was scared of him. But her mom said she liked this guy. What changed?"

"Well, sir, you's right 'bout that. She was afraid of him when she first met him. Hell, I didn't take too kindly to him at first, either. Now Betty Lou had told me she put two and two together and figured that he was some kinda spy or saboteur or somethin'. She said she heard 'bout them U-boats a droppin' soldiers up near Jacksonville and torpedolin' that British ship down Boynton way and 'bout other troubles up and down the coastline, so she figures this German, like any German, cain't be good. That somehow he's mixed up in all that she thought. 'Sides, he did just come from out of the Atlantic on a raft, and I don't care what you say that cain't be good.

"So, he's a standin' there, and then he did what Betty Lou never in her life expected . . . he up and bowed and asked if she's like to dance. He asked her to dance right there in front of God and everybody. Can you believe that? Asked her to dance! Well, sir, Betty Lou figured if'n he was that bold bein' a spy and all, she might as well be bold back, so she just jumped up off that bar stool and told him while lookin' him straight in the eye that she would love to. And they waltzed themselves out on the dance floor, and she said he was such the gentleman that she figured even if'n he was a spy and all that, at that moment, she didn't no more care. She told me she never more feared him, and they danced the night away. Can you beat that?"

"Tell me, Enid, do you know where I can find this German . . . I mean, where I can find Hans?"

"That's just it. He done up and disappeared, and ain't nobody seen him since he left the hotel the night before Betty Lou got killed. I asked around for him after they found her. Figured he'd want to know see'ins how they was" Enid stopped, not finishing her sentence. She stopped before she said something she didn't know if this Frank fella needed to know. After all, she had made promises. Promises she intended to keep. Promises that she knew Betty Lou would want her to keep.

"I heard tell that Hans stayed at the Hotel George Washington down the block. It's owned by some German fella, but I don't recollect his name for sure. I think it's Kloepper; no, that's not right. It's Kloeppel! Yeah, Robert Kloeppel. He's some kinda big hotel owner. Got hotels all over up and down the state. Yeah, that's him, Robert Kloeppel. You go and ask that Kloeppel fella how to get a hold of Hans. I betcha he'll know for sure. I'm sure them Germans stick together now with the war and everythin'. I'd a gone down myself, but they don't like my kind down there." Then Enid muttered something under her breath that Frank couldn't quite make out, but he thought he heard something like "filthy Germans."

Frank stood and thanked Enid for the information she gave him and promised to let her know if he located Hans. Enid said he should know about Betty Lou. Frank wondered if he already did.

11

The Hotel George Washington was within walking distance of the Pennsylvania. Frank decided to stroll down the walkway next to the Intercoastal Waterway and enjoy the salt breezes along with the gentle sound of the tide waters lapping against the jetty seawall and the friendly Laughing Gulls with their kee-agh call that sounded like they were mocking him. He smiled at their playful conversation. Frank rarely smiled nowadays. He was grateful, however, for the occasional shade from the Royal palms scattered along the water's edge. Although the Florida sun is persistent, it is coveted for its vitality. It renews the spirit with its warmth soaking down past the pores into the very soul. Frank thought of the many times he would chastise tourists for lamenting the sun. He never tired of this city and its tropical charms. It truly was America's Riviera.

Frank absently scanned the walkway for a phone booth as he reached into his pocket for his handkerchief to wipe the Florida forehead sweat. He knew he needed to check in with Marla. It was his habit to call her several times a day to see if she needed anything or if a client had called trying to locate him, perhaps. He fingered the coins in his pocket for the nickel to make the call. Frank had forgotten he had put the Judas coin in his pocket with his handkerchief. He felt a tingling in his fingers at the same time he located a booth on the corner of Datura and Flagler. An overwhelming sense of guilt began slowly working its way into his thoughts. He immediately released the coin, but its effect lingered and persisted.

"Frank Lobeck Investigations. How may I help you?"

Frank's mind began to fill with regret for his hesitancy in the relationship with Marla. He couldn't stop it. He slowly spoke into the receiver, "Hey, doll. It's me. Just checkin' in to see if there are any messages and if . . . if you need me for anything?"

Swallowing hard, he already knew what she would say.

"Oh, Frank, you know I always need you," Marla cooed. She waited for his usual quip that he was needed by everyone, and she would just have to take what's left over. But it didn't come.

"Frank, honey, you okay? You sound like something's wrong. Did something happen? Is there something I can help with? Just tell me what to do, Frank."

Slowly, sadly, Frank responded, "I'm fine, babe. Just tired, that's all," but he wasn't sure he convinced her. She knew him all too well.

"Say, I know; why don't you come over tonight, hon? I'm makin' a meatloaf, and I know how much you love my meatloaf. What'd ya say? Six o'clock? I just bought a new Ellington record. We could kick our shoes off and relax on the divan. Sound good, huh?"

Frank almost choked from unresolved regret. "Umh, so sorry, babe. I'll . . . I'll have to take a rain check. Gotta keep workin' since I got some fresh dope on a suspect." Frank almost dropped to his knees in despair. His eyes filled with tears. His hand trembled holding the receiver.

The power of the coin.

Marla could always tell when Frank was lying; he knew that. But he told himself he was not totally lying. He did have a name to run down, and Marla knew when he was scouting a trail that he didn't like to get off of it. When chasing a lead, he often told her he couldn't afford to be distracted, but he never told her that she was a distraction. Frank told his clients that when he was on the case that, his motto was "No gin. No broads." But somehow, Marla always managed to slip by that rule in his loneliness.

Frank didn't like lying to Marla. His shame for this and every moment he held back the truth, the truth that he deeply loved her, settled in his throat, making it hard for him to swallow.

He desperately needed her. She was the only one who filled his voids. She brought illumination into his darkness. Or was it that he was lying to himself and getting too close to Marla made him afraid he could lose her too, just like he had lost Lilly and Beth. Frank believed he could lose his sanity as well, like Lilly, that is, if not for Marla. He believed the pain and sadness would drive him to end his miserable life, much like the first time when he touched the coin. The coin's power had impressed on him his demise was possible.

When Marla was around, when he clung tightly to her in his bed, all his fears, all his demons would recede so far down inside him that he believed they actually were rendered powerless. With Marla, they appeared to have lost their hold on him. He could sleep without waking. And with Marla, he didn't have to reach for the bottle to keep the slumber or to bring it back when it wandered away.

Did he love her? He wasn't sure, but he did know he needed her right now. He needed her more than any possibility. He needed her deeply, way down into the depths of his troubled and darkened soul. That place that all men long to have filled with the consistent reoccurrence of satisfying harmony and contentment that only real love can provide. It's the place that Frank knew used to belong to Lilly, but now that place is mostly vacant and void. Whenever he was there, in that darkness, Marla was there to reach for him and drag him back before it was too late, before the darkness could destroy him forever.

Frank thought often he might as well go ahead and make a decent woman of Marla with an official proposal, not the selfish someday we'll get married that he often relied on late in the evening when he wanted to spend the night and the whiskey wasn't convincing Marla to give Frank a breakfast preference. He knew the reason was not very romantic, but he didn't think he'd do anything for love ever again. He also knew that Marla would have nothing to do with that kind of proposal, knowing that Frank was just trying to get her off his back or onto hers. He would have to mean true love and only true love, or she wouldn't be persuaded. She believed he could get there. She figured her love would hold them until he did mean it. Frank knew the many nights he drank himself to sleep alone and woke to fix his own breakfast convinced him he needed to find love— a real love, a second time around love to fill the hole left by the first. Hell, he was good at findin' things people kept hidden or lost, so why couldn't he find the real love he needed to make Marla his wife.

Somehow, Frank knew that coin would blind him from seeing the truth that love for Marla offered.

In an effort to keep Marla from laying guilt on him by saying everyone's gotta eat sometime, Frank asked, "Has Mr. Wilson called?"

Coolly, Marla said, "No, Frank. I haven't heard from him since yesterday. You want me to check on him?"

"Not just yet. Let me run down this lead, and then I'll go see him myself. Gotta head out, babe. Sorry about dinner. Save me some of that meatloaf. It'll make a good sandwich tomorrow. See ya at the office in the morning."

There was a noticeable silence on the other end of the phone that signaled Marla's frustration.

"Sure, Frank. See you tomorrow."

The Hotel George Washington faced Flagler and the Intercoastal Waterway. It was a stone's throw to the water. Flager was a narrow road. There was a one-story walkway that ran across the front of the hotel and down both sides, supported by arched columns. Across the road was a small marina for the docked fishing boats. It had one long pier. The hotel had 160 rooms, complete with private baths, a large dining room, a lavished courtyard, and a well-stocked bar for the more wealthy patrons. It was whispered that the roof contained red aircraft warning lights that signaled messages to U-boats off the coast. Since the hotel was owned by a German family, this story was accepted as fact by the locals. This, of course, was just a rumor perpetuated by the nervous citizens during the war. No one ever ventured up to the roof to verify it. The hotel staff wouldn't allow it.

Frank entered the hotel lobby and then headed to the front desk to make his inquiries. But his phone call to Marla was compelling him to call her back and apologize. He scanned the hotel lobby for a guest courtesy phone. Frank spotted one and detoured his investigation. He didn't like to admit it, but Marla was more important to him than any case.

Finding Hans would have to wait.

12

When Marla hung up the phone with Frank, she buried her face in her hands and let the tears flow. All the years she had poured into him as his secretary, his late-night sometimes lover, his rescuing savior, they all seemed to no avail at this moment. She knew she loved him, and she wanted to believe it was unconditional; however, she also knew Frank had never gone as far as she had. She believed he could love, just that he hadn't loved her. Not the way he had loved Lilly.

She thought back to the day they first met. She was new in town, just off the bus from Boston. Marla walked over to Olive Avenue and then headed south to Gardenia Street, where she turned west to the Edgewater rooming house like her aunt had told her to. She met Mrs. Johnson, an old friend of her aunt's, who she had been corresponding with through the mail. Mrs. Johnson gave her room six. Marla believed that was her lucky number.

"It's just up the stairs, dear, and all the way to the end on the right. I put you in the room with a kitchenette and a bathroom. I believe it's fortunate that room opened up a few weeks ago, and I've been holding on to it for you because of your dear, sweet aunt. How's she doing anyways?"

But Mrs. Johnson didn't give Marla a chance to respond before she continued with her rehearsed newcomer's speech. "Now, I don't allow no men upstairs here at my boarding house. I got only single ladies up here on the second floor, and they're all respectable good church-goin' girls; the bottom floor is for married couples only, but I don't allow no children, and I don't allow no pets except maybe for a goldfish. I guess that'll be alright. A body does get lonely sometimes and needs something to care for. There's usually no cooking in the rooms, but like I said, I gave you the kitchenette with an electric skillet, a hot plate, and a percolator. Even a small ice-box. It's nuthin' fancy, mind you, but in a pinch, you could put together a simple meal. Now, you will have to do your own laundry. We got a girl that comes in once a week on Fridays to do the linens, and if you pay her, she'll do up your personal things. Now, dear, I lock the front door every night promptly at nine o'clock, so don't be late, or you'll have to sleep on the stoop. I fix a breakfast every morning at six thirty and again don't be late except on Sundays. On Sundays, I allow for folks to sleep in till seven, and the charge is included in the rent. The rent is four dollars a week and for you dear it will start in one week. That'll give you time to find a job. Well, I 'spect you'll be wantin' to go on up and get yourself settled and put your things away and freshen up a bit, then come on back down, and we'll have us a cup of tea and a good chat about that dear sweet aunt of yours. Mercy me, it was just your lucky day when that room opened up. I dare say the city's full of folks nowadays, and there aren't hardly no respectable rooms available anywhere. I dare say it's a whole heap better than some of the awful places down near that dance hall, the Sunset Auditorium. Mercy, the folks that's movin' into West Palm sure is spicin' up the neighborhood. Live and let live, that's what I always say, but I remember the day when folks knew their place, and they lived in it, too. The things that people do down at them dance halls nowadays is pitiful. Bringin' in jazz orchestras from up north and dancin' that jitterbug or whatever they're a callin' it nowadays. Now, I believe if'n the Good Lord had intended his people to carry on that way he'd a put it in the Bible. Best keep away from that side of town. Not a place for a good Christian girl like yourself. You do go to church, don't you, dear? We got us a new priest down at St. Ann's, and believe you me, he don't put up with no shenanigans. Well, look at the time. I got to get supper ready for folks, and here I been standin' a talkin' your ear off, and you probably just want to get yourself up to check out your room and get you a bit of rest before you meet the rest of the folks that room here. Mercy, I got me some good people that live here. Now, go on up, dear go on and mind that step before the landing; it squeaks a might, but don't let that bother you none. I'll get my handyman, Mr. Handran, to fix it one of these days."

Turning and walking into the kitchen, Mrs. Johnson continued to talk out loud as if Marla was still next to her. That woman was a talker, Marla thought to herself as she opened the door to her room and surveyed the quaint quarters that would be her home for a time. She threw her suitcase upon the floral print winged backed chair, drew open the white linen curtains to the only window next to the four-drawer dresser, and then threw herself upon the bed and sighed. The light blue ripcord bedspread reminded her of home.

She was excited but perhaps a bit scared of her immediate future in this strange city with its salt breezes and waving palms.

But she was determined to find her own way and make this a new start. After all, Boston held nothing for her anymore, not now that her fiancé had found his way into the arms of Marla's best friend. Well, she could have him, Marla thought. No man that couldn't hold on to her was not worth the keeping. She'd start over, she said to herself. And this time, Marla knew she'd find a man that needed her more than he needed his own passions.

Tomorrow morning, she'd go out and find a job. Surely, in a town this size, there would be something to do to pay the rent. But for now, the trip was catching up with her, and she closed her eyes. Filling in Mrs. Johnson about her "dear sweet aunt" would have to wait till breakfast. And then she was asleep.

After breakfast of poached eggs and toast with good hot and strong coffee and a longer- than-she-wanted conversation about her "dear sweet aunt," with Mrs. Johnson carrying the conversation, Marla headed out to enjoy the rest of the sunrise along the Intercoastal Waterway. She brought along the half-eaten cheese sandwich she had wrapped in wax paper from the long bus ride to West Palm Beach because she wasn't certain just how soon she'd find gainful employment, and being frivolous with lunch bought at a counter was not prudent on her part. She smiled as she watched the boats moving about on the water. Some were fishing boats headed to the inlet to work for the day's catch. And some were just for the pleasure of dancing with the wind, sailing to nowhere slowly. The gulls and pelicans followed the fishing boats, expecting their breakfast.

She picked up a newspaper sitting on a bench that appeared left behind, which she thought was fortunate, and began to scan the Want Ads. There were various ads for secretarial work, and private domestic help wanted ads. There was even an ad for the

Pennsylvania hotel needing young ladies to clean rooms. The ad said to see Enid. But there was one ad that immediately caught her eye. It was an ad for a private detective. A Frank Lobeck Investigations was seeking a reliable secretary to answer the phone and do some typing and filing. Now, Marla had learned to type at the Katharine Gibbs School of Secretarial Training for Educated Women in Boston. She had graduated with honors, top of her class, along with her best friend, Katherine. They had planned to use their training to secure jobs at a prestigious law firm so that they could meet young lawyers and hopefully land a husband. This is where Marla met her fiancé. This is where Katherine stole him. This is where Marla decided to leave Boston.

The address in the paper took Marla to Banyan Boulevard and a part of the town that never quite recovered from the '28 Okeechobee hurricane, which almost destroyed West Palm Beach. Marla reasoned because of the slow recovery that, the rent was cheap and that this job might not pay all that much now that she saw where it was located. Still, it was within walking distance of the Edgewater, and right now, she couldn't be too choosey because rent was due in a week. She climbed the stairs to the third floor and knocked on the door that had Frank Lobeck Investigations, Licenced Private Detective, painted on the glass part of the door.

Not hearing any response to her knocking, she turned the doorknob and entered cautiously into a small reception area with an old desk that looked to be a rescue from the destruction of the hurricane, complete with matching file cabinets against the opposite wall from the entrance. There was only one chair, and that was behind the desk. Next to the file cabinets was another door that led into an inner office. Stepping close, she could see through that door a small metal fan perched on the corner of another obviously rescued desk with paper streamers giving evidence it was trying hard to stir the air, but all it seemed to accomplish was to flutter the large stack of papers being held in place by a bottle of I. W. Harper whiskey and a half-filled glass. The back of the only other office chair was facing the desk, and seated in it was the back of a man in a sweat-stained, dirty white Oxford shirt speaking in a voice that appeared to be negotiating angrily on the phone with someone on the other end. There was a standing hat rack just inside the door with a brown suit coat and matching Fedora hanging from it.

"I'm tellin' ya I got expenses for followin' your guy. I caught him red-handed with his fingers in the till. I got proof! You owe me a hundred and twenty-five dollars, and I aim to get my money! Come on now, Mr. Jenson, you hired me fair and square and asked me to do a job, and I did it. Now ain't the time to squelch on the ticket. I need my money. You owe me! What's that? Okay, I'll get you an itemized account of expenses sent over this afternoon. My secretary isn't in at the moment, but as soon as she gets back, I'll have her type it up, and I'll bring it by personally. Yeah, you too."

Slamming down the phone, the angry man spun around in his chair and looked surprised to see Marla standing in the doorway. Marla wasn't sure if he was surprised at someone being in the office and overhearing his shouting or the fact that someone was able to come into the office without him being aware. Not a good characteristic for a private eye, she thought. Of course, it could be he was surprised at the fact that a lovely lady was standing there smiling at him. Marla never had any trouble attracting men with her figure and long, beautiful blonde locks. A morning splash of her precious Shalimar perfume was certainly helping. She figured the fan was successful in blowing the scent his way. From his bloodhound sniff, she could tell it was.

Regaining his composure, Frank stood and straightened his tie as he introduced himself, "Well, good morning. You caught me at a bad time. My secretary is out of the office at the moment, and I didn't hear you come in. My name's Frank, Frank Lobeck. What is it I can do for you, ma'am?"

Looking slightly disappointed, Marla replied, "Well, I had come about the ad in the paper for a secretary, but it appears you've already hired one. So I'll be on my way."

As Marla turned to go, Frank moved quickly out from behind his desk and stopped her by reaching out and, grabbing her arm and spinning her around gracefully as if in a dance. He smelled the Shalimar again, and it had him momentarily spinning himself. Stuttering, Frank apologized, "Excuse me, ma'am, but did you say you came by because of the ad? The truth is, ma'am, I just made up that stuff about me havin' a secretary. A guy can't run his office unless he has one, you see. Bad for business. Now, if we could start over, maybe I can redeem myself in your eyes, and we can come to some sort of arrangement. What ya say, ma'am?"

Extending her hand, "Well, you could start by calling me Marla, Mr. Lobeck."

"And you can call me Frank. Please to meet you, Marla. Won't you have a seat?" Frank said as he indicated to the one chair behind the desk. Marla smiled and thanked him, and after she seated herself, Frank sat on the edge of the desk. He had a smile, too.

After some pleasantries and mentioning that she was from

Boston and staying at the Edgewater, Marla asked just what the position required in terms of duties.

Frank looked at the ceiling and began to speak almost as he thought about his response, "First, it would be your responsibility to be here every day to open the office. A lot of mornings, I'm still out on a case and can't always be here." Frank then hesitated as he looked slyly toward her to see her reaction. He wondered if she noticed he didn't always tell the complete truth. The truth was he didn't have that many cases lately, not since the accident and his climbing in and out of the bottle.

"Obviously, I would need you to man the phone and take any messages from clients and to let me know so we can schedule meetings. Like I said, I ain't always here, so you would need to be uh, . . . be creative with the clients to keep them from going somewhere else, if you get my drift?"

Marla looked at him with a smile and a nod that she understood he would not always be faithful, although he expected her to be. She wondered what went on inside this man. He certainly was easy on the eyes, but there was a sadness in his. She remembered the paperweight bottle.

"And finally, can you type?"

"Top of my class. You'll find I can manage your files and schedule with the utmost professionalism and . . . creativity," Marla said with a wink, and then she added, "You can count on me, Frank. So, do I get the job?"

"Yeah, when can you start? I need somebody today if you can swing it. I gotta get a client an invoice this afternoon. It sure would help me from being jammed up, and with what he owes me, I can hire a secretary," Frank said with a smile.

"Just point me to the typewriter," looking out into the front office, Marla couldn't locate one. "You do have another typewriter, don't cha?"

Picking up his typewriter, Frank carried it into the front office and dropped it on what would become Marla's desk.

"I had to hock yours to pay the phone bill last month, but as soon as I get paid, I'll go down to the pawn brokers and get it back," Frank smiled, although Marla could tell he was a bit embarrassed.

"You mean as soon as you pay your secretary, then you'll go to the pawn brokers," Marla said with a smile.

Frank knew he had hired right, and he always had loved the smell of Shalimar.

Marla smiled through her tears as she remembered that first meeting of Frank. She reached for a Kleenex to wipe her eyes just as the phone rang for the second time that day. Marla knew it would be Frank. She knew from experience that he couldn't; he wouldn't let her hang up mad. He always called back to apologize, and then there would be fresh flowers on her desk the next morning. He even made the coffee on those *I'm sorry* days. At the same time, she reached for the phone, a man came into the office without knocking.

"Marla, it's Frank. Listen, babe, you just gotta know I'm sorry about dinner tonight. I haven't got a good excuse except that I let other things get more important than what's really important. You're what's important to me, babe. You gotta know that. I'm the fool for letting the case become an excuse to avoid some alone time with you. I know you are just trying to help. Whatta ya say, babe? Forgive me? Please?"

Frank could hear Marla's slight smile on the phone line, although his senses picked up some concern on her end, something in her breathing. He wasn't quite sure what it was. Maybe it was nothing, just his quilt. It's just that she seemed uneasy. Usually, his apologies were immediately accepted. But something appeared to be off.

Writing it off to his lack of sensitivity, he ventured, "Oh, and speaking of help, I forgot earlier to see if you can dig up anything on a Hans Metzger. You got that, Hans Metzger. Not sure there's anything that can be found on him, but it's worth a try."

"Sure, Frank, I got it. Oh, by the way, Frank," Marla said, lowering her voice with a seriousness in her tone, "there's a man who just came into the office and says he knows you. He says his name is Hector . . . oh, and Frank . . . he's got a gun."

13

Hector Corzo Bazàn was born in Cuba when Mario García Menocal was president of the island. Hector left the island for Florida when Miguel Mariano Gómez became president. Hector was only seventeen years old when he left the Caribbean island. He left behind his mother and his father, seven brothers and two sisters, and a favorite cousin by the name of Patchi, a Basque who loved to play pelota.

He was born in the summer, Hector's mom told him.

"It was the *tiempo muerto,* the dead season. The rains came, the work ceased, and while we waited for the cane to grow and for the rains to stop, you were born," she would tell him often as he lay on his shared wooden bed with blanket-covered iron springs. In the darkness, he would strain his eyes to see her face. He longed to see her smile as she recited the story, showing him that he was truly favored over his many brothers and sisters. But all he saw in the darkness were her distant and dark eyes that never seemed to shine. And lips that never smiled. Perhaps he thought he was, after all, not the favorite. This filled him with remorse. Perhaps, he thought she wished he never had . . .

Life for the *macheteros*, sugarcane cutters, and their families was hard. The cutting and harvesting season only lasted four months, and for the rest of the year, they depended on small gardens and chickens who lived under the raised houses to feed the many mouths that lived in houses too small for families too big.

Hector loved to lay on the beach with his favorite cousin and talk of the many dreams they shared about escaping this life of day-to-day existence. They would lay on the hot sand and stare up at the clouds and imagine each one was able to carry them across the 90 or so miles of ocean water to America, the land of promise.

"There, that one, Patchi," Hector said dreamily as he pointed to the large billowy cloud moving lazily across the expanse pushed by a non-committed breeze that had no interest in being a part of hope.

"That one looks like a big ox. Certainly, we could wrestle it into submission and ride it all the way to the distant shore. What you think, my cousin?" Hector's words were full of hope as he squinted in the sun and thought to himself that it was only here on this beach and only with Patchi that he dared dream his dream of escape.

"You dream too big, *mi primo*," Patchi replied as he turned his head to look at his cousin. "This island has our souls, and that ocean keeps us imprisoned. We will never leave. Never."

"One day, Patchi, one day I shall leave and never return. My life is there," Hector said as he sat up and pointed north out over the small, choppy waves of the blue Atlantic.

"And one day, I will be the greatest pelota player in all Cuba!" Patchi proclaimed as he stood and shouted at the sea while raising his hands towards the clouds, declaring victory. Then, kicking sand on his cousin, he ran laughing down the beach, zig-zagging as he ran to keep ahead of Hector, who jumped up and began to chase.

Stopping at a food cart in the little town along the beach, the boys smiled as they watched the vendor slather up a chunk of fresh, warm *pan Cubano* with guava jam. This was by far Hector's favorite treat, though he rarely was able to enjoy it. Hector's mom would never allow such a luxury. She always told her children, "Eating is what identifies us as Cubans. We eat rice and beans and, when we can, meat. Bread is for the wealthy." But today was Hector's birthday, and his cousin knew that he would not be celebrated by his mother at home, so he treated his cousin to the delicacy to give Hector a moment of joy. He loved to watch his cousin smile.

Hector often did not smile.

"What is there to smile about," he would say. "*Mi madre* would tell me, Hector, today is not the day to smile. We have work to do, or we have no work to do. Smiles only give us false hope that everything is okay, and that is never true."

But that day, with his cousin standing in the small town by the beach, he smiled as he took the first bite of the shared snack. Hector proclaimed, "One day, when I am in America, I will eat guava jam for breakfast every day. This I promise you."

"Do not make promises that you cannot make come true," Patchi declared through a mouthful of the bread and jam. "Remember, our prison surrounds us and reminds us we will never leave."

Turning to his cousin and speaking in a serious tone, Hector declared, "I will leave! Even if I have to swim the entire way, I will leave. This I promise you!"

When Hector turned seventeen years old, he left Cuba. His mother never wished him well.

93

14

He arrived in Miami hiding on a banana boat after escaping the island, thanks to a friend who worked on the docks. His friend was charged with the task of finding and killing any Cuban boas who managed to hide amongst the fruit, but not all snakes are reptiles. Miami, as did many ports, had rules about intentionally or unintentionally unloading and releasing any indigenous reptiles or even insects on Florida soil, poisonous or not. Upon arriving, Hector quickly assimilated into the ever-growing Cuban community there in Miami. On the advice of another friend, he made his way up the coast to West Palm Beach and quickly found work as a gardener at the Pennsylvania Hotel.

This is where he met Nora.

Nora Taylor came to the Pennsylvania Hotel from Jacksonville looking for a place to establish her *business* in the lower part of the state. After all, the state was now the residence of the infamous gangster Al Capone with his home on Palm Island in Miami Beach. Nora figured he would surely not offer any objection to one more brothel in that part of the state. She knew from her business in Jacksonville that the wealthy would often head south to run away from the winters, and their wives and West Palm Beach certainly had its share of wealthy clientele. But one night in the Pennsylvania Hotel, Nora met a man at the bar who owned real estate in Ft. Lauderdale and was looking to unload a prime piece of property known as Sunrise Hall. Nora ever so subtly explained her "business" to him once she was sure he could be trusted not to reveal her plans to the police. Her confidence was sealed when he leaned forward with a smile and placed his hand on her knee. He assured Nora that the area was ideal and that the local city officials could be persuaded to look the other way, especially if they were allowed to partake in the services rendered. They made a plan to drive down the next morning and at least have a look.

After a light dinner in the dining room, Nora felt the beckoning of the beginning night inviting her out into this tropical paradise along the Intercostal Waterway with its salty, warm breezes, swaying palms, and setting sun. Nighttime always had its way with Nora. She loved its romance and seduction. The night offered possibilities that didn't always come easily in the daylight. As she strolled along the walkway, she noticed a tall, dark-tanned man smoking a cigarette leaning against a Royal Palm. The smoke enticed her, and she casually approached him, asking if he had another cigarette.

"I left mine in my room, and I don't see any place to buy some on this walkway," she said with a seductive smile. She had hoped this beautiful man would give her more than a cigarette before the night was over.

Hector had noticed the lovely and well-dressed lady as she exited the Pennsylvania, and he, too, had hopes of an evening of company with this obviously wealthy guest at the hotel.

Since he had arrived in Florida, he had grown into what many women would say, "a fine-looking man." He kept to his duties during his working hours as the groundskeeper but was always conscious of the patrons who frequented his manicured lawns seeking shade amongst the tall palms. He knew that those who chose to stay at the hotel could certainly afford it, but he knew they did not interact with the hired help unless it was to demand some service they felt was to accompany their hefty bill at the end of their stay.

Having showered the day's labor from his body and grooming his dark hair with just the right amount of hair pomade, Hector had put on his one clean Guayabera shirt and took up his nightly position leaning against the magnificent palm to smoke his cigarette and admire the women who strolled by arm in arm in desperation hoping their next escort would stroll them down the aisle. Hector did not mind using his good-looking charms and fabulous smile to his advantage, but he clearly had no design of strolling down an aisle. Tonight, his usual ploy of being a well-to-do Cuban familiar with this paradise appeared to be paying off. This woman hopefully would not notice he was the one who clipped and handed her a beautiful red hibiscus earlier that day at her request.

She smiled, remembering.

Offering her his pack and then smartly striking a match on his penny box of matches, he said, "It's a lovely evening, but you, *Señorita*, have brought the night a challenge to do better tomorrow if it wants to be more lovely."

Nora smiled. She mused to herself that she had heard every line possible in her business, but this interesting Cuban indeed surprised her. Nora thought to herself that she could possibly use a man such as this to join her enterprise. A strong, confident man was always needed to keep order among the more rambunctious customers who thought their money gave them freedoms that were not a part of her services.

"You are very kind, *Señor.* Perhaps we can stroll along the walkway until we find a bar and go in for a drink?"

Hector tried not to let the lovely lady see him finger his coins in his pocket and knew he better get control of the evening quick since his income never allowed for the luxuries of drinking and eating before he attempted to steer the ladies to his room.

"Maybe the *Señorita* wouldn't mind accompanying me to my room, where I have a nice bottle of Cuban rum? What do you say?" Hector said, flashing his alluring smile and hoping that she was as bold as he was at that moment.

Hector was practiced at using his smile and charms on the many women who worked at the Pennsylvania Hotel. His latest conquest was a lovely young girl, barely seventeen, named Tina. But tonight, he had set his designs on this obviously experienced woman who did not hesitate when he suggested retreating to his room.

Nora again smiled as she took his arm and strolled away in confidence.

The morning sun peeked unembarrassed into the one-room apartment from behind the sheer curtain designed only to soften the beginning of another day here in this tropical paradise. For the first time, Hector lingered in the bed next to this woman and, unlike many times before, did not wish for her to rush out the door for his reputation or for theirs.

As he lay there gazing at her mature loveliness, he remembered back to the morning he left Cuba, the morning his mother cursed his name and took back any love she had ever allowed him. It was the same morning she had discovered Hector naked and intertwined with his much older cousin, Lupita, who had promised she would show him what his mother was denying him—love with affection. It was the same morning that this much older cousin jumped up naked from his arms and shrieked, pointing a finger at him, and yelled to Hector's mother that he had forced her to do this terrible and unforgiving act. It was the same morning that Hector's mother shattered against his head his one and only dinner plate from the kitchen table, symbolizing he no longer had a place at her table. It was the same morning that he hid in the bow of the banana boat that brought him to Florida.

He raised himself up on one arm on his pillow and smiled down at her, thinking that he had surely met a woman that he could invite back to his bed without reservations. This was so unlike him. Because of his mother, Hector protected his relationships by not allowing any woman a chance to return on their own design. It had to be because he asked them back. Even Tina had to ask.

Feeling the warmth of the uninhibited sun and the stare from eyes that had certainly an unrequested design on her continual company, Nora opened her eyes and smiled at this truly handsome boy who had reminded her of her youth last night. Knowing what he was thinking, she quickly affirmed her independence and told him, "You need to get that look off your face. This was just a one-night stand, and it is not going to happen ever again."

Then, slipping from the bed, Nora slowly dressed to strengthen her authority over the smitten boy, and using her talent to manipulate anyone to her purposes, she said, "I do, however, have a proposition I would like for you to consider.

What would you say to coming to work for me? I could certainly use a man like you to assist me in my endeavors."

Frowning as he, too, slipped from the bed, Hector then brightened with the possibility that he might be able to convince Nora to change her one-night position if he was near her often.

"What is it that you would have me to do?"

Sitting down in the only chair in the sparsely furnished room, Nora slipped on her shoes and straightened the seams in her stockings. Without looking up, she continued, "I run a service that caters to lonely and wealthy men who are needing a night away from, how should I say, their unexciting obligations to some predesigned societal expectations," then, looking up to make sure Hector was following her she added, "if you understand my meaning? What I would need you for is to maintain order when the excitement gets out of hand. Again, do you understand what I am asking?"

"Si, you are an *alcahueta*, a madame," Hector responded without surprise as he turned from her. Knowing this about Nora explained so much about last night.

Stepping around the bed and facing him, Nora looked up into the disappointed Cuban's face. She could tell he had hoped for much more than just being a part of her employees. She knew she would have to sweeten the pot to snare Hector, and she did just that.

"You will be well compensated for your loyalty and services to me, and from time to time, if you're clever, as I know that you are," she said with a shy grin, looking back at the rumpled bed sheets, "you may even convince my ladies to keep your nights from being, how should I put this," she looked up into his eyes that were begging her to continue, "a solitary evening absent of celebration. And I could see my way to a bonus for any ladies you bring in to serve with us. Now, what do you say to that? Have I enticed you sufficiently?"

Hector smiled.

"Good. Now, I'm driving down to Ft. Lauderdale this morning to look at some possible property. I suggest you ride along with me?" she said as she looked around at the limited quarters that he lived in. "Who knows, we might even find you a possible upgrade in your living arrangements."

Hector reached for his clean shirt.

15

Frank ran up the three flights of stairs to his office. Out of breath but determined to bust down the door if needed, he saw that the door was slightly open.

The office was empty!

Marla was gone.

Inside the office, it looked as if Marla had put up quite a struggle before Hector obviously got the best of her. Her typewriter, the one that Frank had gotten out of hock when he hired her, was nearly across the room, upside down against the filing cabinets by the front door.

The *S* key that Marla had always complained to Frank about sticking had broken loose and was impaled into the wood floor plank by its rib, staring up at Frank as if it were a clue. He smiled slightly as he thought about this slight bottle-blonde lady picking up the heavy machine and hurling it at her attacker. Surely she hadn't learned that from the Boston School of Secretarial Training, he mused. He wished he could have seen the expression on Hector's face as the machine took to flight in his direction. But no matter what surprises Marla had in store for her aggressor, Frank knew this woman he had grown to care for far beyond the employer-and-employee relationship would not be able to fend off the strong Cuban for too long. Her absence assured him of that.

He looked around the chaos in the office and began to feel a weakness, an inability to protect those he cared for. At that moment, the Judas coin in his pocket seized the opportunity and again asserted its curse on Frank's emotions. Its power forced on him a sense of remorse so strong that, with a trembling hand and without forethought, he raised his gun toward his head and thought for just a brief second as the coin whispered that ending his life was best for everyone. It taunted him, suggesting that Marla was probably already dead and, if not, soon would be. The whispering continued, *You've already lost one love, and that was your fault. Now, you are to blame for this loss as well. Do the right thing and rid the world of your worthless life before more people are hurt. It's the right thing to do.*

The moment faded. His unspoken love for Marla and the need to enact vengeance on Hector gave him the resolve to resist the power of the coin. He slipped the gun back into its holster. Falling down hard into Marla's desk chair, he wondered what was he to do. How could he bring her home safely? He lowered his head to her desk, and for the first time since losing his Lilly and Beth, he began to weep. The weeping was hard and gut-wrenching, and it was not just for Marla. It was for all the times he had failed those he loved. How could he keep living?

Frank sobbed heavily. He knew he could love Marla just as much as he had ever loved Lilly, maybe more. And Frank knew he needed Marla desperately. She kept him sane from all the insanity that Frank had experienced since his loss. But then the coin again exerted its power of damnation on his mind and told him Marla would be better off without him. Somehow, Frank found the strength to resist his despair, and he swore the next time he saw Marla, he would tell her how much he needed her.

Damn, that coin!

The phone's ringing jolted Frank's head up, and he quickly reached for his gun without realizing he was alone in the office. Staring at the handset, he knew this had to be Hector, and he had to say the right words to get Marla back safe. He couldn't mess this up. Not this time. Not ever again when it came to Marla.

"Hello, Frank Lobeck," he said as steadily as he could.

"Frank, *mi amigo*," Hector said sarcastically, "How are you? I have someone here who belongs to you. Say hello, *Señorita*."

Holding the phone to Marla's mouth, she pretended to weep to keep Hector off guard, "Frank! Frank, I'm so sorry. I tried to fight him off, but he had a gun—" then, before Hector knew what was happening Marla shouted, "BALCONIES! FRANK! THERE'S BALCO-"

Frank heard a slap, and then Marla cursed out loud at Hector.

"You damn bastard! You busted my lip. Frank's gonna hurt you for that! You don't realize what hell you've released on yourself."

She was not prone to cursing, so Frank figured the Cuban must have really hurt her. She was right; he would hurt Hector and hurt him badly.

Hector yelled into the receiver, "You want this bitch; you got to do just what I say! You understand? You mess up, and I will put a bullet in her pretty little head, that is—after I play with her a bit," Hector said with a sadistic giggle.

Frank never bluffed when dealing with scum like Hector. He

always said exactly what he intended. He believed that that kind of people needed to hear what he was going to do. So, he never tried any negotiation tactics that the police would use to resolve a situation.

"Hector, here's what you can expect will happen. I am coming for you. Your threats mean nothing to me. Each night when you lay down, you'll be wondering if tonight is the night that I sneak in while you're asleep and put a bullet between your damn Cuban eyes. Make no mistake; I am coming for you, no matter how this turns out for Marla. You got that, amigo!" Frank added that last bit with hard emphasis.

Hector momentarily hesitated as he felt the promise of death coming from Frank for what he had done. His confidence was temporarily shaken. But he was used to people condemning him for what he did. His mother had trained him in that. The moment quickly passed. Whatever Frank swore, Hector felt he could meet the challenge. In fact, he then realized his life was a complete preparation for this life of hardness and difficulties. Escaping from Cuba and coming to Florida had readied and shaped him into the man that Nora could trust to do the necessary things that keep her girls safe. Except for that one girl last year, he had not failed to protect Nora's enterprise. He told Nora then that it was not his fault. He said Tina had distracted him that night. He said the blame was on Tina, not on him. Hector never had any trouble deflecting blame when the finger was pointing at him. Nora told Hector that she'd give him that one; however, if it happened again, he'd pay for it with his life. Hector swore it wouldn't. He trusted his instincts could deal with whatever came his way, just like he believed he could face down Frank and come out victorious. He had to. His life depended on it.

"*Señor*, it is you who brought this trouble on yourself. You interfered where you were not asked. For that, you must pay. I think maybe your payment for my humiliation will be the death of your lovely woman. She is very beautiful, don't you agree, *Señor*? I think that will satisfy me for now. What do you say to that? Loss for loss?"

Frank's mind was racing. How was he going to protect Marla from this crazy Cuban who believed revenge was more valuable than life. He had to have a plan, and he had to have it quick.

"You got that, *Amigo*? You hear what I say? She gonna die, *si*, *Señor*, she gonna die."

But all Hector heard was a silence on the other end of the line that began to make him doubt his threats were having the intended effect. Frank had heard enough back-and-forth bantering that never produced the desired upper hand for either party. As hard as it was not to demand Marla's release, he simply used the silence as his response, and then when he could hear the Cuban's nervous breathing on the other end, he simply hung up the phone.

Click!

Hector needed some time to think about his next move, and he hoped Frank would not be smart enough to realize he had left West Palm with Marla.

Hector figured wrong.

Frank lifted himself from Marla's desk with a heaviness in his shoulders that came from the fact that he had not thought ahead to the possibility that Hector could get to him through the only one he cared for. Hector had no way of knowing how deeply Frank needed Marla. Still, Hector must have assumed Frank would come looking for someone connected to him, even a secretary. He stepped into his own office and, reached into the bottom drawer of his desk and grabbed the bottle. He took a long slug of amber liquid courage.

He knew he would need it to do what he had promised Hector.

Thinking carefully, Frank figured that Hector would want some distance between him and his adversary, so it was logical that he would head to a familiar place. It was a gamble, but Frank's gambles often paid off. That was one of the many things that made him a good detective. He always seemed to know which alley to turn down or which door to bust through.

Frank had determined that Sunrise Hall was the one place Hector would go because not only was Hector familiar with the surroundings, but he needed a place where he could make his stand knowing that Frank was coming. Frank had been to Sunrise Hall before for a case, and while he was there, he offered information to Detective Jacobs involving a salesman who killed one of Nora's girls. That's where he remembered Hector from. He remembered now that Hector was the one who guarded the ladies and kept the customers in line. Frank was certain this was where Hector brought Marla.

Frank also remembered that the building was surrounded by balconies on all sides.

Frank pushed the 1940 Willys-Overland 2-door tan-colored coupe as hard as she would go down State Road 140 heading south. He was thankful his brother-in-law had made him such a deal on the car two years ago to soften the blow of losing his only daughter when Lilly ran their car off the bridge and into the inlet at Boyton Beach. The Willys-Overland was only a four- cylinder, but it was fast, and sometimes, like now, he needed that extra speed. He needed to get to the Sunrise Hall before Hector found his courage again and did the unthinkable.

Frank knew the route to get there and used the many back

alleys to avoid the local authorities. He also wanted to avoid Hector seeing him coming straight on.

Pulling the car up an alley behind the Hall, Frank killed the engine and hesitated before rushing in to free Marla. He had to act smart. Hector might be surprised that Frank knew exactly where he had run to, but Frank knew the Cuban would react fast on his feet, and he was capable of hurting Marla or worse. Frank couldn't just bust down the door; he needed to surprise Hector.

Checking the chamber of his pistol, Frank slipped out of his car and made his way to the Hall's lower entrance. He knew he would have to guess which floor and which room Hector had Marla on. If he was wrong, that could be disastrous for Marla. For her, he had to be right.

Working his way up quietly up the stairs from inside the building, Frank got encouragement from some of the girls Hector took advantage of. Several girls gladly pointed Frank to the room where Marla was held hostage. One girl even offered, "You shoot that bastard! He deserves anything comin' to him. You kill him dead, you hear!"

Standing outside the room, Frank leaned his ear to the door to listen for any sound that might give him an advantage when he charged the room. He could hear Hector's angry voice threatening someone in the room. He heard Marla growling back and promising to do things that would end the Cuban's romance of women. Again, Frank mused how he had never seen this side of her before. He made a mental note not to cross this woman whom he admired even more now for her bravery.

How was he gonna play this? If he busted down the door, he might get lucky and get off a shot or two, but there was always the chance that Hector could get one off, too. And Frank didn't know exactly where Marla was in the room. Then, he decided as he holstered his gun and reached for the door handle, turning it slowly and stepping inside with his hands raised.

16

Wilson paced back and forth in his small, cheap hotel room at the Southlands Motor Lodge. Since Frank had left, his worry and depression over the loss of Betty Lou deepened. He sat down again on his bed, which was unmade due to the tossing and turning the night before and not from the lack of housekeeping. In fact, the girl had made several attempts to straighten the room, but Wilson had looked at her through the peephole and refused to let her enter. He thought it would be too hard to see someone as young as Betty Lou alive and vibrant. The more Wilson reflected, the more he knew he had to do something or go out of his mind from grief. Wilson also was aware of the promise he made to his wife. She needed him to get home and to bring Betty Lou home to Ohio.

He needed a plan.

So he stood up and decided to pay Father Peter another visit. It was not just his troubled soul that needed comfort; he wanted to see if the priest had any more to say about this Hans character.

He knew what he had to do.

Splashing some water on his face, Wilson headed outside to his car. Locking his room, he turned to face the day, looking up into the bright mid-morning sun that warmed him in spite of the coldness he felt in his heart. Wilson slowly breathed in deeply the salt air as it blew across the fronds on the Royal Palms growing in the courtyard of the lodge. For a moment, his spirit was renewed, and he stretched his arms out and his neck backward, looking upward, scanning the brilliant blue sky for some unknown creator to express his admiration for the day. But immediately, the darkness crept back in, and then he slouched forward and began to walk slowly with an almost distinct limp to his car. Sliding in from the driver's side, Wilson reached over and, opened the glovebox and removed the Colt .38 Special that he had bought from a friend at the paint factory.The friend said he acquired it from another friend and that Wilson ought to keep it out of sight since it came from some dubious origins.He opened the gun's cylinder and checked its load of five shots. Closing it carefully and deliberately, he placed the gun in his coat pocket, cranked the Dodge, and headed to St. Ann's.

Father Peter picked up his Breviary containing the Liturgy of the Hours and headed back to his small office for more reflection. He was troubled still, and it had been many months since he had a clean conscience before listening to the penitents in confession. In about an hour, the lines of people would begin, and he would be responsible for their absolution, something he himself determined he personally could never receive for his sin.

Hearing the door of the sanctuary open, he was about to say that confessions were not for another hour. Then he heard someone whisper his name.

"Father Peter, you have a moment?"

Turning, he saw it was Betty Lou's father, Mr. Wilson. A cold shudder went up his back.

A hiss escaped his lips.

"Mr. Wilson, is it? How may I help you? I'm in need of preparing for the sacrament of confession. Is it something that can wait?"

Walking toward him, Wilson whispered again, "I am sorry to bother you, Father, but I was wondering if I might ask you if you could possibly tell me anything more about BettyLou's, eh, friend, that German named Hans, or where I can find him?"

For a moment, Father Peter felt the man's pain as if it were a tangible thing. It was a pain that clings to us inside our bodies like a virus. It was a pain that weakens us and robs us of reason. It was something that alters how we view the world and our responsibilities to those around us.

That pain had changed Father Peter.

"Listen, Mr. Wilson, it's like I told that detective, your daughter said she had recently met someone named Hans, and she indicated their relationship was troubled. That's all I can say, so if you would excuse me, I really have other obligations to attend to."

With that, Father Peter turned and started to walk away, but he stopped and drew a deep breath in through his nostrils while his shoulders slumped forward more from disgust and disdain than remorse. Turning back to face Wilson, he said, "You might try the Hotel George Washington. Go to the waterway out front and head south. It's owned by a German. They may know something about this Hans fellow. Now, again, please excuse me. I really do have to attend to my duties."

"Thank you," and Wilson was gone.

The morning breezes had gone away for the day, and the ever-present sun was quickly warming everything it touched. Wilson was oblivious to the Laughing Gulls that taunted him and dared the newcomer to throw something their way. They loved showing off for the tourists their practiced routines of acrobatics that generally resulted in being fed without having to work for their daily needs. A lazy brown pelican sat perched on a barnacle-encrusted piling, ready to steal anything it could from their exaggerated antics.

Wilson enjoyed none of it.

Arriving at the hotel, Wilson drew his own breath and patted his coat pocket for assurance. He then opened the door into the lobby and walked, determined, to the front desk. As he approached, the desk clerk with his back to the entrance was busy sorting mail into the many boxes. He turned and smiled, saying, "Welcome to the Hotel George Washington. How may I help you today?"

"Good morning. I've just arrived in town and was wondering if you could help me locate an old friend who I believe might be staying here? His name is Hans."

Wilson then suddenly panicked, realizing he did not know the German's last name. How was he going to convince this clerk that Hans was an old friend? Then, he came up with a plausible story.

"Actually, it is my daughter's friend, and she asked that if I ever find myself in your city, to look up and meet this friend, umm, boyfriend of hers." Then, leaning forward toward the clerk's face while reading his name tag. Wilson smiled, "You see, the truth is, I have never met this Hans character, and as a concerned father, I felt it my obligation to see just who is dating my daughter . . ." then glancing ever so naturally to the clerk's left hand and seeing a ring on the man's finger, Wilson continued, "do you have children, uh, Mr. umm, Schmidt is it?"

The clerk smiled and raised two fingers with pride.

"Well, then, I bet, as a father, you understand my situation. As fathers, we got to protect our kids. Am I right?"

The clerk smiled again as he drew himself to full height and boasted by sticking out his chest and then jumping into the conversation, saying, as he whispered, leaning across the desk toward Wilson, "I would do anything for my children. Anything!" Then, touching his right index finger to the side of his nose as he nodded the secret nod that all fathers understood, he opened the register and ran the same finger down the list of occupant names and stopped at "Hans Metzger. He is the only Hans we have at the moment staying with us. May I ask just how old your daughter is, Mr. eh?"

This question froze Wilson as he realized that Betty Lou would always be twenty-three.

He choked his answer back for a moment and hesitated in sharing with this stranger what he considered personal knowledge of his daughter. Then, borrowing the clerk's boast,he breathed in his full height and announced, "My name is Wilson, and my daughter was, uh . . . is . . . she just turned twenty-three," stammering with a painful smile.

The clerk did not notice Wilson's uneasiness and responded, "Hmm, that would be about the age of Metzger, Mr. Wilson. I imagine he could be your daughter's boyfriend, although I have not observed him in the company of a young lady. Do you know how long they have been seeing each other?"

"Yes, she mentioned meeting him about four or five months ago. Yes, that's right, around five months. Now, they could have been seeing each other before that, but that's what she said when we found out about him. At least that's what my wife told me. You know, mothers and daughters, when it comes to things about love, they never tell the fathers anything until it is too late for the fathers to do anything about it. All we know is when to come to the church to escort them down the aisle and give them away. Am I right? Of course, I'm right," and Wilson added another painful smile.

Glancing back down at the register, the clerk mused, running the dates in his head and then looking at Wilson with a smile, "This gentleman has been staying with us coming up on five months in three days now. I am quite certain he must be the one you are looking for."

Hiding his anxious nervousness, Wilson asked, "Would it be possible for you to tell me what room he is staying in?"

At that moment, the father-to-father conversation disappeared, and in a professional hotel employee's voice speaking louder while looking around the lobby in case someone in authority was listening, the clerk said, "I'm afraid hotel policy will not permit me to disclose that information. I would be more than happy to leave him a message so that he could contact you. Is there a number or a location where you can be reached, perhaps?"

Wilson had trouble hiding his disappointment, but he managed, "Maybe I'll just wait for a bit in the lobby in case this Hans comes through. Would you mind pointing him out to me? That wouldn't break any hotel policy, now would it? I'll just wait over there," Wilson said, pointing to a couch near the lobby entrance.

The clerk nodded with a smile as Wilson turned and walked slowly to the couch.

Hans entered the hotel lobby, heading to the front desk for

his room key. The clerk looked to Wilson and again touched the side of his nose while nodding to indicate the man Wilson was seeking had just appeared.

Wilson slipped his hand into his coat pocket.

17

Frank took in the whole room at once, and he saw the surprised look on Hector's face that betrayed the Cuban's confidence, but with Frank's hands raised, Hector smiled. Frank interpreted this as false confidence that Hector believed he indeed could handle anything that came his way.

Hector quickly stepped behind Marla, who was still tied to a chair, and held his gun to her head while he kept smiling at Frank. He had not expected Frank so soon, if at all. He was not certain at first, just how Frank figured out where he was. But somewhere in his memory, he finally realized where he had seen Frank before the incident at the Pennsylvania. It was back here at the Sunrise Hall back when one of Nora's girls was killed by that salesman. Hector remembered Frank was there with the police who were investigating the crime scene. He remembered Frank had offered some information that led the police to the guilty party.

Quelling his anger, Frank said when he saw Marla tied to the chair, "Hey, Doll Face. I come to take you home," and he winked, trying to instill confidence in her. Frank immediately saw the blood on Marla's lip and clenched his teeth. He realized the Cuban had a weakness. In Frank's mind, any man who hit a woman had weakness. He remembered the incident at the Pennsylvania with Enid and the girl Hector was threatening, and it reinforced his belief that Hector was compensating for some moment in his past that turned him into someone who felt the need to assert power over women.

He looked into the eyes of his enemy and held them to increase Hector's uneasiness.

Frank could feel and taste the salty breeze blowing through the palms lining the street, separating it from the sandy beach and then blowing across the room, cooling it from Florida's summer heat coming from the open French doors to the balcony.

But Hector was sweating despite the breeze.

Even with her swollen lip, Marla managed to smile at Frank. He felt a sense of pride in her toughness. Tougher than he had ever imagined. If he got her free, he promised himself that he would never let her be in a situation like this ever again. He knew that would be a hard promise to keep in his business, but he knew he could never live with himself if Marla was ever in danger again. He loved her too much. He gave her a wink so she would know that he had a plan. She smiled again.

Speaking to Hector, he said, "I told you I would come."

"Certainly, you must think you are a wise man finding us so quickly, but it is I who has outsmarted you. I have a gun on your woman, and you have your hands in the air. I am the one who is wise. I will kill both of you, and no one here will say a word about it. I will feed your bodies to the sharks, and that will be the end of my problems with you."

Using Hector's arrogance, Frank began slowly to lower his

hands.

"Listen, Hector, it's obvious you outsmarted me. I guess I didn't think this whole thing through. All I could think about was getting my secretary home safe. I don't care about what you do to me; just let her go."

Frank wasn't sure Hector would buy into this display of weakness after he had been so adamantly bold here now and on the phone. But again, he was counting on Hector's vanity, which led the Cuban to believe he was wiser.

Pointing the gun at Frank, Hector said sternly, "Get your hands back up! Do you think I am an idiot? Now, carefully and very slowly, take your gun out of your holster and drop it to the floor. Then slide it over to me. Do it now!"

"Don't you think it's hard for me to slide you my gun with my hands raised? You gotta decide which you want me to do." Frank was hoping that the conversation would confuse Hector and keep him distracted while pointing his gun at Frank and not at Marla.

"Remember who's in charge here! Use your left hand and very, very slowly take your gun out and slide it to me." Then, pointing his gun back at Marla's head, he said, "If you try anything I do not like, I will kill your woman. That I can promise you. Anything goes wrong, she will certainly die."

Very slowly, Frank lowered his left hand. Keeping his eyes on Hector, Frank used two fingers to pull his gun from his holster. He very carefully held it out away from his body and lowered it, dropping it to the floor. It made a loud sound when it hit. This startled Marla, and she looked genuinely frightened for the first time since Frank had stepped into the room.

Hector nodded, flashing his white teeth, "Very good, *Amigo*. You are now getting smarter. Now kick it over here to me."

Frank looked at Marla and tried to reassure her with his eyes that he was still in control. Hector noticed the look and reacted, "Do not think you can trick me. I do promise I will kill her." Then he pushed the barrel of his gun against her temple, forcing her to lean her head almost to her left shoulder. Again, Frank noticed her fear.

Frank looked down at his gun, and then, with his right foot, he slid the gun away from his body. But instead of complying with Hector's orders, Frank slid the gun away from the Cuban so that Hector could not pick it up without stepping away from Marla.

Immediately, Hector's smug smile vanished.

"A big mistake, *Amigo*," he said as he pulled back the hammer on his gun against Marla's head.

Frank shouted, "Wait! You have me at a disadvantage. I have no gun." Then, reaching slowly into his pockets, Frank turned them inside out, showing that he had nothing in them as well. "You hold all the cards. All I got is my last cent."

Frank held up the Judas coin against his index finger and thumb with his left hand. It momentarily flashed its silver brilliance from the reflection coming in from the sun. Frank felt the power of the coin only for an instant.

Then he flipped the coin at Hector.

18

Hans Metzger moved across the lobby of the Hotel George Washington like a man who carried the weight of emotional grief, which generally is intended for someone much older than he actually was. He was only twenty-four years old, yet his gait was like that of one twice or perhaps three times his age. He moved slowly and shuffled his feet as if he were uncertain he could maintain his balance. In his face was the look of remorse. The kind of remorse that leads to despair. Despair unto death.

Metzger was a blue-eyed, fair-skinned, blond-haired man who stood around five foot nine inches tall. That is when he stood erect and proud, but today, he was bent at the shoulders, staring at the ground with his hands stuffed deep into his pockets to restrain their free movement, indicating a troubled attitude. His appearance was not that of a typical German soldier. He sported a dark blonde mustache that grew over his upper lip. This was unusual for a soldier in the German military. Most, if they wore the additional hair at all, groomed it neatly trimmed to the top of the lip. Evidently, Metzger was attempting to hide his nationality by embracing what seemed an American appearance. Many might consider the appearance a rugged outdoors type consistent with the western cowboy look or that of a working man who labored with his back and hands. Maybe he thought the additional facial hair made him look more like a naturalized citizen in this country; thus, he could continue to hide the fact that he was here doing the work of the Third Reich. Besides, Betty Lou had encouraged the overgrown facial hair. She had told Hans she liked his "rugged outdoor type."

Betty Lou.

The memory of Betty Lou a month ago would always bring a wide, toothy smile to the generally stoic officer. He had come to these shores to secure a religious artifact for Heinrich Himmler, who was obtaining by any means as many as he could for occultic purposes and for the eventual triumph of the Motherland over those who resisted German domination.

Metzger never imagined he would fall for an American woman; however, Betty Lou was no typical American woman, he would often say.

"Betty Lou, you are truly the most amazing woman. I love many things about you. I love the color of your eyes and how they sparkle when the sun is on your face. I love the shade of your hair and the way it falls around your shoulders. I love the taste of your lips. It is like tasting sweet cherries!"

Blushing, Betty Lou pushed Hans back away from her on the couch as he leaned in for another kiss. She knew it was not right for him to be alone with her in her room, but he had been there before, and he had stayed long enough to see the sunrise more than once. She just could not resist the charms and dashing good looks of this bad boy. After all, he had admitted to her he was the one she saw landing on the beach that night in the raft and that he had come to America on a mission for the German army. He did tell her that he had forgotten all about his allegiance to his mother country and the mission he had been dispatched for on her shores since he had met her.

But what she didn't know was that he lied.

He didn't lie to deceive her; he never intended to use her for his purposes. He lied because he had already secured the package that he had come for. Hans had met his contact the same night he landed and did not meet Betty Lou until the next day. He often thought that if he had met her first, he might never have completed his mission, and the Judas coins would not be in his possession.

He lied because he didn't want to lose this woman who had captivated his every waking thought. He lied because lying next to her birthed a deeper level of commitment than any allegiance to a cause or country that had been drilled into his head since his youth. He lied because he couldn't bring himself to take away the happiness he saw in her eyes and the love she expressed from her heart.

"Hans, you'll say anything just so I won't push you out the door," she said playfully as she rose from the couch and straightened her dress that was disheveled from the always, ever too amorous German. "Now, let me be so I can get ready for my next performance. It wouldn't do for me to appear on stage with my slip showing, now would it?" She then blew him a kiss as she headed to her bedroom to freshen her makeup and brush her hair. Betty Lou often wondered if management knew what was going on behind closed doors, would they let her go? She loved her job, but as she turned back to look at the pouting young boy on her couch, she knew she loved him even more.

She better, she thought as she patted her tummy and smiled.

Metzger looked up from the lobby floor as he slowly moved toward the clerk at the front desk, and in his peripheral vision, he noticed a man rising from a couch and moving in his direction. Months ago, before the welcomed distraction of Betty Lou, he would have noticed anyone who occupied his space. He would have reacted with caution and anticipated an enemy that might possibly be lurking, waiting to pounce and capture. He would never have let anyone get so close brandishing a gun.

The man spoke with a similar weight that Hans carried, "You that Kraut, Hans Metzger?"

Hans turned to face his opponent. He noticed something familiar about him, although he was certain they had never met. It was something in the man's eyes that reminded him of someone.

Then he knew.

19

As the tossed coin flipped over and over in the air, its silver sheen reflected the light of the sun coming in through the open doors leading to the balcony. Its hypnotic brilliance flashed in Hector's eyes and began its intoxicating allure, drawing him ever so slightly into that area of his brain where his depravity existed, distracting him momentarily from Frank and Marla.

Reaching up with his left hand, he was compelled by some outside lust to grasp the object. Smiling at what he perceived to be Frank's attempt to draw his attention away from Marla, Hector found he couldn't bring his focus back to the events in front of him. He, indeed, was distracted, but it was the power of the coin, not Frank.

What happened next robbed Hector of his ability to control the room.

With his hand firmly closed around the coin, Hector immediately felt a guilty uneasiness coursing along through his veins, driving that guilt into his very soul. The coin's curse began its magic. A powerful sense of remorse began to well up inside of him, capturing his memories and taking him back through the life he had led in flashes like Kodak moments. They took him all the way back to Cuba. Back to where his sins had their origin. To where the *Serpent* spun his original lies to a young boy so desperate for validation. Where the tropical Eden island gave the young boy a promise of paradise before corruption stole that away. As the memories pounded in his brain, he was aware of his role in shaping his history. Tears started clouding his vision.

The thing about remorse is it often lies.

Hector remembered the moment when paradise was lost to him and the early years of starvation from love lying in the darkness on the bedroom floor. Lying there silently crying and watching his mother go from child to child, singing and soothing them in the island heat, yet ignoring him every night. But he couldn't remember why he was the one neglected. He remembered the emptiness in his belly, longing to fill it with her love, but the nourishment never visited him. He remembered the almost daily beatings from his father with the leather razor strap for reasons that made no sense to a young boy. His memories leapt to his attempt to create love by forcing his young cousin, Ines, into his perversion of what love certainly is not. The absence and brutal force that shaped his life still demands women show him his redefinition of love.

Not knowing the coin was driving his thoughts, he relived the vivid brutality of his first killing. He told himself it was only a pigeon, but the taste of blood was still on his teeth from pulling its head off with his mouth on a dare. The blood still tastes in his mind. Hector's mind played out in rapid succession the many killings of people at his hand. They were all pigeons, he rationalized. Their blood all tasted the same.

The coin reminded him of the day he killed his drunken father.

His drunken father who would favor Hector whenever he would come home and needed someone's back to soften the leather of his hard razor strap. It seems his father needed to release the pain from a hard and ugly life on an island that never gave back to its people from the abundance of the beauty it spawned. Swearing and flinching from memory still felt, Hector shouted that the strap would never bleed another child. His ears were deaf to the pleas from his father, to the pleas from his mother! He turned to her, but his longing for her love was nowhere inside of him anymore. For the sake of the other children, he did one good thing—he let her live, but the scars were forever visible on her cheeks. Her smile was never genuine again. Her kisses for her children came with great pain.

Hector left Cuba with his pain.

Memory after memory filled his mind. The lies he told, the money he stole, the women he beat for love all came to him in rapid and unrelenting succession. The memories tore at his mind's flesh, bleeding him inside causing his vision to go darker and darker. Normally, for Hector, darkness gave him a false rest, but in this darkness, there was an untold terror for a deserved punishment and torture coming from an evil presence that he could smell sulfuric in his nostrils. He heard from somewhere inside his hideous torment a screaming that begged as his father begged to be released from the pain and punishment, but no forgiveness came. No relenting of the deserving strap. The torture became more and more brutal to his soul, more and more demanding that his life was responsible for this hell. His mouth filled with the taste of blood. The blood of so many that he tore with his teeth. The blood of his own flesh as he was nailed to a cross for his sins. Hector saw the hopelessness and despair that begged for release from his earthly torment. That begged for his own noose. That begged his own bowels to spill out to the ground.

The Judas coin demanded his life for his life's treason.

Frank saw the distraction the coin brought to Hector. He expected it. Signaling Marla with the wink of his eye and the nodding his head to his left, she smiled, knowing what Frank had in mind. She then leaned her weight to her right in the chair, and as it tipped, Frank jumped at his opportunity for his gun and rolled, firing two slugs into Hector's chest from the floor. The surprised Hector was slammed backward by the force against the railing on the balcony through the doors. His weight and momentum carried him over the rail, and he fell three floors to the parking lot below.

Frank rushed to Marla and quickly uprighted her in the chair, and began to loosen her restraints. "Frank, I knew you'd come for me. I just knew you'd get me out of this," Marla said with a slight doubt in her voice. But once Frank had freed her from the chair, she stood and threw her arms around his neck and began to fill his face with kisses that ended any doubt.

"Are you hurt? Did that bastard hurt you?"

"No, Frank. Outside this split lip, I'm just fine now. Just take me home, please."

Still clinging to Frank's neck with her arms, Marla looked into his eyes and saw the terror he felt about the possibility of losing her. She knew she could pursue that and secure their relationship, but she decided she would wait till they were out of this place and safely home.

Frank gently took her by her once-restrained wrists and lowered them to her side as he moved around her toward the balcony. Marla followed him tentatively, and they both peered over the railing to the parking lot below. Hector lay broken in an unnatural position. Blood ran from his chest. Frank could see Hector was still clutching the coin in his left hand.

"Let's get out of here before the boys in blue show up." Then, with his arm around her waist, hoping she needed his support, Frank walked with Marla to the door. He looked cautiously out into the hallway, both right and left, and then, with his arm still around her waist, he led her to the stairs.

Walking down the hall while glancing ever so carefully from side to side at the closed rooms, Frank noticed a door to his left as it opened slightly. His protective instincts kicked in, and he moved Marla from his left side to his right so as to keep himself between her and any potential danger that might be lurking on the other side.

Trying to sound gallant and to keep Marla from any further worry, he winked at her and said, "Let's get you back to West Palm, Doll."

Marla smiled. She loved it when he called her "Doll."

The door slowly opened. Reaching quickly for his gun, he saw in a moment that it was one of Nora's girls. She had the faded marks of bruising on both her eyes and cheeks. Her lip, like Marla's, was split. With an initial look of terror and possibly mixed with distrust, she spoke slowly and barely above a whisper, "I heard you say you were going back to West Palm, right?"

Hesitating and lowering her voice even more, she spoke with a pleading tone, "Please, please take me back with you."

Marla gently removed Frank's arm from around her waist and stepped toward the girl hiding in the doorway. Reaching out her hand, she said, "Come on, Darlin', let's get you outta here. My name is Marla, and this here gorgeous hunk of a soldier is Frank. Don't you worry none, he'll protect you. You can count on that."

The girl smiled ever so slightly and said in a continued frightened whisper, "My name is Tina, and I just wanna go home."

20

As the three beaten and wounded souls approached the door in the dark hallway to the outside, Frank automatically stepped ahead of the ladies to offer himself up in case trouble still existed outside in the bright Florida sunshine. He didn't know if Hector had others loyal to him. He certainly couldn't be on guard here at Sunrise Hall every day of the week, Frank thought.

Marla, with her arm intertwined with Tina's, turned to her and smiled again, "See, I told you he would protect us."

Tina stared back, disconnected. She had heard those words before.

As expected, the bright mid-day sun momentarily blinded Frank as he hesitated in the doorway before exposing himself to warm salt breezes and any danger that might be outside. Looking to the right and then to the left, he turned back to the ladies still sheltered and secluded in the doorway and signaled them the way was clear. Frank hurried them across the parking lot to the car, constantly searching with his eyes for anyone who might want to make a defense for the fallen Hector.

The parking lot was empty of threats.

After securing Marla and Tina in the backseat of the car, Frank decided he better make sure his vengeance took. He headed to the place in the parking lot where Hector had fallen.

Hector's body was gone.

"Frank, you mean his body just up and disappeared? I saw you put two slugs in his chest. I saw him slam into the rail and fall over three stories down to the pavement. There's no way he could of survived that! Much less just got up and walked away. No way, Frank," Marla said, leaning over the front seat from the back and speaking with a lowered voice in Frank's ear so that Tina wouldn't be anymore traumatized than she already appeared to be.

Tina just sat staring out the rolled-down window at the ocean as it raced along SR 140 back toward West Palm and home. Marla turned and looked back at her and noticed a tear was making its way down her cheek.

"I have no idea what happened to him. All that was left to show I did hit him was some blood on the pavement and that coin I flipped him. Could be someone saw him fall and moved him off before we got downstairs. I didn't have time to look for him. I had to get you ladies out of there. So that's just what I did. Once I get you two safe, I'll head back down and find out what happened." Looking in the rear view mirror, Frank whispered to Marla, "In the meantime, just see what you can do to make Tina know she's gonna be okay and see if you can find out anything about her and where we need to take her. Okay?" Then smiling at Marla and putting a light kiss on her cheek, he said, "I'm just so damn glad I got you back in one piece."

Leaning back in the seat, Marla smiled and said, "Yeah, you're just glad 'cause you can't type or file reports. You'd be lost without me, and you know it, Frank." She smiled and stuck her tongue out at him as he glanced at her in the mirror. He noticed she tenderly licked the split on her lip, then looking at the lost girl next to her with compassion, she put her hand on Tina's.

Tina just continued to stare out the window.

Frank furrowed his brows as he relived the violence Hector committed against Marla. He certainly had no regret in shooting Hector. He only wished he could have confirmed that Hector was indeed unable to harm anyone again. He looked at Marla in the mirror and knew she was right; he couldn't get on without her. But his reasons were far different than what she offered.

For many miles, they rode in silence. It seemed they all needed the quiet to recover from the transgressions Hector had brought to each one.

As they approached Boynton Inlet, Frank held his breath when they drove over the waterway bridge. His hands gripped the steering wheel as if the road was challenging his ability to stay in the right lane. Looking to the east momentarily, he swallowed hard from the memory of Beth. He had wished a thousand times he could have traded places with her. She didn't deserve death so early in her life. He no longer blamed Lilly. He blamed himself.

Marla noticed him tense as they began to cross and then watched as his weary shoulders fell back down while letting out his breath when they reached the other side. She knew better than to say anything that would make that fateful evening more real than it was in his dreams most nights. No matter how tight she held him in her bed, he always trembled and murmured Beth's name.

"Say, darlin', where can we take you when we get to West Palm? You got anybody we need to call?" Marla asked.

After a long silence, Tina answered without turning from the open window. "Just drop me at a cheap motel."

Again and with sympathy, Marla asked, "Don't you got nobody we need to get a hold of?

"Surely someone's been missing you, Sweetheart?"

More extended silence and then, "No one's missin' me. I got nobody. I just got to get away from Lauderdale for now." Then turning to face Marla, "I want to thank you for getting me out of there, but it don't matter where you drop me, he'll find me. He'll come and bring me back. Maybe I shouldn't of left. It'll just get worse when he finds me again."

Frank looked back at Tina in the mirror and realized she must not know that he had shot Hector. She was not in the room with him and Marla, and she couldn't have seen his body in the parking lot since it wasn't there. He decided not to tell her just yet. Frank wanted to see if he could get any more on Hector from Tina, so he looked at her from the mirror and asked, "Say, Tina, how long did you work for Hector at the Sunrise?"

The minute the words came out of his mouth, Frank knew he had not been tactful enough. The look Marla gave him from the back seat and the words she mouthed confirmed that fact. He figured the business he was in had jaded him to most people. For him, everyone was capable of doing wrong; every one that is except Marla, he thought. She often reminded him that his people skills were lacking. Many times, with her hands on his desk, she would lean in close to his face and say, "Frank Lobeck, it's a wonder we got any business at all the way you talk to folks. I swear someday someone is gonna knock your block off, and I won't be around to put it back on." Her look always began as stern, but then she would borrow his wink and blow him a kiss as she sashayed back to her office.

Yeah, what would he do without her?

When Tina finally spoke with the same distant stare, she looked up at the roof of the car and said, "You know we's gonna be married, me and him. I know Hector had his faults, but he had his good moments, too. He mostly treated me right. Not like he treated the other girls. We was plannin' on goin' off to Jamaica as soon as Hector got out from under Nora. He promised we could spend da days just drinkin' rum from coconuts and layin' on the beach without no care in the world. I believed him. I had to. It was the only way I could get outta there even if'n it was only in my mind."

Tina's voice began to choke. Her tears began to shine her cheeks as the sun made its way in from the west side window. Then, turning back to the ocean view, she started again, but this time she didn't hesitate.

"Ya know, most nights when Hector was there, I didn't have to work. It was just me and him. He saw to that. It made the other girls awful jealous, but I didn't care none. I wished he'd been there every night."

Frank interrupted, "Where would he go on nights he wasn't with you? Any idea?"

"He mostly went up to the Pennsylvania Hotel in West Palm. That's where he would get new girls. That's where he found me. He promised me he'd take care of me if'n I'd go with him, so I did. Most girls didn't get the choice. He would just bring 'em. I know he was mostly rough with them, but not with me. With me, it was different. With me, he hardly ever hit me," she said as she reached up and softly rubbed her cheek.

"How often would he go to the Pennsylvania? Did he always go on the same night, or was it just when he decided to go?" Frank needed to establish Hector's pattern of coming to West

Palm. It might lead to someone who could have helped him. Someone who could have gotten him out of that parking lot. Someone who could have gotten him to a doctor if there was any life left in him. Someone who could hide the body and later come after him and Marla. Frank needed to know.

"He was pretty regular on goin' up mid-week. Most times, he was goin' up to meet Nora. Sometimes, it was to get new girls. Other times, I guess it was just to blow off steam. I remember he came back one time not long ago with blood all over him. Said he'd been in a fight, a fight with some girl who didn't want to go with him. He said she wasn't gonna go with nobody anymore. He said he took care of that. Asked me to get rid of that shirt and to tell no one that he'd been gone. He told me to say that he'd been with me all night. He often told me to say that."

Frank picked something up in what Tina was saying. He looked back at her in the mirror and tried to piece it together in his mind. Something definitely was bothering him with what she said. Hmmm, maybe? He hadn't thought of that before, but now it made sense. He wasn't sure, but he needed to follow his gut. It always led him to the guilty party. He looked back at her in the mirror again and asked, "That night he came back with blood on his shirt was, it say, maybe around a week ago? Was it on a Wednesday?"

"Yeah, I think it was. Yeah, it definitely was a Wednesday 'cause that's the night me and the other girls all get together and play us some poker when Hector's gone. He came bustin' in and sent all the girls back to their rooms. Then I seen his shirt and he told me at first it was some guy, some German guy. Then later he told me the blood was some girl's. All I know is Hector was pretty upset that night. I ain't never seen him so scared. It ain't like Hector. Hector, don't get scared of nobody.

Never."

Frank's mind was racing. Ideas were coming. Coming into plain view. Maybe he had it all wrong. Maybe he was focused on the wrong guy. Could Hector be the one? Could he?

Frank remembered Betty Lou's body was found a week ago. On a Wednesday night a week ago.

21

Hans could not stop the trembling that his body now involuntarily exhibited to anyone who happened to gaze his way. The coin he handled while gifting it to Betty Lou and the others stashed away in his hotel room were having a poisonous effect on him that had moved to outward manifestations. He believed the curse had worked its way into his bloodstream; the poison from it caused him to not only shake uncontrollably but to react violently from the deep, searing pain that burned as if his very flesh were on fire. His forehead constantly sweated, dripping down into his eyes, causing him to squint at the world around him. He had no doubt the remorse the curse manifested in his heart pushed him closer and closer to an action that would ultimately leave him hanging from a tree like the coin's original owner. But that action—the action of suicide—Hans believed, because of what Father Peter had told him, would forever separate him from Betty Lou. As long as he lived, he knew he could keep her alive in his memory. In death, Father Peter said they would be eternally separated.

The allure of death, however, was overpowering his resolve

to live, and it openly confronted him now on the other side of a gun.

"You're her father, aren't you? She had your eyes." Hans tried to smile to soften the meeting, especially with that gun pointing at his gut.

Wilson did not return the smile. His eyes blurred with tears at the thought that this man— this animal—looked deeply enough into Betty Lou's eyes that he could see the resemblance.

Wilson vowed in his soul at that moment that he would kill this man, the man who murdered his baby girl. There was no way he would let this German live. No way. Then as he cocked the gun, Wilson muttered under his breath:

"Damn, you, you Kraut bastard."

Shakingly raising his hands as he slowly backed up a step, Hans could see the determination in Wilson. Thinking quickly, he said, "Look, Mr. Wilson, it is Mr. Wilson, isn't it?"

Wilson's eyes did not blink. His gaze bore through this man. He knew shooting Hans dead in this lobby would not bring an end to his torment but would satiate his anger for the present. Wilson was unable to formulate a response to this hideous creature before him. The thought occurred to him to spit on the man's feet, but his throat was dry from the bitterness in his mouth.

Hans stuttered, "I . . . I didn't kill . . . .I didn't kill your daughter. I was the one who discovered her . . . her body. I'm the one who called the police. Why would I kill her and then wait around after calling the police? I couldn't have killed her. You see, . . . I was in love with her; we were going to be . . . we were going to be married!" Hans's eyes filled with tears mixed with the sweat as he strained to see what impact that revelation had on the man with the gun. "You have to believe me. I didn't kill Betty

Lou. I loved her. Everything I ever did was for her."

Wilson began to seethe at the thought of this man pleading for understanding. He wondered if Betty Lou had pleaded for her life before she died. Pushing the barrel of the gun into Hans' belly, Wilson said through clenched teeth, "Likely story. You killed her, and then, to cover your murderous deed, you called the police to cast suspicion off of yourself. I know you damn Krauts, you'll do anything but what is decent and right to folks. Now move over to the bar and don't make any noise about it. I just as soon shoot you right here in this here lobby. I don't care what happens to me now. You cain't hurt me anymore than you already have."

Shoving Hans again with the gun, "Move, I said! Now!"

Hans turned slowly and began to walk to the bar area. His gait was that of a condemned man walking to the gallows. Instinctively, he straightened up his back and almost marched with determination. His training returned to him as he felt the surrender of being this man's prisoner. He realized the coin had found an executioner to carry out its murderous plan.

The bar was empty of patrons since it was still too early for the activity of alcoholic illusions that all was right in the world. However, there was a bartender washing glasses, but with his back turned to the lobby, he did not notice Wilson and the gun. The desk clerk had stepped away, so he, too, didn't have the perspective to notice the trouble Hans was in.

Wilson motioned with the gun for Hans to occupy the booth in the far corner so they would remain out of sight of the staff and anyone else who just might happen to wander through the lobby. Hans turned quickly on his heel as he lowered himself into the bench seat. Wilson stood looking down at the man, and then after another moment more of hesitation, he slid into the opposite bench seat, keeping the gun on Hans from under the table. Hans clasped his hands, placing them on the table while looking down at them so as to not have to look at the coming death across from him. He slowly reached up to his breast pocket and took out his cigarettes, thinking to himself that surely he wouldn't be denied one last smoke. Hans offered one to Wilson, but Wilson just frowned at the thought of receiving anything from this man. Hans fumbled with shaking hands to light it, and then inhaling some timid confidence, he looked up into those familiar eyes, awaiting his fate.

Wilson spoke while looking down at the table himself, "You know she was all we had.

"Me and my wife, we only had the one child. One beautiful child. She was our entire world. Now we ain't got nothin'," and looking up at Hans with more directed anger, "we ain't even got each other anymore. You see, you not only killed Betty Lou, but you killed my wife, her mother, that day. Her grief robs her of her soul. She has nothin' to live for. Not even for me." Wilson looked down at the table again. Continuing with great difficulty and choking back uncontrolled convulsive sobs, he said, "Everything I did . . ." Wilson looked up and stared angrily at the German across the table, "Everything was for my Betty Lou." He swallowed hard, and then, after hesitating for a moment, he steadied himself and continued, "And you took that from me. You took that from us!" he shouted as he slammed his fist against the table.

The bartender, suddenly jarred by the noise, looked over at the corner booth. His reaction was as if, for the first time, he noticed their presence. Looking at his watch, he decided it was much too early to help their argument along with alcohol. He turned back to his dishwashing, whistling to himself to cover any further noise.

Then, leaning across the table, conscious of the man behind the bar, Wilson whispered, "There's no forgiveness for that." He punctuated his words by pointing his index finger at Hans. "There ain't a judge in the world that would convict me for killin' you right here right now! A jury would agree with me that not only gettin' rid of one more damn Kraut is not only justice but to shoot the bastard that murdered my little girl, well, that's just savin' the court time and money. Hell, I'm saving the state a last meal."

The coin's curse grabbed Wilson's impromptu courtroom summation and rubbed the guilty verdict all through Hans' heart and mind. There was no escaping the gallows, Hans thought. The curse giddily welcomed the finality of that rope. It contorted his face into a crooked smile. In fact, Hans didn't even have to make this choice; the decision to embrace death warred against his resolve to live and quickly overpowered his own determination within his conscience.

Again, the coin pronounced him guilty.

The charges of guilt were more than what Wilson accused him of. Hans accepted the guilt of believing all the lies his nation and its leaders propagated. He tried to say he believed the lies because he was hungry as a child and that he was promised food and work. Anyone would sell their soul for food. Anyone.

Hans believed what he was told. He was told that the Jews were inferior and were trying to destroy his people. He had initially believed in a sense of nationalism, and he believed that the people could not think for themselves but had to rely on those in power to reason out the truth for everyone. He bought into the lies that the leaders taught, lies that the truth was as it was communicated to the people. That all other attempts by their enemies to subvert the truth were simply lies themselves and pure manipulation in an effort to destroy the unity the leaders sought to establish.

Hans blindly followed all this, that is, until the day he met Betty Lou. Betty Lou's love was stronger than the coin and its curse. She was the one to open his eyes to what the real truth was despite what the coin would have him believe. Real truth was not some selfish ideology that made some superior over others, but real truth was bound up in caring for those who had less, those who needed more than they could provide for themselves. She taught him all this through the love she freely offered to him. She taught him this by giving of herself while lying with him on her sheets. She taught him by rejecting the prejudice her father so freely spewed at him from across the table at this moment.

It was the one need the leaders did not provide—love.

Love overpowered all that he had created in his blind allegiance to his nation. But now that love was taken from him, the coin worked easily, convincing him that love was the real lie.

Without Hans or Wilson noticing, the bartender had slipped over to their booth quietly and, looking at his watch again, announced, "Gentlemen, the bar doesn't open for another couple of hours yet. Can I get you some water, perhaps?"

It was all the distraction Hans needed. He quickly reached under the table and twisted the gun in Wilson's hand away from him. Surprised, Wilson squeezed the trigger, and a loud shot exploded under the table, splintering the dark wood paneling of the wall. The bartender jumped at the sound and backed away from their booth while looking for someone anyone to intercede in this action. He thought momentarily that he might be shot, so he turned and ran into the lobby for a place to hide.

Wilson lost his hold on the gun to Hans, and Hans stood quickly, pointing the gun at his former executioner.

The coin shouted into Hans's mind to kill the adversary; after all, what's one more crime added to all the others Hans was guilty of. But the power of Betty Lou's love overcame the need for blood, and Hans lowered the gun and spoke quietly to Wilson, "I loved your daughter. I still do. I did not kill Betty Lou. And it is for her memory that I won't kill you. Your wife has lost enough. Do not follow me."

And with that, Hans tossed the gun across the room, spun on his heel, and left the bar.

22

Around 2:15 in the afternoon, Frank pulled into the parking lot of the Southlands Motor Lodge, the motel Wilson was staying at. Frank figured it would be easier to keep all the people involved somehow in the case together rather than scattered all around the city. He didn't tell Tina about Wilson.

"I got you a room. Here's the key," Frank said as he handed it to Tina. "You'll be safe here, trust me," adding one of his trademarked winks, hoping his confidence would ease Tina's outward fear. He wasn't so sure Tina was buying it, so he added, "No one knows you're here— but me and Marla."

Then, turning to leave, Frank suggested over his shoulder to her, "Maybe a shower and some sleep would help. I know that's what I got in mind as soon as I get Marla settled. I'll be back to check on you later. Be sure to lock up behind me."

And then he was gone.

Now, it was Marla's turn. Frank drove her to her apartment, and she insisted he stay while she cleaned up, and then he could take her to the office. Marla had left the bathroom door ajar.

An invitation, perhaps?

Looking back at Frank in the living room, Marla suggested, "You know you could use a shower, too," she smiled as she borrowed one of his winks.

"Tempting," Frank smiled back. He was always tempted when he was around Marla. She was the only one who tempted him anymore.

"Well, if you're not going to join me, you might as well pour yourself a cup of coffee. There's some in the percolator you can warm up. I won't be long . . . by myself," and again, she smiled as she turned gracefully with the agility of a ballerina and all the seduction of a burlesque dancer.

Marla continued speaking over the shower curtain, "I need to work, Frank, to keep from thinking about what happened. It's just the way I am. You do the same thing. Admit it."

Frank stepped into the bathroom doorway, sipping day-old coffee. He didn't even bother to warm it up. He thought how helpless he had made himself with Marla in his life. It's not that he didn't know how to heat coffee; it's that he loved the idea that she would take care of all the little details to make things smoother for him. He missed that most about Lilly, at least the Lilly in their beginning before his big mistake. He didn't want to make any mistakes with Marla, so he argued back over the shower curtain with her, "Listen, doll, you need to take the time to rest up from the whole kidnapping thing. I can handle anything at the office that needs our attention.

"Besides, I need to get back to Ft. Lauderdale right away to figure out what happened to Hector's body."

Frank knew the only way he could protect Marla and Tina was to know where the Cuban happened off to or who helped him to happen off.

"I'm also concerned about what Tina said about Hector's trip to West Palm on a Wednesday. I need to check it out and see if there is any connection between that and the murder of Betty Lou. I figure I need to talk to Enid at the Pennsylvania about it, and at some point, I need to check on Wilson when I get back from Lauderdale."

Pausing to drink his coffee, Frank added with as much sincerity as he was capable of, "I just don't need to worry right now about you alone at the office."

Pulling the curtain open enough to look at Frank, Marla smiled, and using her seductive little girl voice, she mockingly said, "Why Frank, I didn't know you cared, but I'm a big girl now, and I can take care of myself."

Then she stepped out of the shower, dripping water on the bath mat, and asked, "Could you hand me that towel, Frank?" pointing to the towel rack near the light switch next to the door.

Frank tossed her a towel and turned back toward the living room to give her some privacy, although, at the moment, she did not appear to need any or want any.

Marla smiled at what she perceived to be his embarrassment.

Frank sat in Marla's small living room, drinking the day-old coffee laced now with a shot of whiskey from his pocket flask. The living room was more like a nook crowded with a settee, a small coffee table, a single leather wingback chair, a floor lamp, and a buffet to store the extra dishes and food items that the kitchen cabinet couldn't accommodate. From where he sat, Frank had a perfect view of Marla's bedroom with her double mattress iron framed bed, five-drawer dresser, and bedside nightstand. The door to her bath was between the dresser and the nightstand. He felt a little guilty glancing now and then through the open door, but he thought to himself she was the one who left it open, and she would not have done that if she hadn't anticipated a male's peeping tom nature doing what a peeping tom would naturally do.

He studied her as she leaned over the sink, checking the split lip Hector had marked her with. She continued to dry off slowly, glancing his way with her coy smile. Then, wrapping herself in the small white towel, the kind you can procure from the YMCA, Marla moved slowly and deliberately to her dresser and selected her undergarments with care. Frank knew her choice in lingerie was sexier than the typical secretary on a typical secretary's salary, and he was almost certain it was not the lingerie she brought with her from Boston but upgraded when she and Frank became accustomed to undressing in each other's presence. He smiled as she dressed and wondered to himself why he hadn't told her just how much he needed her. He told himself she was the one who could replace Lilly in his lonely world when he developed the courage. He believed she would be able to love his grief over losing Beth away; at least, he wanted to believe that; he needed to believe that. But he knew Marla needed more from him than just someone who replaced someone. She needed him to love her for her. Frank wasn't sure if he could, but he knew he needed to.

"You want me to make you something to eat. I'm sure you haven't eaten all day," Marla asked as she emerged from the bedroom, leaving a scented trail that was intoxicating as she moved into the small kitchenette. Her scent was more potent than his whiskeyed coffee.

"Nah, I got to get going. Maybe later. It'll be pretty late when I get back. I may have to stay the night if things don't pan out for me. I got to know what happened to Hector. I can't keep you and Tina safe until I know. You sure you're okay to go back to the office and then walk home. You know I'll worry."

"Why don't cha come by here when you get back. It don't matter to me how late. The later, the better to get by Mrs. Johnson. You know she don't allow no men in the rooms, so for goodness sake, be quiet. You know how to be quiet, don't cha?" Marla smiled down at Frank sitting in the leather wing-backed chair as she walked into the living room and then continued, "You got your key, right? Just come on in that way you can ease your mind knowin' I'm okay. I'll leave some supper on the stove just in case. And in the morning, I'll fix you some breakfast; that way, I'll know you're okay."

Rising and walking to her, Frank slipped his arm around her small waist and drew her close. He buried his nose in her freshly washed hair and inhaled deeply to remember something that he hadn't remembered in so long. Frank felt the greatest mystery in life was the many scents of a woman. It was the one mystery he never would or never could solve. He was fascinated that just moving a few inches from her hair to her neck to her breasts, her scent changed, and each one was more scintillating than the other. He moved back up to look into her eyes, and for a moment, he was in love. The deepest kind of love. The only kind of love a man could have for a woman. He was sure it was how Adam felt in the Garden when he first came upon Eve standing there naked among the trees. Indeed, he thought this was the great plan God had for mankind.

Finding life's one and only real love. Holding her, Frank felt this was true religion. He wanted to worship her like Joyce's protagonist did in "Araby," believing she deserved worship for all she had done to rescue him. She was his savior.

But at that moment, just before he dropped to his knees in tears and pledged his devotion forever, his remorse reemerged, fueled by the coin's poison, and stole his repentance, replacing it with doubt. Doubt that one like him could ever be forgiven. That one like him could ever be restored to purity and wholeness. That one like him could truly be loved by one like Marla.

Stiffening and stepping back away from her, Frank trembled as the coin's power moved slowly, coursing through his veins. It held him, threatening to crucify him if he resisted. He sensed Marla felt the change in him, too. She looked at him with sorrow in her eyes. She sighed audibly as she realized Frank just couldn't give himself over to her and let her love heal him. She knew it was more than just the loss of Lilly and Beth, but she didn't know how to find the door if, indeed, there was a door to let the pain out and let her in.

"Well, we got to be going. You ready? I'll drop you off and then head back down to the Sunrise Hall. Someone there knows what happened. Maybe one of the girls saw something."

"Alright, Frank. Just let me get my purse. Go ahead; I'll meet you in the car."

After Frank dropped Marla off at the office with one last protest from him that she should stay home and rest up from the crazy Cuban's abuse, a protest he didn't win, he headed back south down State Road 140 along the Atlantic east coast toward Ft. Lauderdale and the Sunrise Hall. Frank finally felt the trail was getting warm. He needed answers. And now he was beginning to ponder the idea of a connection between Hector and Betty Lou.

For the first time since he rescued Marla, Frank relaxed and eased back in the car seat, and with the window rolled down, his left arm hanging out the opening, his fingers tapping a rhythm only he heard in his head, the other hand lightly gripping the steering wheel he began to breathe in the addictive salt air. Frank knew that people born and raised in Florida thrive on the salt air coming in off the water. He thought of it like a drug, something you long for it when it's not around, something you tell others about with fondness in your voice and something like a craving in your soul for its presence. Frank breathed deeply and imagined he was one of the many barefoot mailmen who walked the sands from Palm Beach to Miami in the late 1800s when the highway did not exist. Of the hundreds of times he had traversed this road, each time, it mesmerized him. Each time, it carried him to that place where reality faded into a misty haze and left him with only the sound of rubber rolling round and round.

Frank loved this drive along the ocean. The road calmed him and made him think that living with the sea always at his side was possibly the best whiskey anyone could drink who needed to forget the hardness of this life. The road offered other possibilities. It poured itself into Frank's imagination, and he yielded to its drunken escapes. He saw himself leaving the road and sailing off into the proverbial sunset seeking treasure and fighting battles on board galleons which was far more romantic than dealing with scum like Hector on land.

As Frank sobered, he determined, as many men do, that he was born too late.

This stretch of highway offered the best of South Florida. The road meandered in and out of view of the Atlantic and its blue-green waters. At times, there was nothing but the sand dunes scattered with wild muscadine grapes, saw palmettos, and purslane, also named rose moss by the locals. At other times, the highway slid easily through small beach towns such as Boca Raton and snowbird trailer parks like Briny Breezes and Hillsboro Inlet with its famous lighthouse.

The road worked its magic and made Frank feel for a brief moment there was no pain, no emptiness, and no curse. Then, the road ended.

Arriving at the Sunset Hall just as the Atlantic was disappearing for the night, Frank instinctively patted his heater in his shoulder hostler underneath his coat pocket. He wasn't sure just what would be inside, but he needed to be ready. Nora may already have a replacement for Hector looking out for the girls.

It was unusually quiet for this time of night, and no one was handling the front desk in the lobby. Frank made his way slowly down the hall and hesitated just outside the first open door for a brief moment. Then he cautiously stepped inside and took in the whole room in one quick glance. Surprised by a man standing in the doorway, the young girl mechanically rose with a strained smile, greeting a potential customer.

"Welcome, mister. I didn't hear you come in. What can I do for you?" she said without sincerity, all the while sashaying her hips to a memorized song in her mind that helped her forget why men came. Frank noticed her fear and thought he might be able to use that.

"Name's Frank, Frank Lobeck. I'm a private dick, and I was just wondering if you were here earlier in the day? I'm looking for Hector. You seen him around?"

Instinctively, the girl's expression was guarded, possibly wondering why a private detective was standing in her room and just what he wanted with Hector. But then the guard was softened, and for a very brief moment, Frank thought he saw a plea in her eyes asking him to take her away from all this. The look quickly faded almost as soon as it appeared, and she responded with the rehearsed lines, "Listen, Mister, if you ain't here for some pleasure, then you better be about someone elses. I ain't got time for no twenty questions."

Frank reached into his pocket, pulled out a crinkled sawbuck, and began snapping the wrinkles smooth between his hands with his fingers in front of her. She brightened up and attempted to snatch the bill from Frank, but he quickly pulled it back out of her reach. The girl put on a teasing smile and said, "Mister, I can make all your dreams come true for that ten spot. Just hand it over, and it'll be between you and me. No one has to know what went on here tonight. There ain't nobody guardin' the door, if you know what I mean." She attempted to close the deal with one of Frank's trademark winks.

Frank felt sorry for her as she negotiated with her body. He hated this trade of pleasure for profit, but no matter how much he was disgusted by it, he knew man's depravity would not allow it to diminish. But then the coin reared its ugly head and began to tell Frank that this woman's plight was better than any other life she could now possibly have. So, there was no need to be sympathetic and to just let her do what she was forced to do.

"I might of seen somethin', but my memory is worth a whole lot more than what you're offerin'. I mean, if I'm gonna waste my valuable time on questions from some shamus, then I think that it's at least worth twice or three times, yeah, three times as much. You get my meanin', mister?"

Frank reached into his pocket and, put two more tens with the one in his hand and passed them to the girl.

Suddenly, she became animated and began to talk excitedly as if the money had injected some unseen sexual vitality into her veins.

"Hector's got this cousin from Cuba. He comes here once in a while and visits. They sit around talkin' all loud and drinkin' and tell stories about growing up in Cuba, and then they get all quiet and start whisperin' stuff that I don't hear. But it's somethin' serious by their faces. And Hector gets all mean and nasty with us girls after his cousin leaves. Don't know what for, but we certainly don't like it when that guy comes around."

"You got a name of this cousin?"

"No, it was some Spanish name that started with a P or somethin'. Somethin' like Pashe or somethin' like that. I'm not sure."

"When was the last time this Pashe was here?"

"Well, that's just it. He ain't been around here for a long time. Maybe over a year or so.

"Then he shows up out of the blue."

"What day was that?"

"Why today. Right after Hector was shot."

<h1 style="text-align:center">23</h1>

On the drive back, Frank mulled over what he had recently learned from the girl at Sunrise Hall. He was thirty dollars lighter, but he felt it was worth it. If it helped him be certain about keeping Marla safe, he determined he'd have paid more. A whole lot more. Frank still didn't know where Hector was taken or even if he was still alive for that matter, but one thing he couldn't forget was that name Pashe, as the girl called him. Or was it Patchi, the former Basque pelota player from the Crook Factory Hemingway introduced him to at Kelsey's bar. It could be just a coincidence, but Frank remembered Hemingway said Patchi had family here in South Florida. Family who worked in a brothel. Frank made a note in his mind he needed to see if Hemingway and his crew were still in town. Kelsey would know.

But first, he needed to see Wilson, and he needed to check on Tina.

Banging on the motel door for the third time, Frank hollered, "Wilson, you in there? It's me, Frank Lobeck. Wilson?"

As the doorknob twisted slowly, Frank instinctively stepped

back to one side. He had been in the game long enough to ready himself for any eventuality. His hand moved to his pistol.

"Frank, sorry, I was on the phone to my wife. Come in," Wilson said as he swung open the motel room door wide.

Frank stepped slowly into the room, scanning it as he entered. He wasn't sure why he was being so cautious. Just something in his gut told him there was reason to expect the unexpected from this man. It's true the man had lost something most precious to him, but Frank knew if this had been him and his daughter, Beth, he wouldn't simply wait around for news—good or bad.

Frank noticed Wilson's jacket lying over the motel room chair. On top of it was a pistol. "You been out, Wilson?"

Hesitantly at first, Wilson responded with caution when he saw Frank spot the pistol. "No, . . . well yeah. I did go out for a bit. Getting' kinda cooped up here all day. Had to get some fresh air. You find anything more about who murdered my baby girl?"

Frank moved between Wilson and the gun. He didn't need this guy going all grief crazy on him and takin' to the streets by himself. Then Frank thought maybe he already had.

"You say you went out? Where'd you go? You go for a drive? I noticed your car has been moved since I was last here."

Again, as if he was thinking before responding, Wilson looked over Frank's shoulder instead of Frank's eyes and said, "Yeah, I went for a drive along the beach. Like I said, I just had to get out of here. Went and had a cup of joe at this little diner down the road. Got tired of the motel lobby's mud." Then, looking at Frank, he continued, "Had me a slice of that icebox lime pie you folks is so proud of."

"Yeah, is that right? I like mine with the lattice crust. How about you?"

"Yeah, me too. Damn good pie!"

Moving closer to Wilson, Frank watched his eyes to learn what he could about Wilson's whereabouts while he was gone. He noticed Wilson began to sweat a little, and he looked away, avoiding Frank's scrutiny.

"Where were you, Wilson? Lime pie don't have no lattice crust. No self-respecting Floridian would eat lime pie that way. So what gives?" Turning to pick up the gun and holding it up in front of Wilson, Frank asked, "And what's with the heat?"

Wilson sat down on the edge of the unmade bed. He lowered his head, and with a heavy sigh, he began as he stared at the floor.

"I had to do somethin'. I was goin' crazy just sittin' here wonderin'." Then, looking up, he continued, "I went to that Washington hotel to see if I could find that German bastard. And I did!"

Wilson's eyes began to fill with tears, but Frank noticed a burning anger deep in them. Just for a moment, he thought he might have two murders on his docket. Then he asked, "What did you do?"

"I waited until he came in the lobby and then used the gun to force some answers outta him. But he . . . he got away." Then lowering his head again, Wilson whispered, "I swear to ya, if I get another chance, I kill that somabitch, looking back up, "I swear to ya next time I see that German bastard, I'll put a bullet between his eyes. I swear to ya I will . . . but today I just couldn't do it. I let him get away without shooting him."

Wilson again lowered his head to his chest and sobbed silently.

Frank hesitated, then reached out and placed his hand on Wilson's shoulder. Normally, Frank didn't go in for expressing any emotion with his clients, but he decided Wilson's loss and his were profound enough to warrant this display of affection. He knew Marla would be surprised at his actions. At that moment, Frank envied Wilson. At least Wilson had a real enemy to shoot at. How could Frank get revenge on the sea for killing Beth? He couldn't blame Lilly anymore.

The longer Frank kept his hand on Wilson's shoulder, the more awkward he felt. So, patting him once, Frank stuck both hands in his pockets, moved back, and sat on the motel chair.

"Did you get anything out of him before he got away?"

"All he told me was that he loved her, and he didn't kill her. He said they was gonna be married," then Wilson spat on the carpeted floor. "Can you imagine that, my baby girl married to some damn Kraut? No way in hell would I let that happen. We're at war, for God's sake, with them bastards."

Standing up and pacing back and forth across the room, Wilson wiped his eyes and continued to talk angrily, "That's how I know he did it. He was just tryin' to goad me. He was tauntin' me, tryin' to get me off my guard so's he could get the advantage. Well, sir, I didn't believe a word he was sayin'. Not a word! No, sir. Not a damn word!"

Wilson stopped pacing and looked at Frank, "You goin' after that sombitch? Let me go with you. We both can bring him down. What'd ya say, Mr. Lobeck? Wanna kill some Krauts?"

Frank stood up and crowded Wilson's space as he looked hard into the angry man's eyes.

He's seen this level of anger before in his father-in-law. Wilson surely hated Germans, Frank thought. If the war gave him a chance, he believed Wilson would answer the call. Frank knew he had better be the one to find Hans before Wilson did. But Wilson had managed to scare him away. There's no telling where he ran off to. Wilson was convinced it was Hans who killed Betty Lou. It was enough for Frank to put him back on the list of suspects. He had been so determined that Hector was tied up in her murder that he had let Hans slip from his possibles. He figured among the list of folks he needed to see, he needed to add Enid to that list and Father Peter, too. Enid might have some answers not only about Hans but about Hector as well. Father Peter might remember something more about Hans. But right now, Frank needed Wilson to stay put. He needed to check on Tina and Marla and needed a shower along with some rest. But it didn't look like that was going to happen anytime too soon.

"Listen, Wilson. I got to run down some leads, and you will just get in my way. Now you gotta promise me you'll stay put and not interfere. I know that ain't easy for you to do, but things could get messy, and I don't need to babysit you. Ya, get me? Stay put! Promise me you'll stay in this room and don't even go out for no damn lime pie. *Capiche?*"

Wilson wanted to argue. He believed he had the right, but he saw the determination in Frank's eyes and decided he best stay put.

"All right, I'll stay here. Promise I won't go nowhere. But you better call me the minute you hear anything. And if you catch that Kraut bastard, you bring him back here," then, borrowing Frank's determination, he added, "*Capiche!*"

Just for caution, Frank picked up Wilson's gun and put it in his pocket. Wilson didn't argue.

Frank walked across the courtyard to Tina's room. He knocked on the door several times, but there was no answer. She either was sleeping hard or she had gone out. Frank decided he'd check on her later.

Rather than waste time going to check on Marla, Frank called

Mrs. Johnson at Marla's rooming house and asked if he could speak to her. When she came to the phone, Frank assured her he was fine and that he needed to follow up on his leads. She argued he needed to get a shower and some rest. She said he wouldn't be no good to nobody if he keeled over from lack of sleep. Frank smiled over the phone and told her he'd be just fine knowing that he was protected by her concern. He told her to keep the coffee hot and that he'd see her in the office in the morning.

Hanging up, he headed to the Pennsylvania Hotel. He hoped Enid would have some answers.

24

Frank arrived at the Pennsylvania just as the day shift was leaving. Harry was coming out and headed up to Flagler Drive to his car. Seeing Frank approaching, he waved and said, "Hey, Frank. What's cookin'? How's the big bad world out there?"

"Mostly bad. You still chasin' rich skirts wintering here?"

"You know me, Frank. Gotta pay the rent, and lately, rent's gone up. If ya know what I mean?" Harry said with a wink and a sly smile, tapping the side of his nose with his right index finger.

Frank laughed, shaking his head, remembering his skirt-chasing days before Lilly put an end to that.

"Say, Harry, is Enid still on the clock?"

"Yeah, you know Enid. She don't never leave on time. I just passed her headed up to the room of that chippy what got killed. When you guys gonna close that case and let Enid clean that room? Every day, she goes in there, but as far as I know, she ain't cleaned it up yet. Think it's getting' to her. She always comes out all sad-like and don't want to talk to nobody neither."

Cocking his head to this new information, Frank asked,

puzzled, "Didn't know they were still holdin' that room. I'd a thought by now they would have let Enid set it straight. You say she goes in there every day? Wonder what she's doin' in there?"

"Like I said, I got no idea what she's doin', but whatever it is, she's keepin' tight-lipped about it like she did before that girl got killed."

Frank stepped closer to Harry and lowered his voice as he looked around for anyone who might overhear information not meant for the public; he asked, "You say Enid went in regular to Betty Lou's room before she was murdered? Where they close, do you know?"

"Yeah, they were close. I don't think that Enid took a shine to that German fella seein' that girl. Enid seemed to be motherin' her ever since her own daughter ran off with that Cuban gardener. She don't never take too kindly to any gents around her girls, if you know what I mean?" Harry said, touching the side of his nose again. "In fact, I seen her lay into that German fella as he was comin' outta that girl's room the afternoon before they found her dead. You could hear Enid all the way down in the lobby. I had to go up and tell them to put the kibosh on their fussin'. It was startin' to bother the folk's comin' to dinner. Enid was so mad she looked like she could do that German some serious harm. Never seen her that mad except, like I said, about her daughter and that Cuban groundskeeper. What was his name? Uh, Hector! Yeah, Hector. That's it!" Looking off over Frank's shoulder while thinking about something that he didn't share with Frank, Harry mused to himself, *wonder what ever happened to that guy?*

"So, did you happen to see Hector anywhere near Betty Lou's room that Wednesday?" "Yeah, I seen him hangin' around the hotel that day with Nora, you know that lady that runs that whorehouse down in Lauderdale, but I didn't see him anywhere near her room."

"So, as far as you know, the German was the last one to see Betty Lou, or did Enid go in the room after he left?"

"They both clammed up when I got there and then scramed right away. Enid headed back to the laundry, and I saw that German leave out the front. Didn't see them no more that day."

"And you didn't see anyone go in or out of the room the rest of that day?"

"I don't keep an eye on all the goin's on around here, but as far as I know, that girl never came out till they found her body the next morning."

Frank chuckled at Harry saying he didn't know 'all the goin's on.' Harry knew everyone and everything that happened at the Pennsylvania. His reputation with the wealthy, lonely women who stayed at the hotel depended on it. One wrong name, one misstep about their husband's whereabouts could get him fired or worse. No, quite the contrary, Harry knew everything, Frank said to himself.

"Say, Harry, why do you keep callin' Betty Lou 'that girl'? You know her name. You been workin' here longer than she did."

Harry smiled that sly smile and flashed his white teeth. That smile won many lonely women's hearts here at the Pennsylvania, not to mention all the late-night dinners and the early morning breakfasts.

"Any doll-face that don't recognize my charmin' ways gets no recognition from me," Harry said, raising his eyebrows and nodding his chin upward as he pursed his lips together while combing his fingers through his oiled hair. "Between you and me, I don't, as a rule, normally step out with the hired help, but that girl was a bombshell. Then, squinting his eyes and adding another smile, Harry leaned close to Frank and added, "But she turned me down. Turned me down! Can you beat that? She definitely ain't no charity girl. Handsome Harry, don't get turned down by no dame. Ever!"

"Listen, I know you got to get goin' to whatever doll-face is buyin' your dinner tonight, but just one or two more questions.

"Make it quick. You're right about the dinner."

"So, no one went in or out. Correct?"

"Correct." Harry turned to leave but then spun around and said excitedly, "No one that is except Father Peter. I remember now. He came by that day. I remember it was strange because he went into her room, and most priests I know wouldn't do that. You know, go into a single girl's room. But he did. Anyhow, Father Peter was the last one I saw goin' into that girl's room."

Surprised by this new piece of the puzzle, Frank asked, "Father Peter? You mean the priest down at St. Ann's?"

"Yeah, that's him. I only know him 'cause he became a regular soon after that girl started workin' here. They used to meet regular, you know, and mostly in her room. Kinda strange for a priest, don't cha think?" Raising his eyebrows while leaning in close to Frank and whispering, "You reckon her and the priest?" Then, leaning back, he exclaimed, "Naah, no way!" Shaking his head from side to side, Harry chuckled, then he said to Frank, "I'll probably have to go to confession for that thought.

"Ok, Frank, you owe me, but I'll have to collect later 'cause right now, Mrs. Merrick is waitin' on her young man about town."

Walking away with a swagger, Harry ran his fingers through his oiled hair, then he shouted back over his shoulder at Frank, "See ya later, you ol' gumshoe."

Hollaring to Harry, Frank asked one last question as Harry walked away. "Say, what was Enid's daughter's name?"

Frank was surprised at Harry's response.

"Tina."

Enid had worked at the Pennsylvania now for over fifteen years. She arrived from somewhere up north without a husband and toting a young daughter. Her daughter grew up working with Enid at the Pennsylvania until the day Hector ran off with her.

Enid never forgave Hector or her daughter.

She kept a small wooden desk in the laundry for the little paperwork she did for the hotel. Actually, it was a wooden table that substituted for a desk. Management had offered Enid a room for office space and furniture to go with it, but she said she didn't need to be out of sight of her workers like she was somebody. She always said, "I don't need to go and get uppity 'round my folks what work with me. There's more respect when I'm in amongst them. So, just give me a space in the laundry, and it'll be fine. 'Sides, you give me more, ya'll then gonna 'spect more from me. I got's me plenty to do for ya'll, and this way, I can keep my eyes on my people."

Enid had her head down, occupied with the work schedule for the upcoming month, trying to keep a full staff operating for the demands of the hotel and its guests. She was totally absorbed in the schedule and did not notice Frank enter the laundry until he knocked on the door facing so as not to startle her.

"Hello, Enid. Wonder if I can interrupt you for a minute or two and ask you some more questions?"

Looking up, somewhat surprised that someone had come into her laundry without her notice, she responded, "Look's like ya already have."

Sitting down in a chair across the table from Enid, Frank asked, "What else can you tell me about this Hector fellow? Do you know of perhaps a fella named Patchi that might have had contact with Hector?"

"Patchee? Pat . . . chee? Seems like I do remember there being a fella by that name that came 'round here. He and Hector would often disappear for several days, then Hector would come draggin' his butt back hangin' his head and beg management to give him his job back. Said he was gone on family business or such and didn't have no time to make other arrangements. The only problem was he used that same excuse time and time again. Not a very clever Cuban.

Course that don't say much for the management hirin' him back over and over. Why, you ask?"

"I'm tryin' to locate this here, Patchi. I think he might lead me to Hector. Hector got away from me down in Lauderdale. Now I know that there's a group of men in town runnin' with that writer fellow, Hemingway. One of them is called Patchi, but I don't know if it's the same guy."

"Oh, it's the same guy, alright. I'm sure. I saw them all once in the dining room. Seems that writer fella was holdin' court with them, and I seen that Patchee in the group. I remember 'cause it's the first time I'd seen him without Hector. Hector weren't workin' here then, so I thought at first it was odd, but from what I could overhear, they's all travelin' in a boat back and forth to Cuba. I heard that writer fella say somethin' bout chasin' U-boats or somethin'. I 'spect them folks was up to no good. Cain't get a bunch of drinkin' men together for some charity sake. No, sir. I just betcha that bunch wouldn't give back a shiny new penny what fell outta a blind man's tin cup. I's just grateful they didn't bed down here. Heard they's all stayin' down to the Biltmore that time. Likely, that's where they go regular. They only come here to the Pennsylvania for the drinkin' and a fine dinner once in a while. Seems that writer fella believed the Biltmore it was a hang out of Capone's," then leaning over the table and offering a rare smile, Enid continued, "'tween you and me I don't think them stories is true 'bout Capone I mean. He stayed down Miami way, but I don't think he was keepin' quarters here." Then, leaning back, Enid finished with some certainty, "Most likely, that's where they stay."

Just then, another lighter knock came from the doorway. Enid looked up with surprise as the voice behind Frank said,

"Hello, mama."

Frank turned to see Tina standing timidly, almost cowering in the doorway. A look of fear and a look of sadness was on her face. He turned back as Enid rose from her chair behind the table, slowly punctuating her displeasure by leaning on her knuckles while setting her jaw into a scowl. Frank thought he saw a little sadness in her eyes, but if so, it quickly faded into hardness as Enid looked determined to remain behind the table and not run to embrace her lost daughter.

Slowly, Enid spoke, "Thought I told you never ta come back here when you ran off with that no good Cuban bastard! Ya might as well turn 'round and get on outta here. I ain't got nuthin to say to the like's of you."

Tina began to tear up and did not seem to notice Frank sitting there across from her mother.

"Mama, please. I got away from Hector. I got away from that Nora lady, too. Mama, please, I just want to come back home. Won't you ever forgive me, Mama?"

Tina stepped tentatively into the room and, at the same time, seemed to notice Frank for the first time. She pleaded with him with her eyes to intervene.

Frank remained silent, unsure how to do that.

"Ask this man, Mama. He was the one who brought me here from Lauderdale. Just ask him, Mama."

Turning her attention back to Frank, Enid asked, "Is what she sayin' true? Did you bring her here?"

Frank offered, "I was leaving the Sunrise Hall with my secretary and your daugh . . . um, Tina here asked me to bring her back to West Palm, and I did. I dropped her off at a motel to keep her safe from those folks back in Ft. Lauderdale. Didn't know she was your daughter till just a little while ago. She's tellin' the truth about wanting to get away from Hector. She's the one that put me on to Patchi. I think ya oughta hear her out."

Enid looked down at the table as she seemed to study what Frank had just said. Looking back up at Tina and then back at Frank, she spoke to Frank, "For what you did, I 'preciate. But what's 'tween me and this girl goes way back. It's too hard and too grievous to just up an' throw out forgiveness. Me and her got some talkin' to do, so if'n ya don't mind, I'll let you get to your business of findin' that Patchee fella, and I'll get to mine. Again, my thanks for what ya did."

Frank knew it was useless to remain, and he knew Enid would not talk to Tina with him sitting there. Besides, he didn't want to be in the middle of this family problem; he figured it was their business, not his. So he got up from his seat at the table and tipped his Fedora both to Enid and Tina as he was leaving. He decided he better go by and check on Marla at the office before he headed off to talk to Father Peter. He also decided he would try and get in touch with Hemingway before he just showed up at the Biltmore. Kelsey might be able to help him out there. He was also thinking he could use a drink.

<h1 style="text-align:center">25</h1>

"Well, it's about time you got your sorry behind in here to the office. A gal could go gray worrying about the likes of you," Marla said, trying to conceal her pleasure at seeing Frank safe.

Frank gave her a wink. Then he bent over her desk and kissed her cheek. He, too, was delighted to see she was safe, but he also knew he had to find Hector before he felt she was completely safe from any harm. If he lost Marla, he thought they might as well just shut the lid on his coffin, too.

Frank stepped into his office and took off his Fedora, sending it spinning perfectly through the air to the hatrack standing in the corner behind his office door. He smiled at his precision from the toss. Marla saw the usual action from her desk and pursed her lips in a tight smile while hanging her head and shaking it from side to side slowly. She loved the boy in Frank.

Grabbing her notepad and pencil, she stood in his doorway and asked, "Okay, boss, what's our next move? Any leads on finding that creep, Hector?"

"Yeah, I stopped at the Pennsylvania and talked to Harry and Enid. Enid says that Hector's cousin is this fellow named Patchi, and he runs with that writer Hemingway. Oh, and guess who showed up at the Penn? Tina. And guess who Tina's mother is?"

"Well, my guess is it's Enid," Marla said with a little surprise while raising her eyebrows and, putting the eraser end of her pencil to her mouth and tapping her lips.

"Nice guess. How'd you figure that one?"

"Well, you mentioned you saw Harry and Enid, and I figured it wasn't Harry. Therefore, Enid would be the obvious choice. Was it a happy reunion?

"Not hardly. You know you'd make a good detective, Dollface," Frank said with a smile of admiration at Marla's observance. "Mind callin' Kelsey to see if he knows how to get ahold of Hemingway? I need to know what I'm walkin' into."

"Right away, boss," and Marla turned back to her desk with a flirt in her walk.

Frank unholstered his gun and took some bullets from his bottom drawer to refill the cylinder. He threw Wilson's gun into that same drawer. From his experience, he knew he better be ready and at his best, as well as fully loaded, when he ran into Hector. Besides, he didn't know how loyal this cousin might be. While holding open the cylinder, Frank felt an uneasiness in his conscience with each bullet he chambered. The dark thought of putting the gun in his mouth and pulling the trigger seemed to be suitable for one so responsible for so many sins in his life. He blamed himself for Lilly and Beth. His fingers trembled with the last two bullets.

Damn, the coin. Would its power ever leave him be? Looking up, he saw Marla talking on the phone to Kelsey. Her presence drew him back to a place that was manageable. He counted on her to push away the thoughts of depression, guilt, and unending responsibility for his role in the tragedies of those he loved. He holstered his gun before the thought of splattering his brains all over the window behind him could force an action. While placing the bullets back into the bottom drawer, he saw the bottle of bourbon whiskey. It was a little early, Marla would say, but a slug or two came with the occupation, he told himself. It would ease his conscience for a moment, he reasoned. Besides, he needed the prep since he was going to Kelsey's place. Frank chuckled at the thought of using whiskey to keep from drinking too much whiskey. He wasn't sure Marla would see the logic in his reasoning, but what the hell, he was a grown man with issues, and grown men with issues drink.

Walking back into his office, Marla noticed Frank staring into his bottom booze drawer and saw the temptation on his face. Or was it temptation? She often thought he used liquor to chase demons, and this man had plenty of demons.

"Not a good plan, boss. That stuff's gonna kill you one day."

Looking up, Frank said, "It already has. It's just embalming fluid anymore."

Like a child caught with his hand in the cookie jar, Frank slowly closed the drawer and then asked, "What cha find out from Kelsey?"

"He said to tell you to get your sorry behind down to the bar right now. Said that Hemingway character is there now. Kelsey said he'd keep him as long as he could but that he's already poured half a dozen shots into the guy, and he didn't know how many more the writer could stand. He said Hemingway was pretty tight and that he was about to leave something about having to go pick up his boat from the yard or something like that. You want I should call you a cab, or are you taking your car?"

Standing up, Frank walked over to the hatrack and, reaching for his Fedora, he slid it with ceremony slowly onto his head; then, smiling at Marla, he winked, "No, dollface think I'll just hoof it over on foot. It's only a couple of blocks, and I could use the time to clear my head.

"Besides, I know that Hemingway is just getting started if he's only had half a dozen drinks."

Then, kissing Marla on the cheek again, Frank smiled, looking deep into his savior's green eyes, "You know, doll, I couldn't do this without you. I gotta go chase some other leads after Kelsey's, but I'll make it in time for dinner, hopefully. Wait here for me, and we'll go get some dinner at the Pennsylvania if you'd like. Whata ya say?"

Leaning in for a second kiss, Marla whispered, "I'll wait, Frank, but a gal can't wait forever."

The breeze off the Intercoastal Waterway cooled the sweat on the back of Frank's neck.

He loved this city almost as much as he loved Marla. Between the two of them, he knew he could be happy again.

As Frank opened the door to Kelsey's, he almost ran into a deep-tanned man coming out who looked to be in his late 30s or early 40s. The man smelled of salt and seaweed. His hair was bleached and almost yellow from the sun and in need of a trim. These were the signs of someone who spent time in the ocean water more than on its shores. He looked too old to be one of those teenagers who came to West Palm from the West Coast to surf.

Frank tipped his hat and apologized for the almost run-in. The stranger reacted by side-stepping quickly around him and walking on without acknowledgment, but then he turned and looked Frank up and down as if he were about to point out some flaw he had detected.

Something he possibly sensed. Then, just as abruptly, he turned and walked on without saying a word.

Shrugging his shoulders, Frank went into Kelsey's. The usual crowd had not yet gathered since it was still early in the day. Frank noticed only Hemingway was the lone patron. Kelsey was wiping the bar down, and seeing Frank, he nodded his chin and asked, "A Brooklyn?"

"Yeah, and don't bother dunkin' that cherry."

Kelsey smiled and thought that nothing had gotten past this gumshoe.

Turning at the sound of someone else in the bar, Hemingway greeted Frank in a loud voice that matched the writer's boisterous personality with the level of alcohol that must be in him.

"Frank. How's the detecting going? Say, did you happen to notice that gentleman that just left? Odd fellow. Said his name was Reefer. Strange name. Said he'd been around these parts forever. He told me he saw a damn German U-boat off Boyton Inlet the other night during a full moon while he was doin' that surfing thing these kids do nowadays. No one surfs at night. I think it's a bunch of BS. Kinda like that crap about Old Hitler down around Boca Grande. You know, the twenty-foot hammerhead. Just too hard to believe, but that fella got my curiosity up, so I think as me and my boys head out later today, we'll check it out. You know, about the German sub he said he saw. You remember I told you about that U-boat sinking a transport ship in that same spot last time we met. So there's some credence to what that fellow said; I just don't buy that surfing at night. No one in their right mind would do that. Not in these waters. That's just askin' to become chum bait for the sharks. Ha, maybe even that mythical Old Hitler himself might be out in those waters. Now, that would be a story. Say, come sidle up. Tell me what's doin'," he said, patting the stool next to him.

Kelsey set Frank's drink on a bar coaster as Frank settled onto the stool with familiarity. Pushing his Fedora onto the back of his head, Frank turned and, raising his glass to Hemingway, offered the accustomed salutation, "Salute."

"Kelsey here's been plying me with drink to keep me from leaving. I suspect it was till you got here. So what's on your mind? Make it quick. I've got to head up to Rybovich's boatyard to pick up the *Pilar*. Me and the Crook Factory are headed back down to Cuba this afternoon."

"You mentioned last time that Patchi fella had a relative here in West Palm. Do you know if he ever contacted him since you guys have been here this time?"

Throwing back his drink in one swallow, Hemingway slammed the glass on the bar to get Kelsey's attention, and with the same loud voice he greeted Frank with, he ordered, "Two more here for me and my good friend. And Kelsey be sure to put Frank's drinks on my bill. There's a good sport," he said smiling at the bartender.

Frank thought he'd better go slow. He knew he was no match throwing back drinks with this famed writer, although he thought it would be fun to try. Marla certainly would not like this.

Following up on Frank's question, Hemingway said, "You know, I believe he did. We're making camp at the Biltmore, and Patchi had a fellow that went by the name of . . . what was his name? Hector! That's it, Hector. He didn't look too well when Patchi introduced us, but I didn't pay him much mind.

But I do remember Patchi said they grew up together in Cuba and asked if we'd give the bloke a ride back to Havana when we shipped out. Told him as long as he pulled his weight, it didn't matter none to me. He was a serious chap. Didn't make much conversation. But he stayed with Patchi last night, and they are all getting packed up to leave as soon as I get the *Pilar* down to the dock. What business of yours is this Hector fellow anyway? He involved in that case with that murdered lounge singer, bub?" Hemingway said with a wink while raising his glass.

"I can say he's definitely a suspect at this time. But the real reason I want him is the other day he kidnapped my secretary, and I put two slugs in his chest for doin' that. Those shots knocked him over the balcony. I thought I finished him, but by the time I got down to him, he up and slipped away. I'm guessin' this Patchi fella happened upon him before I got there and brought him to the Biltmore. Sure would like to get my hands on him before you guys leave town."

Hemingway again slammed his glass down on the bar hard and slapping Frank on the back while standing up; he shouted, "Well hell man, let's go get this son-a-fa-bitch. My crew ain't no choirboys, but I don't tolerate anyone who messes with a fella's secretary," winking at Frank with some inner knowledge that most men share, "that's just not done. Kelsey, let's settle up. Me and Frank have to go and get us a Cuban son-a-fa-bitch."

"Wait a minute," Frank said as he grabbed Hemingway by the Swiss tabs of his rolled sleeves on his sweat-stained jacket. "I got an idea. I need to get this Hector away from the hotel where there's less folks around that could get hurt. Maybe you should get him loaded on your boat and wait for me at the docks. That way, he'll be easier to grab. I got to run down one more lead, and that'll give you time to get everyone on board. Whata ya think?"

Slapping Frank again on the back, Hemingway smiled broadly and, in his usual loud way, said, "Excellent idea! That's what I like about you, Frank. You're always thinking. Puts you one step ahead all the time. Now I'll go collect the *Pilar* and then grab the boys and meet you at the docks. And mums the word. That Hector fellow won't know a thing, but if he gets suspicious, I'll detain him with a forty-five. Excellent plan! I just love all this cloak-and-dagger stuff, don't you? You know, if I hadn't become a writer, I could see myself as a private dick. You know all Nick Charles and such."

Frank smiled at the thought of this writer sleuthing about. He certainly could drink the part, but he drew too much attention to be unnoticed when necessary.

Kelsey slid Hemingway's tab across the bar, and Hemingway pulled out his money clip to settle.

"Here's a couple of sawbucks for your trouble," tossing the tip on the bar. "Kelsey, my man, it's been a real pleasure, and until next time I bid you adieu. Frank, see you at the docks."

As Hemingway headed for the door, Frank turned on his stool and hollered, "Which docks?"

Without turning around, Hemingway responded with his usual loud manner, "The one across from the George Washington. Don't be late. Expecting a strong north wind, and I want to get out before the tide."

And he was gone.

Using a brisk pace, Frank covered the distance to St. Ann's, hoping to speak with Father Peter. He knew from his last visit that the priest would not give up anything voluntarily, but Frank had to try. He had too many suspicions, and he needed to know if, indeed, it was Hector or if it could still be his first suspect, the German Hans? Maybe the priest would slip up and let something fall out for Frank to pick up. He believed it was worth a try. Frank often went back over and over with people of interest who had connections to a case. He knew from experience that people would often answer the same questions, and sometimes, they would not knowingly add a bit here and a piece there. Frank needed some bits and pieces.

Frank found the priest just as Father Peter exited one of the confessional booths. From the other one, a known bookie came sheepishly out and looked around to see if anyone saw him. He went by the name of Big Bennie. Big Bennie was often found on the corner of North Haverhill Road and Okeechobee Boulevard. He was given his moniker because of his enormous belly, which was produced by his unquenchable thirst for whole milk. Bennie could be found most days wandering the blocks around a local dinner, talking to himself and swigging milk. Folks tended to ignore Bennie, and most believed he was a bit off, but the man could make book. If you needed to place a bet on the ponies or the dogs, Big Bennie was your guy.

Bennie looked nervously at Frank as he recognized the private detective and seemed genuinely embarrassed that he was seen coming out of the confessional. Frank smiled casually and tipped his chin toward the man and offered a wink that assured Bennie his secret was safe with him. Big Bennie hurried past without acknowledging Frank but stopped at the sanctuary door, bending down to retrieve an open gallon of milk left in a corner and turned to Frank and tipping his chin, guzzling half the container, he wiped his mouth with the back of his forearm and then was gone.

Father Peter saw Frank and tried to slip away unnoticed from the detective while Frank was preoccupied with Bennie.

Noticing the reluctant priest, Frank hollered, "Excuse me, Father Peter, you got a minute? Just a few questions."

Appearing startled as if the priest had not noticed Frank, Father Peter turned and gave him a soured look as if to say, You again.

"Frank Lobeck, is it? I told you last time I don't know anything about that young girl, and what she told me in the confessional is privileged. So, if you don't mind, I have duties to get to."

"Please, Father. It'll only take a moment. It's about that German fella you told me about. His name was Hans, if I'm not mistaken. I need to know if you ever saw him during mass? Perhaps he, too, came to confession. Anything will help me solve Betty Lou's murder. I really need to talk to this Hans. Please, help me, Father. It's for the family. They need answers," Frank pleaded with false sincerity. He hoped that that last bit about the family would work on the heartstrings of the priest, but Father Peter's face didn't show any sympathy.

With a very loud audible sigh that appeared to Frank to be more of disgust, Father Peter slid into a pew and gestured with his left hand for Frank to sit down next to him. The gesture was more of a command. Frank complied slowly. He didn't want the priest to think he had control of their meeting.

Father Peter began by softening his voice to appear more empathetic, but it didn't convince Frank. Frank knew from personal experience with Archie when a man of the cloth was not being honest. He noticed the priest appeared a bit more perturbed than the last time they met. Father Peter clearly didn't want to have this conversation. Frank needed to know why. He believed the priest knew more than he was willing to give up, and Frank suspected it was not from some moral duty.

"To answer your question, Mr. Lobeck, no, I never noticed this . . . Hans, is that what you said his name was? This Hans, I do not remember ever having seen him during the mass. My congregation is small, and the parishioners are mostly locals, with a few faithful tourists now and then. I am very observant of anyone new during the mass. I think a blonde-haired German with a mustache and glasses would have stood out to me."

Frank looked the priest directly in his eyes. He looked for that tell-tell sign that people give when they are lying. They cannot hold your gaze and generally look away.

Father Peter looked up and away from Frank. "Why are you lying about never having met Hans?"

Startled, Father Peter looked back into Frank's eyes, and Frank saw an anger not expectant for a priest. He slowly exclaimed, "I assure you, Frank, I am not lying. Why would you suggest such a thing? Here in God's house, a priest speaks only the truth."

Frank lowered his head and his voice to a whisper, at the same time raising his eyes to look up at the priest, "In my experience with the clergy, that is not always true." Frank paused, looking carefully for the priest's reaction. Then, slowly and with a slight smile, knowing he had caught Father Peter off guard, "You just described a man you said you never met or saw, but I never said anything about Hans having blonde hair, and I especially never said he had a mustache or wore glasses. The only way you could have known that is because you've met him before."

Wide-eyed and stumbling over his words, Father Peter looked even more disgusted than before. Perhaps Frank thought it was because the priest realized his mistake revealed something he did not want Frank to know.

"I just—I just assumed, being German, that he had blonde

hair. Don't all Germans have blonde hair?"

Frank knew now he had him. "You don't."

Father Peter shrunk down and away from Frank as if he had been dealt a blow to the stomach by this detective. He quickly regained his composure and asserted, "What makes you think I am German?"

"Your name is Peter Heinrich. Father Peter Heinrich. It says so on the marquee out front. Now you wanna tell me why you don't want to admit you know this Hans fella?"

Quickly rising from the pew, Father Peter stared down at Frank with a surprising fierceness that made Frank instinctively reach inside his jacket to feel for his caution.

"This conversation is over! Now, if you'll excuse me, Mr. Lobeck, I have duties to attend to."

As the priest turned to move away, Frank reached up and, grabbed him by the wrist and pulled him forcefully back down onto the pew.

"This conversation is not over, Father! Now you're gonna do your own confessin', and I'm gonna be your priest. And you better convince me this time that what you're sayin' is true 'cause I don't give away no Hail Marys."

26

"Alright, I met this Hans a few times at the Pennsylvania hotel when I went to see Betty Lou. She had called me and asked if I could help her with some questions on morality. I told her she needed to come to the church for counseling, but she said she couldn't get away at a convenient time during the day. I saw this Hans fellow in the lobby a few times, and of course, he was the subject of Betty Lou's moral dilemma. And that's all there is to it. Are you satisfied, Mr. Lobeck?"

"Just call me Frank. Mr. Lobeck sounds like we ain't friends."

With a refrained snarl, Father Peter said reluctantly and with a forced smile, "Frank."

"You said you 'met' this Hans a few times. That's not the same as you 'saw' this, Hans. So which is it? Did you actually speak with him?"

"Now, wait a minute, Mr. Lo . . . I mean, Frank. What I meant was that I saw him. Met him is just a figure of speech. Don't go and try putting things together that never happened."

"So when I go to the Pennsylvania and question the staff about you and this Hans, they'll tell me you *did not* speak with him at

181

any time?"

Looking up again and away from Frank, Father Peter was visibly flustered. Then, very slowly and deliberately, he began again."It is possible I passed pleasantries with the man, but I did not engage him in conversation. I was there to see Betty Lou, and that was it!"

"But isn't Hans the reason you went to see Betty Lou? I can't understand how you could counsel Betty Lou and not have some conversation with Hans. Remember, you are the one who described him from memory. That indicates some sort of association or time spent in his presence now, doesn't it?"

Exasperated and with clear anger in his voice, Father Peter almost shouted, "Alright! Yes, I may have suggested he make his intentions clear to Betty Lou and to keep the relationship proper and decent. Young men nowadays do not often conduct themselves as they should. They can lack restraint when in a public place. Or they can put pressure on the young lady for, shall we say, 'favors' that are not solicited. You're not married, are you, Frank? And your secretary Marla she's not married either, is she? So, you see what I mean. Men today must show restraint when alone with women. Wouldn't you agree, Frank?"

The intention was clear coming from Father Peter. Frank was not sure how the priest knew he was not married and that his secretary's name was Marla. But he did know that Father Peter was clearly attempting to go on the attack. Frank figured he had backed the priest into a corner, and he came out fighting. He most definitely was hiding something, Frank thought.

But what?

"I'm sorry if you think poorly of me, Frank. It's as if you suspect me of some crime. I assure you that all I did was counsel a young lady in distress and advised her boyfriend to show more restraint. My only crime is that I did not mention my having spoken with Hans in order to keep the confessional sacred for Betty Lou. Now, if you do not have any more questions for me, I really do have to be about my duties."

Rising from the pew, Father Peter looked at Frank with a confidence that he had won the battle. Then, to throw the last punch, he asked, "Say Frank, when's the last time you came to confession? You know it's never too late."

Again, Frank wondered why Father Peter assumed he was Catholic. How is it that this man assumes to know more than he should?

"I'm not Catholic, Father, but I do have one more question, if you don't mind?"

The priest straightened his posture to appear bigger than he was waiting for the next punch.

"Tell me, Father, why is it you went into Betty Lou's room at the hotel and didn't meet with her in a public setting. Why didn't you insist she come to your office? Did her father, Mr. Wilson, know about you seeing her in private in her room? Now, before you get all defensive, I got several witnesses that saw you on multiple occasions enter her room alone. Doesn't that appear to be a bit inappropriate in and of itself, Father?"

"You seem to be insistent that I did something wrong, but my duties as a priest sometimes have me meeting with parishioners in private and even in their rooms. There was nothing inappropriate about my seeing Betty Lou. I resent the fact that you are trying to make Betty Lou's murder about me. That somehow I was involved or had knowledge about the crime. I really think it is time for you to leave, Mr. Lobeck. I have nothing further to say to you."

As the priest turned to leave, Frank smiled to himself. He

knew he had Father Peter against the ropes. Frank decided he needed to give the priest some room to wiggle before pressing him again. But he would be back and press harder next time. He needed more information before delivering the knockout blow. Father Peter was definitely hiding something, and Frank was determined the priest was going down.

In the meantime, Frank headed to the docks to meet up with Hemingway. It was just a short walk to the docks from St. Ann's.The *Pilar* was no where in sight, so Frank assumed he had arrived early. A dock worker noticed Frank as he walked up and down the slips and came toward him.

"You the private dick Frank Lobeck?"

"Yeah, that's me."

"Mr. Hemingway said to give you this note when you got here and to tell you he couldn't wait because of the tide."

Handing the paper to Frank, the worker turned to leave when Frank called him back. "Hey, here's a little something for your trouble," Frank said, handing the man a couple of bucks.

Raising his hands to Frank, gesturing a refusal to accept the tip, the man said, "Mr. Hemingway already took care of me. And quite generously, I might add. He said to be sure and not take anything from the good detective. Thank you, but no thanks." And then he left.

Opening the note, Frank read:

Couldn't wait. Damn tide. I'll deal with the package. Hope it doesn't float.

Yours respectfully,
E. Hemingway

<h1 style="text-align:center">27</h1>

Frank knew that the hour was running out for dinner with Marla, but he couldn't bring himself to offer another excuse with the promise for another day. He often thought that his relationship with her was ticking away and nothing he could do could rewind the clock. She would not wait for him to find peace with himself forever. So he called Marla and had her meet him at the Pennsylvania for a late dinner.

As they were seated, the waiter informed them, "Folks, the kitchen is closing soon, so if you don't mind, you might want to put your order in pretty soon."

Frank looked up, and, snapping the menu closed quickly, he said, "Just give me somethin' simple. How about steak and grits. Make the steak medium rare. And does the cook know how to make a decent bowl of grits," he asked with a smile.

Smiling back, the waiter responded, "He's from Georgia, so I reckon he does. We don't get no complaints ever."

Marla smiled at Frank and then stuck her tongue out at him for ordering ahead of her.

Usually, he was more considerate and let her order first.

Something must be on his mind, and she thought that maybe the case must have him preoccupied. It seemed lately he was always preoccupied with something other than her.

Looking up over the menu at the waiter, she ordered, "I'll just have a salad. And could you bring me some oil and vinegar, please?"

"Listen, babe, you don't need to refrain from eating for your figure," and Frank threw a wink at the waiter.

Smiling. "It's not for my figure. It's late, Frank, and I don't need anything heavy before bed." Then Marla threw a wink at Frank.

Frank wasn't sure if she was just being flirtatious or just sensible. He knew she worked hard at courting him, but he just couldn't make the commitment right now, so he didn't always pick up on her suggestions. His pain and guilt over Lilly and Beth wouldn't relent, especially now with the coin in his pocket working its curse. The coin refused to allow Frank's senses to believe confidently that love, the kind of repentative love that Marla offered, was indeed possible again. It constantly told him that there was only one way out of this guilt and shame, and that way did not involve Marla's love. It did, however, involve his pistol.

Sensing Frank had slipped into his depressed thoughts, Marla changed the subject, "So, how did the meeting go with Father Peter?"

Coming back to the moment, Frank responded with, "Well, I got a suspicion that he's definitely holding something back. I caught him in a lie several times. Can you imagine that—a priest lying? He tried to wrangle his way out, and he even tried to throw me off the trail by providin' some personal information that I can't for the life of me figure where he got it. He knew you and I were not married and was suggestin' that we had far more than an employer and employee relationship."

Smiling, Marla replied, "Well, we do have more than a working relationship, Frank," then she reached across the table, took Frank's hand, and kissed his knuckles tenderly.

Using his signature wink, Frank smiled back, "I know that, and you know that, but how does the good priest know that? I haven't ever discussed us with him. Why he even tried to rattle me and throw me off the trail by asking when was the last time I had confession. Told him I wasn't Catholic, and I believe he already knew that also."

Sitting back in her chair with both hands on the edge of the dining table and with a flush in her cheeks, Marla took a deep breath and confessed, "I think I may know how Father Peter knew about us. The other day, I was talking to Mrs. Johnson, you know my landlady, and she asked about our relationship. Seems she saw you leaving early one morning down the back steps, and she reminded me of the no men in single women's rooms rule. And I didn't think of it till just now, but Mrs. Johnson goes to St. Ann's." Then, removing the flush, Marla snarled a bit to herself as she mused out loud, "Why that little gossip. And she was getting on to me."

"That explains the relationship items, but what about the whole Catholic confession item?

"Did you talk to Mrs. Johnson about my lost soul?"

"Now that, Frank, I have no idea. Maybe Father Peter was just trying to get at you for some reason with the whole private eye reputation. You know what they say about those in your profession, all whiskey and women. He probably assumed your soul was in need of saving because of what you do. I mean, it's true you do drink a bit of whiskey now and then," Marla said as she dipped her chin downward and then looked up at Frank while raising her eyebrows; she continued, "and you do consort with a woman of questionable repute," smiling, "that is, according to Mrs. Johnson." Then, leaning forward with her elbows on the table and her hands clasped under her chin, "If I'm going to be known as a loose woman, at least I'm loose with a private eye. My private eye," she offered with a smirk. "I'm quite sure my reputation was a matter of discussion with the good Father. Evidently, you're not the only one in need of confessing."

Marla pouted her bottom lip as she batted her eyes at Frank, hoping to get some consolation from him. At the least, he could come to the aid of her reputation, she thought. But Frank missed her intent.

"You mean that's all people think of when they think of private eyes is we're a bunch of drunks and fraternizers? Hell, people read too damn much Hammett nowadays. His Spade and Nick Charles gives folks the wrong impression about what we do. I ain't no cartoon in a book. I'm the real deal! Like to see anyone of them walk around in my loafers for just a day and deal with the sorts I deal with every day."

"Why, Frank, I do believe you're upset about what people think about you. I've never known you to worry about what others think. What's gotten into you lately? I've noticed you've been a bit on edge. Is it the case? You still brooding about the whole Hector thing, or is it something else?"

Frank had not told Marla about the coin and its curse since he found it in Betty Lou's room. He decided he needed to wrestle with its power on his own, not realizing that this idea was the coin's influence on his conscience. He knew Marla would have had him get rid of it, but the coin had become a kind of dope to his soul, not letting go and refusing to acknowledge the need for help. The coin became Frank's private hell, and he didn't want Marla anywhere near it. Like most addicts, he believed he could handle it on his own.

"Frank? Frank, are you listening to me? Tell me what's going on, babe. I can help. Let me help. Is it the whole Lilly and Beth thing again? You know, dear, that wasn't your fault. You've got to believe that, Frank," Marla whispered as she reached across the table and took Frank's hands again in her own. But her words always seem to fall on deaf ears no matter how bright the torch burned for him. This time, the coin made sure of that.

Walking Marla back to her room at the boarding house, Frank kissed her cheek and said he didn't want to upset Mrs. Johnson tonight, so he was going back to the office to work. Marla protested, but Frank tipped his Fedora and gave her a wink as he turned and left Marla standing alone.

She whispered to herself, "Frank, you're always leaving me standing alone in the dark." She watched him walk off till she couldn't see him anymore and then turned and went inside.

Frank unlocked the door to his downtown office but did not turn on the light in the reception area. This was Marla's area. This was her chapel. He somehow convinced himself that the area deserved a reverence. His influence would only spoil the sanctity of her sanctuary. She had taken over the room when she came to work for Frank. Even in the dark, he could sense her distinct personality in the way she simply placed a single flower vase on the corner of her desk. He could smell her distinct perfumed scent that constantly clung to the air around her desk, where Frank and others enjoyed lingering. He knew many of his clients came to him simply for the pleasure of watching her. Even if, just for a moment, Frank knew his clients would often fantasize about losing their burdens by just sitting and gazing at this goddess. And if he could only free himself of his past, she would willingly be his goddess.

But right now, Frank didn't need the distraction or the unrelenting frustration. He needed to focus on the case. There were too many pieces that needed to be put together. If Marla were here, her presence would often sidetrack him from the puzzle. So tonight, being alone was opportune for the case. Stepping into his hallowedless office, he flipped his Fedora at the coat rack and made a perfect toss in the dark. Moving around to his desk, he turned on the chocolate brown colored brass Art Specialty desk lamp with the 40-watt bulb, which gave him enough light to think. Reaching down to his bottom whiskey drawer, he pulled out the bottle of bourbon and a glass. Pouring an ample shot, he sipped the whiskey, letting it breathe in his liver.

Maybe Hammett was right.

Frank pulled a legal pad and a pencil out of the middle desk drawer. He had a habit of listing what he knew and what he needed to know. It's the one thing he remembered his teacher from sixth grade, Miss Greer, taught him that he found useful today. It was his way of working through a case and maybe exposing a trail or connecting some evidence that either he or the police overlooked. He began to jot down in order what he knew thus far about Betty Lou's murder.

Being alone in the dimly lit office, Frank would often talk to himself out loud. He knew Marla would tease him if she overheard, so he tried to remember to do this only when she was not around.

"I'm sure she would think I was quite ready for the looney bin, and before this case is over, maybe I will be. Hmmm, so now let's see, first, Betty Lou's body was discovered in her bedroom."

Frank wrote his first heading:

1. What is known about the body and the crime scene? Underneath, he wrote:
2. Autopsy report.
3. Strangled.
4. Stabbed lower belly after death.

"That would explain the enormous amount of blood at the crime scene," Frank said. He thought that there must have been a tremendous amount of rage on the part of the killer based on the brutality of the crime. Strangling was not enough. So the culprit had to be one with a lot of rage against Betty Lou or women in general, Frank surmised.

Next, he wrote: Who was near or around the body before it was discovered?

5. Hector
6. Tina confirms Hector at Pennsylvania on Wednesday
7. Abused Tina physically.
8. Enid confirms Hector uses rage against women.
9. Eyewitness to abuse.
10. Marla kidnapped by Hector.
11. Abused and threatened her.
12. Harry confirms Hector seen at Pennsylvania on Wednesday.
13. But not near Betty Lou's room—important!

Again, Frank spoke out loud as if he were outlining the known facts to someone across his desk. "Hector was known as an abuser of women and capable of tremendous rage, and he often returned to the Pennsylvania to recruit girls for Nora."

Frank placed a checkmark next to Hector's name at the top of his list.

The problem now, Frank thought, was Hector couldn't be questioned since Hemingway and Hector's cousin, Patchi, spirited him back to Cuba on the *Pilar*. Frank figured that Hector probably would never set foot on his home soil if Hemingway indeed had his way. Hemingway had indicated so much at Kelsey's. So, Frank said, "If Hector is the guilty party, Hemingway may be the one to bring the justice. But I can't place him in the room only in the vicinity. So, who's next?"

14. Hans
15. Boyfriend/Finance
16. Wilson confronts Hans.
17. Confirms Hans Betty Lou's boyfriend/finance.
18. Background
19. German.
20. Betty Lou tells Enid about Hans landing in raft at Breakers.
21. Hemingway confirms someone landing at Breakers.
22. Gregory.
22. Confirms FBI interest in Hans.
23. Harry confirms Hans near Betty Lou's room.
24. Enid confirms Hans near Betty Lou's room.

Pouring another ample shot of bourbon, Frank said, "However, there was no evidence of any rage in Hans. Hans told Wilson that he's in love with Betty Lou and would never hurt her. Hans said they were going to be married. But Enid didn't like him. Harry saw her yelling at Hans outside Betty Lou's room."

A check mark went next to Hans' name.

Frank then listed

25. Father Peter.
26. Harry confirms seeing Father Peter multiple times going to Betty Lou's room.
27. Confirms Wednesday entering Betty Lou's room.
28. Confirms last one entering room.

Thinking out loud, "Just what is Father Peter keeping from me. And why does he go into the girl's room? Maybe he ain't an upright priest after all."

Frank made a mental note to check out Father Peter's background.

Placing the pencil down next to the legal pad and refilling his glass with some more bourbon, Frank leaned back in his chair as his eyes became heavy with sleep.

Swallowing his whiskey, the night's darkness swallowed Frank.

28

I didn't have the heart to wake him. It was not the first time in his long narrative that Frank had dozed off. I decided to take the unplanned opportunity to closely examine the rooms that Frank held so obviously important by his refusal to move anything since 1942. Or was it that he somehow fell for this lovely young victim who had tragically been robbed of her life? That happens now and then to folks in our profession. We get so intimate with our clients or the loved ones of our clients, and our emotions align with those who have been hurt. It's happened to me.

Unfortunately, it happened when my secret mistress—alcohol—was ruining my reasonings, my emotions, and my marriage. I didn't plan it, nor was I looking for it, but there it was, beckoning me to its candle-lit cloister of lies. Hidden in the guise of love, luring me by its hidden web that tangled me and held me so tight I couldn't get loose. I tried, but it lied and told me that love is able to overcome any and all oppositions and truths. Deceit told me that no one would get hurt and that the pleasure would be greater than the guilt.

Becky, my wife, or should I say my former wife, was the real victim. Looking back on the alcohol-driven misdeeds, I felt remorse.

I looked at the still, mostly full whiskey glass I had poured from the bottle Frank said was for him and my grandfather. Frank had polished off two or more pours, I think. I lost count. I, however, was still on my first. Guess the virtues of AA were still intact.

Well, mostly intact.

My observation of the front living area was primarily complete. I had scanned the room thoroughly while Frank filled in the back story along with many incomplete clues. What I didn't know much about was the bedroom. As I said, the trail of the lady's clothes throughout the living area heading to the bedroom indicated that the young girl was excitedly rushing either to change for something or someone or she was disrobing for that special someone. Quietly standing so as not to disturb Frank, I made my way to the bedroom. As I entered the dark room, it almost felt like a sanctuary, a hidden cavern of secrets. I felt I was violating some private world that only those invited were allowed. Feeling the inside wall for the light switch, I hesitated before exposing all of Betty Lou's most intimate thoughts.

It's interesting when we bring light into darkness how we tend to stumble backward as if repulsed by its brilliance. But the truth is it takes a moment to adjust to the exposure, having grown accustomed and comfortable to what is not seen. Light shows us the truth,and sometimes, we just don't want to know the truth.

The first truth revealed was that the bed had not been disturbed since that fateful night so many years ago. Frank, I thought, must be sleeping on the cavernous couch. He certainly was not sleeping on the blood-stained bed. That is unless he was some kind of pervert, but I quickly ruled that out by the impressions made in the sheets from someone lying back on the bed from the foot of it. The impression of wrinkles also indicated that the head of that person was about middle way up the bed, showing that this was the victim's position. The height indicated by the impression made it evident that the victim had their legs bent over the end of the bed and dangling toward the floor.

The next clue the room revealed was the pattern of the blood stain. I knelt at the foot of the bed and noticed there was a saturation of dried blood going through the sheets and deep into the mattress. It was an unusual amount of blood for just a stab wound. I surmised the body cavity would have had to be opened to allow that much blood to be released onto the mattress.

Reaching into my front pocket for my penlight, I bent down to observe if any of the blood had made its way through the mattress and onto the floor to confirm my suspicion. Even though the blood had run over the end of the bed, the blood on the floor under the bed indicated that someone possibly pushed hard into the body, creating a collecting pool from the indention made by force under the body. The blood's weight held the impression, and as it dried, the impression became permanent. This indicated that the murderer not only stabbed the victim but used an unusual amount of force as if they were cutting more than simply stabbing. From a previous case, I remember this extreme brutality was perpetrated on the victim for the purpose of cutting something out of the victim. What kind of animal would do such an act on a simple lounge singer?

Was Betty Lou perhaps a victim of some savage cult? Was the murderer leaving behind some cruel message of some perverted righteousness on chastity? According to Frank, Betty Lou was strangled, and the stab wound was delivered after she died. I needed to see the final autopsy report.

Standing back up, I noticed the bed impression wrinkles also confirmed the impression of the head as if someone was pushing against the victim at the neck, indicating that the strangling was done while Betty Lou lay back on the bed looking up. That meant she was looking at her attacker.

Looking around the rest of the room for clues as to what happened that fateful night, I noticed a lamp had been moved close to where the body had been lying. The overhead light evidently was not enough for the murderer to see closely what they were doing. So, the stabbing was not just a simple act of violence; the murderer was being careful to cut into the victim and needed more light to execute their perverted procedure. The lamp made me think of a doctor and an operation. Did the murderer have medical knowledge?

Next, I noticed bloodstains on the carpet, indicating someone kneeling at the foot of the bed. Obviously, they knelt to see more carefully what they were doing to the victim. This convinced me beyond any doubt that Betty Lou was violated surgically after death.

Frank never mentioned that. Maybe he didn't know, or maybe his unplanned infatuation with the victim clouded his perspective and his ability to see what was directly in front of him. Again, I know from experience how that can happen. I knew this might be a sensitive fact, but I was determined to ask him about it when he woke from his age-imposed slumber. Then I froze with the horrible realization that maybe Frank had left out some of the details of the crime.

Maybe his timeline of events was faulty because he came upon the scene much earlier than he said. Could it be that Frank was the brutal mutilator? Had this occupation gotten to him as it had gotten to me? Had that Judas coin he talked about finding completed its mission and turned him into the monster he so often spoke of? As quickly as the thought came, I just as quickly dismissed it. I shook my head to clear it of the thought. I definitely have been in this business too long. Everyone is guilty nowadays to me. However, at this stage of the game, no one can be ruled out as a suspect.

29

"Gee, I must have dozed off. Sorry about that, bub. It comes with the age," Frank smiled yet seemed embarrassed by it. "Not sure where I left off."

"It would help if you could fill in some answers to some questions on your primary suspects. For instance, could you tell me what happened to the Cuban Hector? Did you ever hear from Hemingway about him? Speaking of, you actually met Ernest Hemingway, the Ernest Hemingway, the writer?"

"Yeah, I met him, but he's no big deal. Lot of hot air and self-publicity if you ask me. He actually chased U-boats up down the coast with the . . . what did you call them—the Crook Factory?"

"Yeah, that's what he called them—the Crook Factory. And it was one of them, Patchi, that was the cousin of Hector." Then, pointing with a shakey and bony finger at the credenza that displayed the whiskey bottle, Frank said, "I actually got a letter from Hemingway some months later where he told me what happened to Hector on the way back to Cuba on his boat. I believe the letter's in that drawer on the left somewhere. Take

199

a look and see if you can find it in there."

While I looked through the stack of unorganized letters, I noticed there were several from Marla. I figured I needed to ask Frank about her since the letters all had a Boston return address. But I filed that away for later.

"Is this it?" I asked, holding up a letter in an old envelope with a Cuba postmark.

"That's it. Go ahead and read it."

The letter was written on yellow legal paper. The penmanship was not what I expected from such a celebrated author, nor was the spelling. At first, I thought it might not be from Hemingway, but it was signed at the bottom, *E. Hemingway*. It appeared to be written in his minimalistic style. The letter was dated December eighteenth nineteen forty-two. It began:

Frank,

Well, I imagine you are wondering about that Cuban sonsabitch. After chumming the water, we through his ass in the drink. Seems he can't swim that good, at least not with the sharks nibbling on his toes. While he treaded water, I asked him if he was the one who killed that girl, and he said it wasn't him. Funny thing, I believed the SOB. Then I asked him if he kidnapped that lady of yours, and he admitted it. I started to throw him a life float, but something pulled him under. He never came up. Patchi never did try to stop me. He just turned and went below. Guess he got tired of taking care of his bastard cousin. Sure wouldn't want to be related to Patchi. Anyway, guess you can close the books on that Cuban.

E. Hemingway

Looking back at Frank, I asked, "What do you think? Did you close the books on Hector?"

Frank leaned his head back into the couch and sighed. I thought maybe he was regretting the loss of a prime suspect, but he then leaned back forward and stared at me as if he was just hearing me for the first time; he responded, "No. I don't regret what happened. In fact, after I got Hemingway's letter, I ran into Nora, Hector's old employer, and she confirmed that Hector couldn't have killed Betty Lou, although she said it sounded like him. She told me that Hector tried to date Betty Lou a couple of times, but she flat refused him. He didn't take kindly to that. Nora then told me that she had demanded he leave Betty Lou alone. It seems Nora had met Betty Lou down in Lauderdale when she first came to Florida looking for work. Nora told me she sent Betty Lou up to the Pennsylvania to see Enid 'cause she didn't have any business workin' for the Sunrise Hotel. But Nora did tell me that at the time Betty Lou was murdered, Hector was with her at the bar of the hotel having a drink. The autopsy report confirmed the time of death was the same time Nora was with Hector. Harry confirmed seein' them at that time as well. So, it appeared Hector was not the one who murdered Betty Lou. That left the next prime suspect, Hans."

"Now I thought you said Hans was Betty Lou's boyfriend or fiancé? Doesn't seem to me at first thought that he would kill the woman he supposedly loved, and according to Betty Lou's father, they were going to be married. What made you think it was him?"

Frank leaned forward from the couch with great effort. It appeared his body didn't want to yield to the stretching and bending he exerted to reach for the bottle of whiskey on the coffee table. Standing, I walked over and obliged him by placing the bottle within his reach. He struggled to pull the cork but finally managed to pour himself a double shot.

Taking a long pull from his glass, he began slowly, "Later, I dismissed him like you for the very same reason; however, my first instinct was he killed her because she most likely knew he was a German spy, and with the FBI on his trail, he probably decided it was better not to have any connections to his real activities."

"How is it you believe Hans was a spy for the Germans?"

Pointing again to the credenza, "That same drawer has Betty Lou's diary. Take a look at that."

I located the small red leather-covered diary with a metal clasp. On the cover were imprinted the words across the top— Every Day and in the lower left corner, it was embossed with the words *Five Day Diary*. The clasp no longer held, so I opened it to the inscription page, and it said it was presented to Betty Lou Wilson on the day of her graduation from high school by her mother. As I quickly flipped the pages, I observed that Betty Lou had kept an almost complete record of day-to-day thoughts and emotions. The diary ended with a last entry on the morning she was murdered.

"Turn to the date March 16th. Read what she wrote. Then look at March 19th."

Flipping the pages, I found the sixteenth and read aloud, "Today, while walking on the beach, I observed a man in uniform landing a raft behind the Breakers Hotel around sunset. "

Strange.

"March 19th: While I took a break from my singing set, the man from the beach approached me at the bar of the Pennsylvania Hotel. He asked me to dance, and from that moment on, I knew this man would be important to my life. I believe he is a spy or something possibly worse, but at that moment, I didn't care. No one had ever danced me the way he danced me. He has the bluest eyes. His name is Hans."

"Now read March 28th."

"Hans came over tonight all excited about meeting with his friend from up north. He showed me a bag of old coins but made me promise never to touch them without gloves on. Hans put on a glove, reached in very carefully, took one of the coins out, and placed it in an ashtray on the end table. He told me the coins were over two thousand years old. He told me he loved me for the first time and wanted me to have one, but again, he made me promise never to touch it with my bare skin. He said it would diminish its value. I never touched the coin. I told him I loved him too."

"So, based on this, you believe Hans was a German spy who came here to Florida to pick up some two-thousand-year-old coins from some contact that met him from up north? Do you have further evidence for this fact?"

Frank tilted his chin toward the diary and said, "Take that with you and read it. Betty Lou writes about Hans and what he told her about his mission here. It's all in there. You ever hear of Hitler's top dog, Himmler? Hans told Betty Lou that he was sent by Himmler himself to pick up these Judas coins and bring them back to Germany. Read the diary. It should give you the same insight I got as to who this German was, and it will most likely convince you as it did me that he was not the murderer. As to what happened to him when he left the Hotel George Washington after being confronted by Wilson, we may never know. Betty Lou was dead at that time, so she doesn't leave us with any information that could lead us to his whereabouts. I did read of an account of a fishing boat—don't know if it was the *Pilar* or not—that sited a U-boat in the area behind the Breakers around the night or soon after Wilson confronted Hans. Maybe he got away back to Germany. I checked with Enid, and she said she never heard from him again after that night she argued with him. She wouldn't tell me what they argued about, although I gathered it was a pretty intense discussion."

Frank suddenly looked at the clock on the end table and announced, "Shit! It's three- thirty; I've been talking all day. It's almost time for dinner. You know I have it delivered to this apartment each day. You wanna stay and eat a bite?"

Rising while placing the diary in my back pants pocket and using this as an opportune moment to exit, plus the fact that eating dinner at four o'clock in the afternoon was not anywhere on my schedule, I responded, "No thanks, Frank. I need to get back to my hotel and check on some things, and now I got this diary to go through. How about I come back tomorrow, and you fill in whatever else you can remember about the case. I still need to hear about any other suspects you might have suspicions about, and I am curious about this Father Peter character. Do you know if he's still around?"

"To my knowledge, he is, but then time has passed. Guess you could check at St. Ann's."

"I'll do that. So, shall we say until tomorrow, say around ten o'clock?"

"That works for me. But it's okay to come by earlier; I'm an early riser. I don't sleep much through the night since I take so many damn naps. It comes with the age."

"Let's keep it ten o'clock; I want to stop by the police department and check on the autopsy report."

"See Officer Benson at the front desk. Use my name. He was

an acquaintance of Officer Gregory before he passed. Say, you need a little snort before you go?" Frank said, straining to reach the bottle.

Looking down at my half-empty glass, I said, "No thanks, I'm good. See you tomorrow."

Lifting a frail hand to his eyebrow, Frank saluted, and then, with a wink, he said, "Until tomorrow."

30

Back at my hotel room, I slipped into my swimming shorts and took the diary out to the green and white webbed lounge chair by the pool. There were moms on vacation with kids who needed to play to release the pent-up energy from riding all day in the back seat. Those moms lingered around the shallow end. There were dads who needed a vacation from work, from the never-ending bills that come with marriage and family, and the kids who had pent-up energy from riding all day in the back seat. Those dads lingered around the deep end, drinking beer, smoking cigarettes, and telling war stories about their respective factory jobs up north. Dads lied about wanting a relationship with the neighbor's wives. Moms lied about the relationships with their neighbor's husbands.

For me, reading Betty Lou's diary was like eavesdropping on a private conversation. I didn't belong there in her world, but I had to go in. Be careful, I thought; pass no judgment. Once inside, it gave me a glimpse into the young girl's life through her most intimate thoughts written only for her eyes. She would have died all over again knowing some stranger was peeking in. I blushed out of respect for her secrets.

I began to read the passages that revealed Hans:

March 29—I woke up in love for the first time. The most wonderful part is that Hans said he loved me too.

March 31—Hans stayed over for the first time last night. It was incredible! I'm definitely in love. How did I ever live before meeting him? I didn't.

April 2—Hans told me about his coming to America for the purpose of getting the coins. He told me he hates this war. He told me I must keep his purpose a secret from everyone. I told him I would never betray him. He told me again how much he loves me. He made us coffee for breakfast.

April 3—Hans told me that after he gets the coins back to Germany, he will return and never leave me. I hate this war!

April 7—Called Mom today, and I told her about Hans. I didn't tell her his real purpose. I told her he came to escape the war. I don't think Dad will like him because Hans is German. Mom agrees. Dad hates anything that has to do with Germany. I hate this war!

April 13—Hans and I ate in the dining room of the hotel for the first time yesterday evening, where everyone could see us. Enid told me she does not like him. She says he will bring nothing but trouble for me. What does she know about love?

May 4—Hans says his superiors are pressuring him to return with the coins. He says he can put them off a little while longer, but he must make contact with his associates up north to arrange for a pickup in a U-boat.

May 16—Hans is tired tonight. He is tired most nights. Not sure what he does to tire him out so much. Most of his life is still a secret to me. He mainly talks about the time before the war, never about the war.

May 17—Today, Hans told me before the war, he was always hungry. He told me Hitler promised to feed the people. He joined the Party so he would not be hungry.

May 20—Hans could not come over tonight. Maybe tomorrow I'll be able to give him the good news. I told Mom; she said it best not to tell Dad just now. She reminded me how much Dad hates Germans.

May 21—I'm so excited today! Hans asked me to marry him. I told him I would.

May 30—Hans spends most nights with me now. He looks older and worn. It must be the war. He told me he has to go away for a while. I cried all night in his arms. I think he cried a little, too.

June 14—Hans is due back tonight. He's been gone for two weeks on business up north.

June 15—He's aged. He says it's the coins. I didn't realize his mission was such a worry for him. He says he has to get the coins back to Germany so he can be free, and then he will marry me. I hate this war!

July 3—Tonight, we both waited on the beach for the U-boat to take Hans back to Germany. It never showed. Secretly, I was glad it didn't show. As he lies next to me, I watch as he struggles to breathe. He has to get those coins back to Germany. I told him to just get rid of them, but he said it's his duty. I don't understand.

July 17—I dusted today while cleaning the apartment, waiting for Hans to arrive. I lost the coin he gave me. I'll find it later. I hate those coins.

August 1—Today is my birthday! I hope Hans can make it. He's been so tired lately and so full of regret that he hasn't gotten those coins back to Germany. I worry when the U-boat comes, will they take him away from me forever? He says it's his duty. He says when they come, he will have to go. I don't understand.

August 31—We waited on the beach last night. I'm torn. I didn't want Hans to leave, but I hoped this time the U-boat would come and get this over so Hans could come back to me.

Again, the U-boat didn't surface. Hans is so very, very tired. He keeps telling me it's the coins. I don't think he is telling me everything.

September 4—Hans told me he has to leave again to meet his associates up north. He says he will be gone for the rest of the month. He says it's the last time, and when he gets back, he will be leaving on a U-boat. He says he will arrange for it to pick him up at Boynton Beach. I will miss him, but he promised it was almost over, and then we can be married. I cried all night when he left. Father Peter came by again this morning. I think he knows about Hans and me.

October 2—Hans called and said he would be here in the morning. I am so excited! I haven't sung in the lounge for three weeks now. I'm afraid they are going to fire me. Mom wants me to come home. She told Dad. She said he's brooding and threatening to come and get me. If only Hans were here.

October 5—Hans has arranged for the U-boat to pick him up tomorrow night. This is our last night together.

He doesn't know how long he will be gone, but he promised it would not be forever. I can't hide in the room for much longer. Enid is constantly arguing with Hans about me. She has given me work in the laundry for now. When will this war end?

October 6—Harry let me borrow his car to drive Hans to Boynton to meet up with the U- boat. Hans made me leave; he said they must not see me, or there would be trouble. I drove back to the hotel. I cried all night. I hate this war!

October 7—Slept in this morning. I can't believe Hans is gone, but I will just keep busy until he returns. I do hope it won't be too late. I never knew one could miss someone so bad.

Maybe I should go home until Hans gets back. He said he thought it would be a good idea. He said at least I would be with family during this time. I'll call Mom for the bus fare later.

I closed the diary. It was Betty Lou's last entry.

31

I got up early the next morning, determined to stare down the continental breakfast in the hotel dining lobby. I needed some java since the small one-cup pot in the hotel bathroom made coffee like house whiskey poured in a bottle of fifteen-year-old scotch. It looks nice in the package, but it's just not the same when you drink it. Besides, the only packet was unleaded. I never understood why anyone would want to drink decaf. What's the point? The lobby's coffee was, indeed, stronger, and it was hotter, but the store-bought Danish on the stacked Plexiglas trays was stale and lacking aroma. Not sure why they call it continental. I'm sure the French had fresher fare in mind. Seems to me the wafting of baked goods under the hotel room door always enticed hungry patrons from their rooms to gather and peruse the local newspapers and occasionally have conversations about the weather and local attractions with like-minded coffee hounds seeking a donut that didn't have to be dunked to soften the bite. My mind was on the schedule I had planned out for myself. First, I needed to check with the police department about viewing Betty Lou's autopsy report. Frank

211

had told me to see Officer Benson at the front desk since Officer Gregory was forevermore absent from that position. After that, I needed to head back over to see Frank at the Pennsylvania to ask about some of the characters from his previous day's long narrative. I also was curious to know what happened to Marla.

Since the police station was only a few blocks from my hotel, and with the South Florida weather beckoning me with its salt-laced breezes, warm, moist sunshine, and migrating laughing gulls whose laughter would stir my Buffett's pirate imagination carrying me away aboard a wooden galleon bobbing gently on ocean waves, I decided the walk was mandatory. Besides, I needed a well-thought-out scheme to convince Officer Benson to allow me to see that report. I didn't have a legal claim to the information, but I was hoping since the case was still open, although cold, the police would be more than obliging to someone who could possibly shed some light on the absent facts. I would definitely use Frank's name in hopes that the aging detective still had a respected reputation around the station.

"I'm looking for Officer Benson. Could you please tell me where I can find him?"

"You're talking to him. How can I help you, Mr. uh"

"Brunson, Thomas Brunson, I'm a private investigator working with Frank Lobeck on an old case, the Betty Lou Wilson case. Frank told me to see you about getting a look at the autopsy report. Can you help me out?"

"Frank Lobeck. Well, now there's a name I haven't heard in a while. How is ol' Frank?"

"He's doin' okay for his age," I said in a lowered voice as I placed both hands on the dark walnut-stained chest-high counter and leaned up to whisper to Officer Benson so only he could hear. "But between you and me, he's getting a bit feeble.

Not moving about much. That's why he asked me to come into the case and be his eyes and ears, so to speak. He hardly, if ever, gets out of the apartment anymore." I felt I was laying on the "feeble" part a bit heavily, but I needed Benson's sympathy if I was going to get a look at that report.

"Yeah, I'd heard he was slowing down a mite. Shame. I also heard in his day, he was the best. Not a case he couldn't solve," then, realizing what he had just claimed, Benson sidetracked with a lusty grin as he turned toward the records room, saying, "I also heard he had the hottest secretary around. Let me go pull that file. Be just a minute."

While Benson left to retrieve Betty Lou's report, I looked around the lobby of the police station. There was a wall of archiving photographs of the past and present captains. I saw that Captain Jacobs was now the presiding officer in charge at this local precinct. Struck me as interesting, and I wondered if this could be the same Jacobs who disliked Frank back in the day.

What are the odds, I thought. If it was indeed him, he must be pretty long in the tooth, being he was in Frank's neighborhood as far as age is concerned. Didn't know police hung around that long.

I didn't have long to find out. Accompanying Officer Benson, according to the photo on the wall, was the station captain. He didn't look happy to see me, and he was mighty gray with what hair was left. I made an assumption.

"You Brunson?" he asked. Then, straight to the point, "I'm Jacobs. Captain Jacobs," he emphasized that last part for the authority it brought. He didn't extend his hand for the customary shake, which gave me further evidence that the feud between him and Frank was still burning.

All of a sudden, I saw my chances fading of seeing that report.

"You got a warrant from a judge to see those classified files on an ongoing case? We don't just give out information to any Tom, Dick, and Harry that happens to wander in here looking for the details they haven't discovered by hard investigating themselves. We work for our information." Again, that last bit was meant to belittle me so I could pass on to Frank that Jacobs still was mad as hell with him. I wasn't sure why all the hatred; Frank only told me of that one time he solved the case for Jacobs of the murdered hooker down at the Sunrise Hall. This feud sounds like a whole lot more than just that one case.

Hoping to defuse the obvious bitter rivalry between Jacobs and Frank, I offered in my best conciliatory manner, "I do not have any legal right to the information; I just was hoping for some professional courtesy between our respective professions on an ongoing case that recently has been brought to my attention. I believe the autopsy could shed some light on the case and maybe lead us to a conclusion and possibly an interesting suspect. I assumed the police would be glad of any assistance in closing a cold case. Was I wrong?"

"Anyone or anything," Jacobs sneered, "associated with that sonofabitch Lobeck is in my book up to no good. And unless you have a warrant, I won't grant you even the possibility of spit-shinning my shoes, much less access to that report. Good day to you, Mr. Brunson, and you can tell that Frank Lobeck he can kiss my . . . well, you can just tell him Captain Jacobs is still in charge around here."

And with that, Captain Jacobs spun on his heel and walked off. Age hadn't diminished his agility any. Officer Benson just stood there looking embarrassed and shrugged his shoulders, indicating it was out of his hands, then looked back at the disappearing Jacobs till he slammed his office door.

I realized then it wouldn't do any good to pursue the matter with Jacobs further, so I thanked Benson with a handshake and headed back outside. I hadn't gotten down the station steps when I heard someone from behind hailing my name.

"Mr. Brunson. Mr. Brunson, wait up, please."

Turning around, I saw Benson running after me down the steps two at a time.

As he closed the distance between us, he stopped short, almost toppling over on me, and then he looked cautiously around to see if anyone was paying attention to our meeting. Reaching up inside his lightweight desk uniform jacket, he pulled out a manila folder marked *Classified*. Since he was standing so close, he used his body to shield the passing of the folder to me. He then whispered, "I could get in big trouble for this, but I think it is important you see what's in here. Besides, Frank is a good man, despite what ol' Hard Nose thinks. I'm not sure what all went on back then that got Jacobs so all fired up against Frank, but Officer Gregory thought an awful lot of Frank, and so do I. Read it quick. I got to get it back before anyone knows it's missing.

"You need to know about six months ago, a forensic expert came through and updated all our cold case files. She left a note containing new information pertaining to the examination of the body. It's on page six of this report."

While I scanned the pages, Benson kept a vigilant stake-out of the station doors behind us. When I got to page six, I couldn't believe what it said. I looked up at Benson with astonishment. Benson smiled, knowing he did good. Frank hadn't given me that detail, and I wondered if he actually knew it for himself. Handing the folder back to Benson discreetly, I thanked him with another hardy handshake and told him, "I appreciate this, and I can tell you Frank appreciates it too. Now, you better get back inside with this before ol' Hard Nose knows it's gone. Thanks again."

I then walked a few blocks to the Pennsylvania, wondering if I needed to tell Frank what I had discovered. The gulls mocked me with their call-like laughter. It was as if they knew this information changed things quite a bit. By the time I got to the hotel, I had decided that if Frank had indeed formed an unhealthy mental attachment to Betty Lou, it was probably best at this point that I keep the new information from him, at least until I figured out how this revelation fit into the case.

Walking through the lobby of the Pennsylvania, I noticed an elderly hotel bellhop watering the plants with a small watering can. His once classic hotel-issued burgundy uniform had seen its day and was in need of an update. The man was clearly approaching retirement age or perhaps recently passed it, but his lively step, the twinkle in his eye, full head of snow-white hair, and his gleaming white teeth that accompanied his broad smile told me this man was not thinking of giving up his position anytime soon. The bellhop whistled and flirted with the early morning sun worshipers who made their way to or from the hotel pool. I even saw the bellhop lightly smack the barely covered and barely legal backside of one of the sun worshipers. She turned with a smile and admonished the "old pervert" by wagging her finger at him and then walking away, wiggling the object of the bellhop's slap.

This must be Harry.

Walking over to him and extending my hand, I questioned, "You Harry?"

Looking down at the gold-colored name plate with black

letters pinned to his right breast pocket, the bellhop responded with his bright white teeth, smiling, "I must be. At least, that's what the name tag says. But you know, when I got up this morning, I did feel like a different man and the beautiful lady lying next to me in my sheets said I was not who she expected either. Still, there's something familiar about my face this morning in the mirror while I was shavin'. And who might you be?"

"Name's Thomas Brunson. I'm a friend of Frank Lobeck."

"How is the old coot? Haven't checked on him today yet. I usually get by once or twice a week to reminisce. How is it you know Frank?"

"He is a friend of my grandfather who just recently passed. I came to bring him the news, and he got me involved in the Betty Lou Wilson case. Seems Frank and I are both in the same business."

Harry looked up from his watering of a large stone pot that contained a peace lily. I could tell by the concerned look on his face that Betty Lou was a name he hadn't wanted to speak of in quite some time.

I noticed Harry looked a bit sad. An unusual look for a man who just moments ago seemed to be celebrating the day.

"Man, Frank just ain't never goin' to give up on her. You know he moved into her room before they even got around to cleanin' it up. He said to leave everything just as it was the blood… " Harry stopped and swallowed hard as if he remembered that day vividly, "the blood and all. He said there must be somethin' he missed, and I think it drove him just a bit nuts. He just sits in that room and never comes out anymore, runnin' the case over and over in his mind. When I stop in, that's all he talks about. It cain't be good for him. I try to get him to at least come down and eat in the dining area, but he just sits on that couch day in and day out. You know, I think he even sleeps on it too. It'll be the death of him yet, I'm sure."

"Say, tell me, Frank said that you were one of the last to see who was coming and going to Betty Lou's room that day. Could you tell me just what and who you saw? I need to check it against what Frank told me. Do you mind?

"Let's have a seat over there," Harry indicated with the watering can in his hand and moved to some pastel-colored floral cushioned wicker chairs that faced each other and were separated by a wicker coffee table with a glass top. He set the watering can on the table glass but then snatched it up and looked around to see if anyone noticed.

With a chuckle, he said, "Still cain't get used to the idea that Enid ain't around anymore. She always got on to me for settin' my water can on the furniture and leavin' a water ring. She's been gone now for years, and I still see her ghost in this place. She was a legend and a saint. I miss her still."

Then, relaxing with a heavy sigh as he leaned back into the cushion's softness, Harry closed his eyes as if he were focusing on that particular day. Opening them, he turned his head toward me without lifting it from against the cushion and began:

"Sometimes things just get stuck in your head, and you don't never forget. Like what happened well before that day, I remember telling Frank that I saw Enid and that German boyfriend of Betty Lou's, Hans, arguin' to beat the band. Not sure what about, but it made me curious, so I slipped up to the level they were on to see if I could overhear what the fussin' was all about. When they saw me, they both just took off in different directions. Hans just sorta disappeared after that for a while. However, I did hear something before they knew I was there. They were talkin' about Betty Lou being in a fragile state and that she was really worried about something. I never heard just exactly what Betty Lou was worried about, and Enid never talked to me about it—ever. All I know is Enid really didn't care for Hans or the way he was treatin' Betty Lou. Betty Lou hadn't been out of her room for pretty close to a month or more at that time. She worked for a little while for Enid, but then she just holed up, and I didn't see her at all. Just Enid would go into her room. Oh, and sometimes Father Peter would come by and go in to see her. Guess he was offerin' comfort. I thought maybe that German was doin' her wrong, you know," and Harry held up his fist when he said this, "You know that ain't right. No man should beat on a woman. Hector did, and Enid ran him off. Now, like I said, I never saw Betty Lou in bad shape 'cause she didn't come out, but I don't know what else to think. I think Frank thought so, too. And that's pretty much all I remember before that day. Now, as to your question, on the day of Betty Lou's murder, I saw only Father Peter and Hans, but not together. Guess Hans had come back from wherever he had been, and I ran into him on the back stairs, but I didn't see him go up to Betty Lou's room. He just left by the back door. Now I don't remember seein' Enid that night. I had gone home that day before anyone discovered that girl's body. I didn't hear about it till I got to work the next morning. That was the saddest day ever around here. She was such a sweet kid."

Harry turned his head back away from me and closed his eyes again. Then, with another heavy sigh, he sat forward and then stood up, grabbing his watering can. Turning to look down at me, he said, "Anything else I can do for you there, Mr. Brunson?"

Standing and offering my hand, I said, "No, Harry. You've been a big help. Thanks for letting me bring up the past."

Walking off toward Frank's upstairs room, I stopped and turned, "Say, Harry. Thanks a lot for checking in on Frank. I know he appreciates the company. You're a good man, Harry."

"Yeah, that's what all the ladies say." Then, smiling as he turned away, he caught the sight of a sun-worshipper heading to the pool and yelled after her, "Say, Miss, can I get you a towel and maybe rub some of that suntan lotion on your hard-to-reach areas? My name's Harry. You know they are serving an excellent swordfish here tonight for dinner."

I didn't catch the rest of Harry's lines, but I'm sure he continued to cast until he hooked his catch.

32

I knocked on Frank's door several times, but I couldn't hear a response even when I put my ear to listen. I decided he must be asleep and was about to leave when I thought I ought to try the doorknob, and to my surprise, it opened. My first thought was that Frank had gone out this morning and left it unlocked, anticipating my return. But when I stepped inside, I saw Frank was still in the same position on the couch, still coaxing heat from the small heater at his feet, still wrapped in the same sweater as yesterday. Harry was right; the man needed to get out of this room and get some air and sunshine. I determined before I left West Palm that I'd get him out even if he had to be carried.

"Frank, you takin' visitors? Thought I'd come by and pump you for some more information about your case."

The old detective turned his head toward me, but the recognition wasn't there. A detective is dead when he can no longer put the pieces together. Frank was dying, I thought.

"Frank, it's me, Brunson. We met yesterday. I'm Farley's grandson, you remember?" He smiled and nodded his head slowly up and down. Then he gave me a wink.

"I remember you. It just takes a while nowadays for all my parts to come together for a response. Come on in and grab a seat. While you're at it, go crack open another bottle I got back there in the cupboard above the sink. Seems someone finished off that bottle from yesterday from your grandfather," Frank scolded me with a wink. I noticed my unfinished glass still sat on the end table where I left it. Frank didn't.

After retrieving the bottle, I broke the seal and refilled Frank's glass, then set the bottle down within his reach. I thought that most folks would admonish Frank for drinking so much, but hell, at his age, what's it gonna hurt. It's not like he's driving anywhere.

Sitting back in the same seat, I picked up my glass and swished the whiskey around as if the pour was recent. I asked, "So, Frank, I read Betty Lou's diary last night and then went by and saw Officer Benson at the station. Jacobs sends his love."

Frank looked up from his glass at the name of Jacobs being mentioned and chuckled between swallows, draining his glass as if it was the day's last drink. He reached for the bottle, making sure it wasn't.

"That sonofabitch was always jealous of me. I probably solved half of his cases, if truth be told. He always thought I was out to get him, but I wasn't. I was just better at the job than he was. I think he knew that that's probably why he has resented me for so long. That and the fact that he tried to date Marla, but she wasn't havin' anything to do with him. She told him their relationship could only be professional. Did ya learn anything from the diary or the autopsy? You know they never let me see that report. Damn, Jacobs. I'm surprised they let you. You must not have told them you was workin' the case with me."

CHAPTER 32

I decided to keep the new information from Frank at that moment, especially with him sluggin' down whiskey right after breakfast. I assumed he had eaten breakfast. I was certain he wouldn't take the latest news well.

"No, nothin' you already didn't know. But I did run into Harry down in the lobby just before I came up here. He told me he thought that Hans was beatin' on Betty Lou. He said you might have suspected that, too. Is that right? Did you have good reason to think Hans was abusin' Betty Lou?"

Frank stopped mid-motion, raising his glass, and held it there as he contemplated what he had just been asked. Then, finishing the motion, he downed the drink in one big swallow.

Slowly, he said, "I always thought that initially, it was a possibility. But when Mr. Wilson had his encounter with Hans at the George Washington, I began to be convinced that Hans really did love Betty Lou and couldn't have been doin' what Harry thinks he was. Enid told me once, when I pressed her about it, that Hans was not beating Betty Lou. She said that was not how he was hurtin' her. But she never told me just what she meant. You might try and talk to her daughter Tina. She may know more about it than I learned. I got her address in that book over on the credenza."

He pointed a shaky, bony finger in the general direction of the credenza. Then he poured another drink. Frank seemed exhausted already, and it wasn't even noon yet.

I decided I needed to leave him to rest, but I had one last detail I selfishly had to know. "Frank, you mind me askin' what happened to Marla? I saw some letters postmarked from Boston. If you don't want to answer and if it's none of my business, I'll understand, but it just seems that you two were destined to be together from all you've told me about her."

Frank's eyes began to tear up as he stared at the bottle. Then, with some hesitation, he reached for it and refilled his glass again. Then, staring off into that place where one stares when one doesn't want to make eye contact, he began:

"I never could get over what happened to Lilly and especially Beth. I drank a bit too much, which kept me from lettin' Marla help carry my burden. She finally got tired of walkin' home alone, even when I was with her. And that damn coin just kept destroyin' any chance of my forgivin' myself. So one day, this travelin' office supply salesman came by, and she up and followed him to Boston. She wrote me a few times tryin' to see if I would come after her, but finally, she ran out of stamps. I got a letter a few months ago from her sister that she passed away. I sent flowers. First time I ever did that."

Frank lowered his head and set his whiskey glass in his lap. His breathing became slow and regular. I got up slowly and closed the door without a sound, taking Frank's address book with me.

33

Leaving Frank's, I walked north down Olive Avenue and turned west on Clematis Street. Frank had scratched out Enid's name and wrote in Tina's above the address. According to his address book, Enid had lived in a small apartment behind City Hall. From what Frank told me, Tina now lived there alone since Enid had passed. I later learned that Tina and Enid had patched things up between them at least enough that Enid convinced Tina to move in with her to care for her in her last days. I walked up the pewter gray painted concrete steps to the pewter gray painted concrete porch that was sparsely occupied with occasional Woodward Orleans wrought iron bounce rocking chairs. The constant westerly salt breezes dulled the powder-coated turquoise finish and was in the process of eating away at the part of the curved legs that made contact with the concrete where it scraped the paint off, leaving scant traces of rust. Three pastel- green painted wood doors, also weathered by the salt breezes, opened onto the porch. Frank had written a note in the address book indicating that Tina lived on the northerly end of the porch.

I rang the doorbell but didn't hear any reassurance coming from inside that the bell was operational, so I knocked. Evidently, the bell indeed did work, or perhaps the woman who answered the door before I could finish my customary three hard knocks was aware of someone standing on her porch. The shades were pulled, so I didn't see any movement until the door slowly and tentatively opened. Before me stood a slight woman with weathered, worn, premature facial wrinkles that lied about the supposed years that had gone by.

There was no greeting; there was no smile.

Tipping my attempt at gumshoe-days-gone-by-Fedora to the hard-looking lady standing there, I asked, "Excuse me, mamm, I'm looking for a Miss Tina Alexandre, the daughter of Enid Alexandre. Would you happen to know if she still lives here?"

Eyeing me suspiciously, she replied, "And just who is it that's a askin'?"

Removing my hat, I introduced myself, hoping that this was Tina and that she remembered with fondness Frank's rescue of her from Hector and the Sunrise Hall; I said in my best disarming tone:

"My name's Thomas Brunson. I'm a friend of Frank Lobeck, or I should say that Frank was a good friend of my grandfather. Frank's the one who gave me your name and told me I might ask you some questions from the past concerning your mother."

"Whatcha wanna know 'bout my Mama? She been dead goin' on four years now. Ifn' she owed you money, you's too late to collect. I ain't got nuthin' left after the buryin'. Hell, I had to pay for the marker outta my own pocket. And believe me, it weren't nuthin' special. You can go down to the Evergreen Cemetary and see for yurself. Now get off my porch."

Realizing that Tina was cautious for so many reasons and

possibly others I did not yet understand, I quickly tried some more disarming to lessen her overly cautious fears.

"Believe me, Miss Alexandre, I am not here to stir up any trouble. I am helping Frank on an old case of his that involved a girl who worked for your mother at the Pennsylvania many years ago. Her name was-"

But before I could finish, Tina ended my sentence, "-Betty Lou Wilson."

"That's right, Betty Lou Wilson. Would you mind if I ask you a few questions about your mother and her association with Betty Lou?"

Lowering her shoulders as her demeanor relaxed slightly, she responded with less grimance, "Long as you drop the Miss Alexandre. I ain't gone by that since I was a child. It's just Tina. Might as well come on in so's people walkin' by don't get to thinkin' I'm back in the business."

Then she opened the door wider, and I stepped into the purposed darkness. It took a minute for my eyes to adjust since the shades were pulled down, blocking out the very reason tourists come to this state, and as they adjusted, I noticed a room sparse of memories. Either Enid was not sentimental, or Tina removed any memory of her mother except one picture leaning up against a wooden cross that I assumed was Enid in her younger days placed strategically on a flat white painted brick fireplace mantel. I quietly laughed at the ridiculousness of a fireplace in South Florida. Winters here were never below seventy degrees. I guess the builder was hopeful.

The young, slender girl, possibly not quite yet a teenager, in the black and white photograph was standing barefoot on a beach with blurred palm trees frozen in movement behind her, wearing a light-colored shift with a ragged hemline that appeared to be handmade. She had a slight shy smile, but her eyes looked like they were full of dreams for a different life. I thought she might possibly resemble Tina before Tina's life got hard. But I hadn't met Tina before the hardness, so I wasn't sure. It was just a thought.

"That's my Mama. If anyone is, she's Miss Alexandre. Enid Rose Alexandre. That in French means defender of mankind. That she was, my Mama. She was born in Haiti. She came to this country when she was just barely a teenager. I 'spect right before that picture was taken. She always dreamed of a better life for herself, and she often hoped out loud for me. Guess she got her first dream."

Tina sighed slightly as she looked longingly at the picture, then motioned me toward the only chair in the room next to the well-worn, flowered patterned couch, where she lowered herself heavily despite her lightweight thinness. I deduced the heaviness was emotional for the life her mother never saw materialize for Tina.

With the lessening paranoia, she quickly stood back up, possibly from remembering something earlier taught, and asked, "Can I get you some ice tea? Just made a pitcher this mornin'. It's got slices of oranges and lemons in it the way my Mama made it. Sure is refreshin' in this part of the sun."

"Sounds delicious. Wouldn't mind a glass one bit." Then, rising from my training, still holding my hat, I asked, "Can I help you with anything?"

"Keep yur seat there, Mister Brunson, is it? I'll fetch it."

"Most just call me Brunson. Not sure why, but folks don't use my first name or the Mister either. I don't mind, though, you calling me Thomas. It's funny how people refer to you, don't ya think?"

This brought the first smile to Tina that I had noticed since we met on the porch. Maybe my charm was getting through, although my ex-wife always said I left that at the altar. I suspected Tina was not used to much charm from the male sex. Just demands. According to Frank, Hector had robbed her of any potential charm for her life. I determined to use it often this morning if it softened Tina's caution.

Returning with a Mason jar full of more fruit and ice than tea, Tina handed me the sweating glass as I rose instinctively again and bowed slightly with a thank you and a grin, and I saw my second smile that morning. The charm was working.

Sitting back down with her own sweating glass, she asked, "So what is it ya wanted to know? I don't know if'n I know that much about Betty Lou. I only met her a couple of times since while she worked at the Pennsylvania, I was mostly in Lauderdale." Tina frowned and looked away. I imagined she was wondering at that moment just how much Frank had revealed to me about her.

I distracted her by complimenting the tea, "This recipe of your mother's sure is tasty. I got to remember this next time I make some tea."

Another smile. Damn, I'm good.

"What I really want to know is, did Enid talk any about that day they found Betty Lou's body. I don't mean to bring up bad things from the past, but it would help me to put some of the pieces together that Frank may have left out or was not aware of."

"Not to be disrespectin' Betty Lou, but that gal is the least of any bad memories in my life." She stopped and looked again away momentarily, then she returned to the conversation.

"Mama told me about that day when she came on the body.

She said she found Betty Lou stretched out on the bed, and from what it looked like, she was just a breath away from dyin'.'"

"Wait a minute. You say that Betty Lou was still alive when Enid found her? The autopsy report said she was dead from strangulation and made no mention of your mother finding her.

"But you're telling me she was still alive?"

"I'm just tellin' ya what my Mama told me. She said that gal had a bad heart. Always did.

"She said that someone did strangle her, but stranglin' her must of caused the heart attack, and whoever it was what was chokin' the life outta her must of thought she was as good as dead or got spooked or somethin' and left for whatever reason before she drew her last breath. That's when Mama came on her. She said Betty Lou never spoke about who it was that was a killin' her. All she said was, 'Save my baby.' So Mama did."

"The baby lived! There's no mention in the autopsy report about that. In fact, the report never mentions the baby at all. Just that Betty Lou's injuries were consistent with a crude C-section. I only guessed at a baby from examining the crime scene."

Surprised, Tina asked, "Surely Frank must a told ya 'bout Betty Lou's baby?"

When I said that Frank never mentioned it and suggested that perhaps he didn't know, she followed up with, "Maybe he didn't know 'bout Betty Lou bein' heavy with child when she was killed or even before that. She did hide out from everyone, Mama said, once she started showin'. She quit her singin' job at the hotel, so then Mama gave her work on the night shift; that way, she could work without bein' seen by the rest of the hotel folks. But like I said, Mama knew all along. I suspect she kept it from everyone outta respect and love for that gal. Mama often fussed with that German man of Betty Lou's, tellin' him to do the right thing by her. But that German kept sayin' somethin' 'bout havin' to get somethin' done before he could make an honest woman of Betty Lou, but now Mama she wouldn't stand for that puttin' it off. She never did like that man; she always said so, but I think she knew that Betty Lou loved him, so she was gettin' used to the idea of them bein' together. She didn't like most of the men in her girl's lives. She was right 'bout mine. That Hector was a no good, worthless piece of . . ." then, turning her eyes toward the cross on the mantle and looking down, she caught herself before she uttered the word, then continued, "I just couldn't see it at the time. But by the time I did, it was too late.

"Mama saw it. I just didn't listen to her. Anyhow, Betty Lou was expectin' real soon, so Mama was keepin' a careful watch on her with her bad heart and all, and when she found Betty Lou, her first thought was for that baby. Like I said, Betty Lou was still breathin' her last, and Mama said Betty Lou made her promise to get the baby out and to see after it. So Mama delivered the baby right after Betty Lou's last breath."

Now, some of this was the new information that Officer Benson had disclosed to me that I kept from Frank. But the report never said anything about a bad heart or having a heart attack. As I thought about it, this was a piece of the puzzle that Frank never put together. Since it was not in the original report, Frank assumed the death was simple strangulation with a single stab wound to the abdomen.

"You say your mother delivered the baby. Was she a nurse before coming to work at the Pennsylvania?"

"Nah, she just knowed how to deliver babies. In her raisin'

back in Haiti and when she lived here in Florida early on, she learned to bring them babies out. There was always someone who was a needin' to birth in places she grew up in. She told me she even learned to do that C- section. Said it weren't no pretty thing like they do at the hospital, but it got the job done. She done told me that it was just a special miracle the baby survived. Mama told me she ran into the other room, got a steak knife off the dinin' tray, and used that to bring the baby out. She said she wrapped the baby up in a pillowcase and snuck her outta there afore anyone knew 'bout Betty Lou. She later took the baby to St. Ann's and the nuns there for her to be raised."

"So the baby was a girl?"

"Yeah, Betty Lou had told Mama earlier that she was gonna name the baby Rose after her if'n she had a little girl. She said she chose that name outta respect for the kindness Mama showed to her all their days together. So the baby got the name a Rose. Mama was real proud 'bout that. She always said no one ever brought so much honor on her than that Betty Lou. She looked on her as ifn' she was her own daughter 'cause she would say that she lost me when I run off with that Hector." Tina again looked at the picture and the cross on the mantle as tears began to slip out onto her cheeks. Wiping them with the back of her hand before she turned back to face me, she smiled slightly and whispered, "And that's 'bout all Mama ever told me 'bout that day."

Swallowing a big swig of tea after hearing all this new information from Tina, I began to wonder what else Enid might have told her. So I started:

"Now, let's back up a minute, Tina. You said your mother came into the room, so the killer could have been hiding in there somewhere. Enid's coming in could have been what spooked that person, so they didn't finish the job. But I don't see how they could have gotten past Enid without her seeing them unless they snuck out while she was preoccupied with delivering the baby or they slipped out after she took the baby away."

"Mama didn't say she saw anyone in the room, but she did say it felt eerie, like someone else was there or had been there right before. She wasn't sure. Just somethin' that gnawed at her. Ya know, kinda like when the hairs on the back of yur neck get to standin' up when somethin' just ain't right. Mama said when she got there, she knocked on the door, said she heard movement inside, an' thinkin' it was Betty Lou; she waited, but when no one came to let her in, she let herself in with her passkey. Remember, she was a checkin' up on Betty Lou 'cause of Betty Lou's delicate health bein' with child and bad heart and all. Now, Mama did say when she left the room with baby Rose wrapped up in that there pillowcase, she stopped at the rail to the mezzanine to look below into the lobby to see if anyone was around so she could slip out of the hotel without bein' noticed. She said mostly the lobby was empty, 'ceptin' for a few workers, including Harry, who Mama said she could count on to forget he saw her that night, but she did tell me she saw that priest, Father Peter, leavin' the lobby, but then that didn't strike Mama as odd since he had been a frequent visitor as of late to the hotel. Mostly to see Betty Lou. What was odd, she said, was that as he was a leavin', he bumped into a man comin' in, and she swore that man was that German fella of Betty Lou's. The reason Mama thought it was odd is 'cause Betty Lou had told her that he was gonna be outta town for a while and most likely couldn't get back before the baby was born."

I now had more pieces to the puzzle that would help me get a clearer picture of that night.

Taking Tina by the hand and in my most sincere voice, I said, "Thank you, Tina. Your information sure has been a big help."

Another smile.

Stopping me before I could stand, Tina continued, "Mista, there's one more thing you gots to know 'fore you go. My mama was a good lady. She didn't do nuthin' what it wasn't for to help someone. Even me. Me and Mama made up for all the shenanigans I pulled with me goin' off with Hector and all that I done," Tina stopped and hung her head, then continued, "and my Mama was awful hard on me, and rightly so. But she did forgive me at the end, and we was good. Yes, sir, we was alright."

Satisfied with what I had learned from Tina, I handed her my still-sweating tea jar; I rose politely and thanked her for her time and the refreshment. This gave me my fourth smile.

Settling my hat on my head, I moved through the living room to the front door and stepped out onto the concrete porch. Tina followed and, stopping at the door, she asked, "You gonna tell Frank about baby Rose?"

Turning around to face her, I was struck by the difference in Tina from when I first met her there on the porch. She seemed softer somehow. Almost angelic. Like she had found some peace talking about her mother. Maybe Tina had found some form of redemption from all the remorse due to her past with Hector. Surely, taking care of Enid in her last days gave Tina a new meaning for her life now. Maybe she had become Tina Alexandre after all.

Smiling at her, I said, "Not sure I need to tell Frank everything we've talked about just yet. Still, you've given me some leads to run down. But it sure was nice meeting you, Tina. I wish you all the best."

Then, tipping my hat, I turned and walked away from one more smile.

235

34

Walking east back down Clematis toward the Pennsylvania to check on Frank, I realized I was not that far from St. Ann's, and it would be helpful to visit and check on the whereabouts of Father Peter. If he indeed is still around, he could possibly fill me in about the man Tina's mother said she saw him run into that fateful night. Was it Hans? Harry had told me earlier he couldn't confirm they actually ran into each other, although he did say they both were there that night. Harry also told me he didn't see Hans go up to Betty Lou's room, but the possibility of returning after Harry's shift still existed. So, turning left on Olive Avenue, I walked a few blocks to the church. As usual, the soft salt breezes accompanied me. But the gulls no longer laughed.

Curious.

The rectory was located adjacent to the church building across the alley. From my limited knowledge of the Church's practices, I remember reading somewhere that most priests retire by the time they are seventy-five at the latest. Frank was in his eighties, so I was guessing Father Peter was similar in age.

That meant finding him still living in the rectory was unlikely. But perhaps if he indeed was still alive, someone there would know just where he was residing.

Knocking on the door to the rectory, I was greeted by a young priest who invited me in when I inquired about Father Peter.

Putting his finger to his lips, the priest whispered, "Father Peter still lives here. We keep it to ourselves since he retired and had no place to go. He has no family but us, you know. He's gotten a bit more feeble lately, and he no longer is able to see very well, but he is still lucid and always willing to share in the rectory's history. The man is an institution around here, having been among us since the forties. Also, he's a great cook. Let me take you back to his room. Just follow me if you will."

From the doorway, the young priest cleared his throat, waking the old man bent at the waist, chin to his chest, in an oversized bright flowery stuffed chair, which, I guessed, was probably donated to the rectory since all the other furnishings were plain in appearance.

Snapping his head up quickly, maybe out of embarrassment for being caught napping, I observed the old man had very little hair, except around his ears, and it was the color of new snow. Raising a trembling hand in need of a manicure, he motioned to the young priest to enter. Moving his head in our direction, I observed the man's eyes were glazed and cloudy with cataracts, and I surmised that visual recognition would perhaps be very difficult, if not impossible, for the aged priest. But with clarity in his still strong voice, he asked:

"Forgive an old man, but slumber seems to come upon me when I least expect it. How may I help you?"

"Forgive me, Father Peter, but there is someone here who wishes to talk with you. His name is . . .". Then, turning to me, he stated, "I'm sorry I did not catch your name."

Facing the young priest, I said, "I apologize; my name is Thomas Brunson." Then, turning to speak directly to the old priest, I continued, "I'm afraid we have never met, Father Peter, but you might remember a friend of mine, Frank Lobeck. He's invited me to work with him on an old case, and your name has come up a few times. I thought if you would allow me a moment of your time, I might ask you a few questions. Would that be okay?"

Father Peter looked away from our direction for just a moment as if he was recalling a memory long lost.

"Hmmm, Frank Lobeck. Now, there's a name I haven't heard in many a year. It's been so long since I met the detective that I'm afraid I don't remember much of our meetings. Oh, but where are my manners, Mr. Bunson? Please have a seat wherever you can find room," he said, sweeping his trembling hand across the room.

Looking around the room void of luxuries and furnishings, I sat on the edge of the bed since Father Peter occupied the only chair. He turned his body in my direction, knowing exactly what the room had to offer, and continued:

"I do apologize for the lack of accommodations. I have so little needs these days and fewer visitors. So tell me, how is ol' Frank? Now, mind you, I did not know the man on a priestly basis, you see. Believe he was Episcopal. In fact, it seems to me that the few times I did meet Frank was when he had a question about a case he was working on then. Let's see, if I recall correctly, it was about a young girl who briefly became a part of this parish; what was her name? Betty something. Miss Betty Lou Wilson. That's it! I believe she was killed, poor girl, and Frank was busy trying to solve the case. He seemed convinced that her boyfriend, a German that went by the name of Metzger. Hans Metzger. Yes, that's it. Frank suspected this Metzger fella had something to do with her death. It was such a great tragedy taking the life of that poor young girl and her baby with a steak knife, of all things. So ghastly! Who would do such a thing? Just horrible. Simply horrible."

"You know, for a man who doesn't remember much, you sure retained a lot of details. I think you know more about the case than I do," I said with a smile, then realized Father Peter didn't see my attempt at humor.

Father Peter responded quickly, "Mr. Brunson, I live alone in my darkness and spend my day in quiet meditation to our blessed Mother Mary, so I tend to reflect on the work here at St. Ann's and the people of the parish. Guess I remember because it's all I have to do."

I observed the old priest momentarily lost his smile. I wondered if perhaps it was from some past neglect of some parish purpose or person. Having been at the same church for so many years, there certainly existed the possibility of many disappointments that could have accumulated. Getting to know his parishioners so intimately through confessions would possibly compound his sorrow when they passed on. Maybe the weight of losing Betty Lou, who was new to the parish, disturbed him more than he would like to admit. At that moment, I felt sorry for him.

"I have a witness that said you were at the Pennsylvania the night Betty Lou was murdered. They said you were seen leaving the lobby after you left Betty Lou's room and that you ran into someone they believed was Hans Metzger. I only ask because I need to establish Hans's whereabouts. So tell me, Father Peter, do you remember seeing Hans that night? "

Father Peter leaned back in his chair, clasping his hands behind his head. But before he had a chance to respond, there was a knock at the door. The young priest who met me when I arrived stuck his head in and apologetically offered:

"Please excuse the intrusion, but Father Peter, if you are going to make your doctor's appointment, we need to leave pretty soon."

"Thank you, brother. I'll be with you momentarily. We were just finishing up our conversation. I will grab my sweater and my cane and meet you at the van."

Smiling, Father Peter then rose while feeling for his sweater on the back of his chair and then extended his hand in my general direction. I gave him a firm shake as I rose and then commented, "I do hope we can continue this conversation. I sure need to know about that night and Hans. Do you mind if I call again real soon?"

Still gripping my hand, he offered, "Well, I can answer those questions right now. I did not go to the Pennsylvania that night. Therefore, I could not have been seen coming from the girl's room. I had, on occasion, gone to her room for confession since she was not able to come to the church, but not that night. And it stands to reason, therefore, that I could not have run into Metzger either that night. Whoever said they saw me there must have been mistaken. In fact, if memory serves me right, someone told me Metzger had returned to Germany either before or right after that night, and to my knowledge, he never came back to America. I hope, Mr. Brunson, that satisfies your questions?"

"Thank you, Father Peter. You've been very gracious with your time. I appreciate your honesty and clarifications. I hope that I haven't brought up too many bad memories of the past.

Perhaps if I have further questions, you might allow me to return in the near future."

Father Peter feigned a conciliatory smile and said, "Certainly, my friend. Always glad to help. Just check with the rectory deacon about my availability if you would." Then, with a nod toward me, he continued, "I do nap a lot more nowadays." Smiling, he made his way to the doorway and reached for his walking cane leaning against the doorframe; he stopped and, turning back in my general direction, added, "It was nice visiting with you, Mr. Brunson. Good day."

35

After leaving the rectory, I decided to head back to the Pennsylvania to talk things out with Harry. It helped sometimes to say
out loud what's in my head with someone directly or indirectly
related to the case. Harry struck me as a man whose mind
was still sharp, and he was in a unique position to observe the
comings and goings at the hotel. I needed to see that night in
my head, along with the facts. I had to keep reminding myself
that Frank was old and he drank way too much for precise
memory. Whiskey often steals our memories and promises.
I know it did mine. And then there was Frank's story about
some ancient curse on a coin I hadn't even laid eyes on yet.
Frank believed it; I wasn't so sure. As for Tina's story about
what Enid saw that night, it was certainly revealing, but a third-
person account is hardly conclusive for my business. I needed
something more concrete. And Father Peter, well now, his
account was puzzling. He denied the other's testimony three
times. Someone was lying. I hoped talking it out with Harry
would clear up some of the inconsistencies and put some pieces
together. Besides, I needed to check on Frank. For some reason,

I was growing more and more concerned about his well-being lately. It wasn't just this so-called coin-induced remorse he claimed or his slumber from too much whiskey, but something was gnawing at me in my gut, saying that Frank wasn't long for this case and, for that matter, not long for this world.

Entering the hotel, I saw Harry across the lobby with his constant watering can. I wondered if that's all Harry did for the hotel—water the plants? He had been a staple for the Pennsylvania for over fifty years, an institution, and so far, all I've seen and heard of is that Harry waters the plants and flirts with the female patrons. I smiled and thought, why can't I get a job like that?

Harry was looking around the lobby, most likely for some evening companionship or some butt to slap, when he saw me enter. He nodded and anxiously motioned me to him as he moved across the distance quickly. I could tell by his expression that something wasn't right. I was hoping my gut wasn't right either.

"They took Frank to the hospital! It doesn't look good. Apparently, he's had a massive stroke."

Harry could see the expression on my face that said I needed questions answered and fast.

But before I could ask, he began:

"It happened about an hour ago. I had gone by his room to check on him like I try to do several times a week. He didn't answer my knock or my calling to him, so I let myself in. I found him slumped over on the couch, and he wasn't responsive at first. I immediately called for an ambulance and then tried to revive him by sitting him up and talking to him. I noticed an empty whiskey bottle on the coffee table. At first, I just thought he had drunk himself into another stupor like many times before. But he just looked at me as if he didn't recognize me or even know where he was at. And it was as if he couldn't speak or at least couldn't speak clearly. I got really worried then and kept talking to him until the ambulance got there, and then I realized I probably should get ahold of you, but I didn't know how to reach you. Fortunately, you walked in."

"Where'd they take him?"

"To St. Mary's. Like I said, they just left less than an hour ago. I gave them the hotel number, but no one has called yet. You wanna go over there? I'm in the middle of my shift, but I bet the boss will let me go to check on him, and I could drive. My gosh, it's Frank, for Christ's sake."

"See if you can clock out."

Harry parked in a reserved doctor's spot in the Emergency lot. I didn't mention it to him, and he didn't seem to care. We both rushed in the back door as if we belonged. I headed straight for a nun behind the admittance desk. Her white-and-black-lettered nametag indicated she was the nursing administrator. She looked up, unsurprized by our anxious, hurried arrival. She probably saw anxious, hurried arrivals every day.

"I'm Sister Mary Rose; how may I help you?"

"They brought in a man in his eighties suffering from a stroke about an hour ago. His name was Frank Lobeck. Any word as to his condition?" I asked with the same anxiousness in my voice.

"Let me check. Frank Lobeck, you said?" Running her finger down the admittance log, she continued, "Yes, Frank Lobeck admitted at 9:13 this morning. Apparent stroke. Dr. Martin is the attending physician. Let's see, they took him to intensive care." Pointing with her finger, she said, "That's down this hall to your left. See the nurse at the station."

Then, reaching across the admittance desk while smiling gently, she touched my arm and declared with genuine sincerity, "I'll say a prayer for you and Mr. Lobeck."

With the same anxious, hurried stride, we headed down the corridor following the good Sister's directions. There were two nurses at the intensive care desk; one was busy going through paperwork, and by the look on her face, she was desperately searching for information that seemed to elude her. She was moving in and out of an office behind the reception area, and the other was busy on the phone with a conversation with an unknown party that appeared to require a quiet and sensitive nature. She looked up and raised a finger to indicate she would be with us momentarily. It appeared Harry felt she was taking too long, or he may have decided the conversation was not as important as our quest, so he interrupted rudely by reaching over the counter and placing his index finger on the button of the handset cradle, disconnecting the call. The nurse looked up with her mouth agape while Harry flashed his charming smile, hoping it would defuse the situation. For once, Harry's smile was not working. The nurse rose with her fists planted firmly on her desk and leaned forward toward Harry across the counter, but before she could lay into him, I quickly stated:

"We're looking for Frank Lobeck. We understand he's here in intensive care."

Turning toward me, the nurse took in what I was asking and quickly adjusted her attention to my request. Looking down at her chart by the phone, she scanned it and then looked back up, concentrating solely on me with a concerned look. Then, without a word, she turned and walked back to the office behind to counsel with the other nurse. Their tones were hushed and solemn, much like the tone she had used on the phone before Harry hung her up. They both came toward us at the counter, and the other nurse asked, "May I ask how you are related to Mr. Lobeck?"

Again, before I could answer that we were friends of Frank's, Harry chimed in, "I'm Mr. Lobeck's brother, and this is his best friend, Thomas Brunson."

I looked at Harry with a look of satisfaction for thinking quickly on his feet. I thought it must come naturally for him with all the years of practice with the ladies at the hotel. I also thought that somewhere deep inside, a part of Harry cared for the aged detective more than just a room check twice a week.

Then, pointing to his name tag, not thinking his last name and Frank's were not the same, Harry continued, "I work at the Pennsylvania Hotel where Frank lives. I was on duty when the ambulance came and brought him here. Now, please tell us what his condition is, and can we see him now?"

With a very sincere look, the nurse on the phone turned to the other nurse for reassurance. The other nurse then lowered her head, appearing to study a chart and making it awfully obvious to me that she was stalling with some bad news.

Looking up, she said solemnly, "I am so sorry to have to tell you this, but I'm afraid Mr. Lobeck passed away from complications involving the stroke. Apparently, he suffered a major heart attack in the ambulance while en route. The doctors did their best; however, they could not stabilize him, and he passed away about thirty minutes ago. We apparently did not have anyone to contact when they brought him in except for the place where he lived."

Then the nurse on the phone looked at Harry and said without emotion, "I was on the phone with the Pennsylvania when you disconnected me."

Harry looked at her and exclaimed, "Baby, I am the Pennsylvania."

Staring at the two nurses with shock and disbelief, I finally was able to say, "Is he still here? Can we see him, please?"

The other nurse looked at me and said, "Follow me."

Frank's body had been moved out of intensive care into a private room. The nurse pulled the sheet down from his head and then left the room, saying she would give us a moment. Harry stood over in the corner, refusing to come near and pay his last respects. He mumbled something about it being unlucky to see a corpse.

I moved to the side of the bed and looked down at Frank; I suddenly was struck with emotion as I thought about what brought me here to meet Frank in the first place. I knew that later, I would lift a toast to both him and my grandfather. But for now, I was thinking that Frank's death was the worst possible death for a private detective dying with an unsolved case.

Leaning over to whisper in his ear, I felt the only thing I could say at this moment was, "Frank, I swear to you I will find Betty Lou's killer. I promise you that."

As I stood up, the other nurse came in with a box of Frank's personal items. She handed the box to Harry, who was still in his corner.

Turning and speaking to me, she said, "These are the personal possessions that Mr. Lobeck had on him when he passed." Then, reaching into the box and picking out an envelope, she handed it to me. "This has your name on it, Mr. Brunson. He had it in his pocket."

The other nurse then covered Frank's head with the sheet

and motioned us to the door.

She smiled at Harry, stepping through the doorway bringing him out of his corner. Leaning toward her with a slight smile and a nod of his head, Harry said, "Thanks, babe."

I knew as I slipped the envelope into my pocket it contained the Judas coin. Frank had finally let it go.

Turning to Harry, he flashed me one of his famous smiles. Then it struck me. I'll be damned! It was then I knew Father Peter and I would finish our conversation.

36

Harry dropped me off at St. Ann's on his way back to the Pennsylvania. All the while driving there, I was bothered by something I heard Harry say to one of the nurses. It nagged at me. It was something that didn't seem right when it came to the case. It was something I needed to clear up with Father Peter.

After knocking on the rectory door for the third time, I tried the doorknob and found it unlocked. Opening it up, I stuck my head inside, calling for anyone who might be around.

"Hello? Anybody home? Hello, it's Thomas Brunson."

Getting no response, I decided to let myself in and walked noiselessly down the hallway back to Father Peter's room. I found the aged priest again asleep in his oversized chair. I hesitated at first to wake him because, for a moment, he reminded me of Frank nodding off due to his age or perhaps all of his whiskey drinking or maybe even a little of both. Now, I assumed, unlike Frank, Father Peter's frequent naps were simply because of his age, not because of drink. But then, I decided the conversation couldn't wait, so I let out a cough. The aged priest didn't stir, and his breathing continued regularly, so I cleared my throat. This caused him to wake. He lifted his head in the direction of the door and asked, "Is that you, Brother Andrew?"

"No, Father Peter. It's Brunson. Sorry to wake you. I knocked at the front door, but no one answered, so I let myself in. Didn't find anyone about. I'm guessing you're all alone?"

"Brunson? Sorry, I wasn't expecting you. Everyone here has gone to a program at the school, but I was feeling a bit tired. It's been a long day for me, so I stayed behind to rest. Please come in and have a seat," the aged priest said, pointing toward the bed.

Damn, his memory is good.

"Listen, Father Peter, I need you to clear up a couple of minor points in my investigation about your whereabouts on the night Betty Lou was murdered. It's imperative that I establish Hans Metzger's comings and goings. Evidently, whether or not he did go back to Germany, he had returned. You see, I have an eyewitness; in fact, I have two eyewitnesses that put Hans in the lobby that night. Those same witnesses put you there as well, but you told me earlier that you had not gone to the Pennsylvania that evening. Perhaps you were mistaken about just which night, or perhaps, let's see how do I put this delicately? You know, as we age, our memories are not quite as sharp as they used to be. Although I don't think that that is your case, could it be that you just don't remember being there that night? Is that possible?"

Leaning forward in his chair to emphasize his statement and wagging his index finger at me, "Again, as I told you earlier, I was not there that night, as your so-called eyewitnesses claim. I do not know why anyone would want to accuse me of some wrongdoing. Maybe someone has something against the

Church or something against priests, but I think it's time you leave. I've had enough of these questions."

Keeping my seat, I leaned toward the priest and responded with a tone that worked hard not to be accusatory, "No one is blaming you of wrongdoing. It's just that the story doesn't add up. And possibly it's because of one other sticky point. It came to me earlier when Harry, the fellow who works at the Pennsylvania, and I were at the hospital. He called the nurse 'baby.' Now, that's just Harry. He calls every woman baby. However, that struck me as odd, and it got me to thinking about what you said earlier to me about Betty Lou and her baby and the use of a steak knife to deliver that baby. That's information, not anyone could know unless they were somehow privy to the updated autopsy report. No one has seen that report because Capt. Jacobs won't allow it. Even Frank didn't know those details. Now, here's what I'm thinking. There is another possibility of how someone might know those specific details, and that is that someone had to be there that night and they saw what went on in that bedroom. I could imagine that seeing those particular details of an improvised C-section could traumatize one so as to not want to remember the details, but it is crucial that you be totally honest with me. So tell me again, Father Peter, just where were you the night Betty Lou was murdered, and how did you know those particular details?"

The old priest looked even older as the color drained from his face. His eyes stared darkly up toward the ceiling for perhaps some intervention from some higher power. None appeared to come. He fell back into his chair as if the weight of leaning forward had become a burden. Then, with hardly a whisper, Father Peter confessed, "Forgive me, Brunson, for I have sinned. I haven't told you the honest truth."

"The truth about what? Where you were that night?"

Looking toward my voice, he began with a slow, steady pace as he unfolded a tale I was not ready for:

I read the headline on the Marietta Times newspaper stand outside the Harmar Tavern, and it was still the same as it was two days ago: "Japanese Bomb Pearl Harbor - United States Declares War!"

I was new to the country, having just arrived from Germany only three weeks ago. I had learned to speak English in my native land, so I naturally fit. This small town in Ohio has a considerable community of Germans, but we kept to ourselves and did not reveal our allegiance to the Motherland since the events now propelled the United States into this war. It wouldn't be safe for us if people knew.

The crowd that night at the tavern was rowdy because most were from the local paint factory, and their shift had just ended. It was, after all, the weekend full of backyard grilling and all-night beer drinking that came with remodeling bragging rights and the occasional secret affair that found itself smiling ever so slyly across the fence. I moved to the far side of the barroom and sat at a table quietly, drinking my beer while waiting for a friend to arrive. It was not hard to listen in on the conversations:

"Hey, Wilson. Heard Betty Lou up and moved to Florida. Whereabouts down there?"

"She moved to West Palm Beach. She got a job singing in the Hotel Pennsylvania. She's doin' real good. Me and the missus plan on goin' down for a visit next summer."

"That's wonderful! She always did have the best voice. Listen to me; you know you better be careful; I hear the Krauts are patrolling the coastline with them damn U-boats. If I were you, I'd get my girl outta there and back home here where it's safer."

"Ain't nuthin' gonna happen to my, Betty Lou. She's as safe there as she is here. Besides, we been blowin' the smithereens outta them

Krauts lately. Why, just the other day, one of my aircraft, a U.S. Army Air Corps bomber, dropped depth charges on one of their U-boats off the coast of North Carolina. Sent the bastards all the way to the bottom and straight to hell."

"Wilson, you talk like that was you in that plane. We all know you're too damn old, and the Army wouldn't take you, so whatcha talkin' about 'my aircraft'? I know for a fact that you was right here mixin' paint with the rest of us."

"I may have been here, but it was my paint that painted that aircraft that sunk that sub. So I kinda see it as my way to get in the war and kill me some Krauts."

I glared at the one known as Wilson from across the barroom floor. That U-boat he was bragging about sinking had my two brothers, Franz and Karl, on board. My family ended on that day. I knew in my heart that I would find a way to make that man pay. I'd bring the righteous judgment.

I thought about the reason I came to these shores: to receive my sacred orders and then minister through the Church among my people in that small town. All of a sudden, those religious orders became less and less important. My whole being cried out for revenge because of the total destruction of my family. I was now alone in the world. But now I had a greater purpose—to exact punishment on the one guilty. What I needed was a plan.

I could no longer stay in the presence of all that hatred that night. So I finished my beer and left without waiting any longer for my comrade. As I stepped outside, I pulled my jacket tighter around me because of the wind and cold, but it did not warm the coldness in my heart. At that moment, I had a plan. I would travel to Florida and find this man's daughter, Betty Lou, and bring to him more devastating pain than what he brought to me.

I currently was serving as a deacon prior to my Rite of Ordination.

The Ordination would have to wait. Surely, the Holy Mother would understand that my new mission was more divine than any commandment.

The wicked must be judged and punished.

I left Ohio that night and made my way down south to Florida by bus. I had decided that I would need to blend into the community there so that no one would get excited about a German immigrant new to town. The local parish could help conceal my determined intent. From the bus station, I walked north to the Hotel George Washington. A local on the bus told me it was owned by a German, and that seemed as good a place to stay as any for now. The man at the registration desk told me of St. Ann's, which is just a couple of blocks from the hotel. He also informed me that they were in the process of establishing a new priest.

My plan was evolving.

I applied for the position at the church and told the bishops that I had recently been confirmed the Rite of Ordination, but the ordination papers had not yet been forwarded. There was one bishop who, for some reason, distrusted my story, and he took it upon himself to check me out. When he heard from the parish up north that I still lacked completing the Rite, he confronted me. Since he was the only obstacle to my plans for revenge, I saw no other choice but to silence him. The ocean's full of silent voices. Without his opposition, the rest of the bishops installed me as St. Ann's new parish priest.

The next step in my plan was to locate Wilson's daughter, Betty Lou. I remembered the talk at the bar said she was working at the Pennsylvania. But the Blessed Mother smiled on me, and that girl found me first. She showed up one day for confession and then a Mass. I now had a face to go with my plan. I went to the Pennsylvania to watch her perform and followed her to her room, but I left without being noticed. The time was not right for my plan. For many months, she did not return to mass. Then, one day, I received a message from her that she wanted to have confession but asked that I come to her room at the hotel.

Again, my plan was evolving.

On the night she died, I had gone to her room to hear her confession. She was in her housecoat as if she hadn't expected me that soon, or perhaps she was expecting someone else. I had learned she had become pregnant by her German boyfriend, Hans, and was not appearing in public since she was showing well. She confessed that Hans had taken a sub back to Germany and did not know when he would return. She was thinking of returning to Ohio to have her baby with the help of her parents. Suddenly, I realized all the planning and scheming would be for nothing if she returned home. So, when she went into her bedroom, I followed. All the pain of losing my family overcame me again, and my sense of divine judgment rose up, and I grasped her around the neck and began to choke my vengeance out on her. She began to shake violently, and at the same time, I heard someone knocking on the apartment door, calling for her. As her resistance now lessened and my vengeance began to abate, I threw her on the bed and slipped into a closet to conceal myself from whoever was at the door. With the closet door slightly ajar, I watched as this cleaning woman tried in vain to revive the strangled girl and then beheld the ghastly attempt to deliver the baby with nothing but a steak knife. While this woman was intently preoccupied with the makeshift surgery, I slipped quietly out of the closet and the apartment and out of the hotel through the lobby.

Father Peter appeared to me surprisingly content as he finished his tale. I'm not sure how I knew that other than a look on his face, a look I would describe as even more than contentment, it appeared to be a look of relief. Not something I expected from someone who just confessed to murder. Although I now saw all the pieces coming together, what I couldn't understand was how anyone could intentionally take the life of another without a hint of remorse. To me, remorse is a part of our nature, or so I thought. Without remorse, I sensed we'd never find our way to recognizing our failings toward one another and toward ourselves. Remorse is what breaks down our reluctance to genuinely feel sorry for our actions to the point of changing our direction. It's what causes the guilty to finally take responsibility for their crimes. Without remorse, how do we ever get to right again?

The old priest was not broken over his actions. In fact, he smiled slightly at the judgment that he had passed on Betty Lou. It appeared Father Peter saw no reason for repentance; he saw no sin. Without remorse, Father Peter could never have the opportunity to be free from that which could torture him forever—the betrayal of his holy vow of obedience to Christ. This was the very vow that would have prevented his actions against Betty Lou.

It was then I reached into my pocket and took out Frank's envelope. Tearing it open pronounced my verdict. In the priest's mind, he saw himself as God's vengeance and self-appointed righteous executioner for the crimes against his family. In my mind, I saw my decision somewhat contrary to the priest's position, at least at that moment. So, standing, I moved closer to him and, without remorse, said, "I have something for your apostasy. It's something I believe Frank kept just for you. Hold out your hand, please."

Father Peter held out his trembling hand. I dropped the Judas coin into it.

Later, sitting at the bar at Kelsey's, I ordered three separate shots of I. W. Harper bourbon. Taking the first one, I held it to my nose to smell the taste. Raising the shot, I said out loud, "To Grandpa Farley for believing in me," then placed it back down again on the bar, untouched. Then, I raised the second shot, "To you, Frank, for trusting me," and with a wink at the glass in my hand, I placed the drink back on the bar with the other. Turning on my bar stool and facing the barroom patrons for witnesses, I thought of my own apostasy. Many would ask how was it any less than the priest's? This time, I swallowed the whiskey. Before I did, I simply proclaimed,

"To Peter."

OBITUARY

Lobeck, Francis (Frank) Abbott, 86, of West Palm Beach, passed away on July 22, 1994, after a heart attack. Frank was born on December 15, 1908, to Harold and Francine Lobeck in Jacksonville, Florida.

After Frank graduated from Newton Knight High School in 1926, he worked for the Atlantic Coast Line Railway for many years, bringing him eventually to West Palm Beach, where he would settle for almost 60 years as a private investigator.

In 1936, Frank met Lilly Forester at a local dance and were married soon after. Frank and Lilly had one daughter, Beth, who passed away at the age of four. In 1942, Frank moved into the Pennsylvania Hotel and spent the remainder of his life residing there.

Frank was predeceased by his father, Harold, and mother, Francine, wife, Lilly, and daughter, Beth. He had no other known family.

Services to be held at Holy Trinity Episcopal Church on Tuesday the 26th at 9:00 am.

Metzger, Hans Ludwig, 72, a long-time resident of the Hotel George Washington, finally gave up his battle with cancer at St. Mary's Hospital this past week.According to his only daughter, Sister Mary Rose, nursing administrator at St. Mary's, her father came to the United States to escape the war in his native country of Germany. It was in West Palm Beach that he met his wife, Betty Lou Wilson, who died due to complications in child-birth.

Services will be held at St. Ann's on 27 July 1994 at 11:00 am, officiated by Father Peter Heinrich of St. Ann's parish.

Warfeld, Marjorie Anne, 93, of Jupiter, sadly passed away on Saturday, the 23rd, of natural causes.

Marjorie was the daughter of Herschel and Anne Chapman, originally of Tampa, Florida. Marjorie worked at the post office in Jupiter, where she met her first husband, George Lacy, and they were married prior to him being sent to Europe for WWI.

George was killed in battle, and soon after, Marjorie married George's younger brother, Marvin. They were married for over 60 years until his passing 3 years ago.

Mrs. Lacy is survived by one son, two daughters, 7 grandchil-dren, and 5 great-grandchildren. She also had many friends and was a well-loved member of the community in Grandview Heights.

Funeral services will be held on Monday the 25th at 9:00 am at Quattlebaum Holleman . . .

Acknowledgement

How do you tell a good friend thanks for all the work they put into a project, especially a project of this size. We spent over a year meeting via Zoom almost every week to discuss the latest chapter. Those discussions were about the impact of the words, the adding and subtraction of the words, the clarity of the words, and occasionally even the spelling of the words. This friend read not only the original drafts but the revisions as well. Week after week, this friend kept encouraging me to write, even when I was stalled and could not find any more words to put on the page. Without this good friend, I would never have completed this project. Thanks, Paul, you indeed are a good friend. Let's have a round of applause for Paul Juhasz, everybody.

Next, let me say thank you to an old friend from our high school days at John I. Leonard High, Michael (Mike) Rybovich. Mike was our senior class president of the graduating class of 1972 in Greenacres, Florida. While doing research for this novel, I ran across some information that suggested Ernest Hemingway knew and used Mike's grandfather, John Rybovich's boatyard, for repairs of the *Pilar*. I contacted Mike, who now owns the boatyard named Rybovich and Sons Custom Boat Works in Palm Beach Gardens, Florida, and he faxed me two pictures of his uncle and Hemingway to verify the information.

Thanks, Mike. Can't wait to put this book in your hands.

I also need to say a heartfelt thank you to Dr. Mark Shipman. As my professor and for the last 23 years my colleague, you put the love of Hemingway into me. It is indeed an honor to call you my friend. And thanks for helping me fill my concert bucket list and taking me to The Who. Rodger still has a fantastic set of vocal pipes after all these years.

Once again, I want to say how grateful I am to have Fine Dog Press with Roxie and Terry Kirk as my publisher. As long as they'll have me I'll keep coming back.

And finally, I saved the best for last: Kelli, my beautiful wife who let me spend so much time cloistered away in my office to complete this work of fiction. I promise I'll write the ultimate love story one day all about you. Now, about all those unfinished chores.

About the Author

Woodstok Farley is often told his life resembles the many fascinating stories he weaves on the page. In many ways, parts of it are true. Born on the Atlantic side of this fantastic land down in South Florida, he spent his youth riding the waves and running amok through the swamps. He then headed out across this vast country with his faithful German Shepard in a VW Beetle until it broke down in Oklahoma. He tried to blend in with the locals, but this long-haired former beach bum was finally asked to leave, so he headed south to Texas. Texas let him stay. He married, raised a son, and buried his faithful companion.

Then he wrote it all down. Well, some of it.